THE OUTCAST: GOLD TOWN

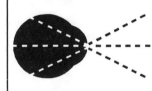

THE OUTCAST: GOLD TOWN

LUKE CYPHER

WHEELER PUBLISHING
A part of Gale, Cengage Learning

Detroit • New York • San Francisco • New Haven, Conn • Waterville, Maine • London

GALE
CENGAGE Learning™

LIBRARY OF CONGRESS CATALOGING-IN-PUBLICATION DATA

Cypher, Luke.
    The outcast. Gold town / by Luke Cypher. — Large print ed.
      p. cm. — (Wheeler Publishing large print western)
    Originally published: New York: Berkley, 2008.
    ISBN-13: 978-1-59722-912-8 (alk. paper)
    ISBN-10: 1-59722-912-1 (alk. paper)
    1. Clergy—Fiction. 2. Large type books. I. Title. II. Title: Gold town.
PS3555.I23O984 2009
813'.54—dc22   2008045486

Published in 2009 by arrangement with The Berkley Publishing Group, a member of Penguin Group (USA) Inc.

Printed in the United States of America
1 2 3 4 5 6 7 13 12 11 10 09

For Leone

Then came the third rider of the Apocalypse upon a black horse. He held a pair
of scales in his hand, but the scales
weighed against those who labored with
their hands for wheat and barley, taking
triple weight for a coin of gold.

My Lord, watch over the ways of the righteous and guide them along the path away from the wicked and sinners and mockers. Lead them along green paths to cool water, safe from the wicked who are like chaff that blows away in the wind. Give them the strength to stand against evil and the wisdom to understand their fellow man. Can he who hates justice govern? Or those who seek to do harm to their fellow man? Men cry out under the burden of oppression and the strong prey upon the weak. We know, O Lord, that You have a time for all things, even a day of disaster for the wicked.

Prayer of Amos Hood

1.

He rode slowly down the mountain and into the dark valley where shadows from the mountains on both sides of the valley still masked the day. Night was not the time for riding, but at times, his dreams came back to haunt him, dreams of when he was Tom Cade, a marshal who had been swift with his gun before giving up his name to become an itinerant minister, following in the footsteps of his father and grandfather. It was when the nightmares came that Amos Hood rode Sheba, a gray filly with a streak of white down her nose who tolerated only Hood but no others, into the night, guiding himself west by the stars while bullbats swept and darted overhead. Riding helped put the night demons to rest. They were still there, but not as vibrant and alive as they were when he was trying to sleep, or even when he was sitting around his campfire.

Now, Hood could see a tiny string of yellow lights where the night met the edge of the earth, and he relaxed the reins, letting Sheba find her own way. He could not see the gray wolf, Sam, he had rescued as a pup after someone had killed his mother, trotting beside him or ranging out in front to find an unwary rabbit, but he sensed Sam there, moving silently with him. Night sounds came to him: the call of an owl, the shriek of a nighthawk dropping down to its prey, bullbats dancing and squeaking as they filled themselves with fireflies, the warning rattle of a sidewinder when he or Sam came too close. They were familiar sounds and comforting sounds and he sat slumped in his saddle, content with the night and his movement through it.

He watched the lights come closer. He hadn't anticipated them. He didn't know where exactly he was — someplace in the Sangre de Cristo Mountains, he thought — but it didn't matter where he was. There might be a church needing a minister and he felt a certain calling, a tugging at his senses, that brought him toward the lights. He grinned in the dark. Then again, he was nearly out of beans and dried meat and he had drunk the last of the coffee three days ago. Now, he needed to refit his supplies before being a wanderer in the wasteland southwest in the mountains at the beginning of the desert between New Mexico and southern Colorado.

Pale streaks of gold, lavender, and pink streaked the sky over the western side of the valley as he came near enough to the town to recognize buildings, and faintly he thought he heard a piano played badly but fast enough that no one minded the missed notes. Then, he heard gunshots followed by rebel yells, and he straightened in his saddle, his senses coming alert. Sheba's ears pricked forward and Sam gave a single bark of warning from beside his left stirrup. Hood's hand strayed automatically to the left saddlebag where the ivory-handled Schofield .45, with which he had earned a reputation as a gunfighter and the marshal of Walker, a railhead town back in Kansas, rested in the bottom of the saddlebag. In the other saddlebag was his father's Bible and the silver cross his father had always worn when he preached in his church back in the Tennessee hills. The saddlebags also held clean white shirts and his grandfather's watch, which his father had carried into the pulpit when he had preached in the same church as *his* father. Hood's black coat and pants were folded neatly and tied behind the saddle, wrapped in a stained brown leather coat. He wore a pair of gray cotton pants, a blue shirt, and a black bandanna tied around his neck. His black Stetson was pulled down low over his eyes. He wore black boots without spurs.

Almost reluctantly, he brought his hand back from the saddlebag and rested it on his saddle horn, near the sheathed Spencer .56 tied to the saddle horn, as he neared the edge of town. He watched the town as he approached, and the gold and lavender streaks disappeared and the sun leaped into the sky, seeming to bake the ground with its arrival. Perspiration began to slip down Hood's face and back. He took a handkerchief from an inside pocket and wiped his face. He sighed and felt the early morning heat enter his lungs.

He reined Sheba in and rested for a moment, stretching himself in the saddle while he read the bullet-riddled sign announcing the town's name, GOLD TOWN, beneath which some wag had listed the population, crossed out and rewritten seemingly as the population decreased and increased and decreased. The sides of the mountains were clear now. Denuded of all vegetation, with the remains of trees black and standing lopsided on the mountainsides like canine teeth. Mud seemed to be the new face of the mountains as miners and placers dug and washed for gold. Ugliness was everywhere, the hastily thrown-together town sprawled out and along the north side of Jedediah Creek — named after Jedediah Smith, the famous mountain man and explorer, some said — while the south side of the creek ran along the valley cliffs on its way to the Colorado before the Colorado plunged through the red cliffs and deep canyons, with places like the Crossing of the Fathers and stony lay-bys, spotted with old campfires, where travelers could rest.

A wry smile crossed Hood's face. He remembered hearing about the gold strike somewhere in a nameless town that had joined other nameless towns in back of his wandering trail, and now he knew that Gold Town in front of him was a town without a minister and a town without a church. It was too new to have the luxuries of a church and, he reflected, a school.

Gunshots continued to split the air, punctuated by yells of cowboys racing their horses through the street. He sighed and nudged Sheba with his knee, riding forward into the town, keeping purposely to the right to avoid being caught up in one of the rushes the cowboys were making back and forth in what must be the main street of the town.

He dismounted in front of Bledsoe's General Store, and draped Sheba's reins over a hitching rail near a water trough. He slapped the dust from his clothes with his hat before he entered the store. Sam came to the door with him, glanced inside, then dropped down next to the door, propping his head upon his paws, yellow eyes gleaming, watching.

Hood paused as his eyes adjusted to the light inside the building before moving forward to the counter. He waited patiently while three ladies conferred over a bolt of red satiny cloth. The younger one glanced at him. He noticed her hair, an unusual shade of blond that came from the continued use of peroxide. Her eyes were cornflower blue, but there was no softness to them, although her smooth and unlined face lent an expression of innocence to them. She smiled, the corners of her lips curving into deep dimples. He smiled back, and the older woman caught his smile and rapped the younger woman sharply on the back of her hand with the knuckle of her forefinger.

"Sally, pay attention," the older woman said. "You need a new dress after that cowboy tore your last one. We need to

16

decide what kind so Hermione" — she nodded at the woman on her other side — "can get it sewn before you go back to work again."

Hermione's eyes had tired purple circles under them and her cheeks looked pinched in, her lips thin and colorless. She nodded and touched the satin cloth.

"This one will do just fine," she said. "With black satin for the top and edged in green to match her eyes. We've still got trim from Sally's last dress that we can use. If I can get started now, I might have it finished by nine tonight."

"You hear that, Sally?" the older woman said sharply. "You decide or I'll decide for you."

Sally's eyes turned back to the cloth. "This will do," she said indifferently and shrugged. "One is as good as the other."

"We'll take three yards of this and two yards of the black," Hermione told the man behind the counter.

He nodded and unwrapped the bolt, measuring it against a wooden yardstick nailed to the back of the counter.

"And some black buttons — the large ones — and a spool of black thread," Hermione added.

"You new here?" Sally asked, turning

toward Amos. "I can't remember seeing you around before."

Hood removed his hat and nodded. "Just rode in. Thought I'd pick up a few things before getting a room."

"You'll play the devil to try and get a room in this town," the older woman said. She extended her hand. "I'm Alice Bank. Folks call me Squirreltooth Alice. I don't like it, but it's followed me around long enough that I'm pretty used to it."

"Alice," Hood said, taking her hand.

"Well," Alice said, placing her fists on her ample hips. "You're a different one. But every room is taken in this town. Sometimes three or four men in one. And some rooms are used by different men when the shifts change in the mines."

"I hear Missus Hargrave has a room to let in her boardinghouse since that young feller from back East went and got himself killed over at the Texas Saloon the other night." The storekeeper nodded at Hood. "It'd be better if you run down there and get it if it ain't gone already before you do business with me. You'll find it on the edge of town. The only house that's got white paint on it. That is," he added, glancing at Hood's hips where a gun normally would rest, "if you plan on staying around some."

"Thank you," Hood said politely and stepped toward the door. "I'll be back shortly."

"Come and see us when you get settled," Sally said. "We're at the Nugget across the street."

"Perhaps," Hood said gently, and stepped out the door.

Sam jumped to his feet and waited on the boardwalk as Hood picked up Sheba's reins and swung smoothly into the saddle.

"Come on," he said gently. "Let's go see about getting a room."

Sheba tossed her head and turned with Hood's gentle pressure on the reins.

A string of cowboys rode by, whooping and hollering and shooting their pistols into the air. One of the cowboys noticed Sam and pulled up in front of Sheba.

"I'll be damned. A wolf," he said, and grinned. He pointed his pistol at Sam.

Hood slammed his heels against Sheba's sides. She reared, her front hooves lashing out at the cowboy and horse in front. The cowboy ducked, and then Sam had him by the hand with the pistol and dragged him from his horse. The cowboy landed heavily and lay still, blinking owlishly in confusion. Then his face twisted in anger and he started to rise, but Sam placed his front paws on the cowboy's chest. His lips curled back from his teeth and he lowered his head within inches from the cowboy's throat, a threatening growl coming from deep in his throat. The cowboy dropped back to the ground and lay still, his face white beneath black beard stubble.

"Hey!" he said, glancing up at Hood sitting patiently in his saddle. "Get him off me!"

"Sam," Hood said quietly. Immediately, Sam stepped away from the cowboy and went to Hood's stirrup beside Sheba.

"I'm gonna kill —" the cowboy said loudly and reached for his pistol.

"Sam," Hood said, the tone of his voice changing threateningly.

Sam leaped forward and grabbed the cowboy again by the hand reaching for the pistol. His jaws closed and even from his saddle, Hood heard the bones crunching in the cowboy's wrist before the cowboy cried out in pain.

Sam growled, braced himself, and shook his head from side to side, grinding the cowboy's wrist harder and harder.

"That's enough, Sam," Hood said. Sam backed away and crouched, facing the cowboy, his lips turned back, a harsh growl coming from his throat.

The cowboy sat up and rocked back and forth in pain while holding his hand close to his stomach. He looked up at Hood.

"You should have let him be," Hood said. "Come on, Sam."

Obediently, Sam slipped to the right side of Sheba and trotted alongside as they moved down the street. He glanced back, eyeing the cowboy, but the cowboy didn't move, his attention full on his broken wrist.

They rode down to a neat two-story house freshly painted white. Small lilac and wisteria bushes had been planted on the sides of the porch. A bed of flowers had been planted a short distance away from the front of the house, but the flowers had been trampled by horses and now lay wilted and torn on the ground.

Hood dismounted and dropped the reins over the front railing of the porch. He climbed the steps, removed his hat, and knocked on the door. It opened immediately and a robust and cheerful woman in a pearl gray dress stood before him. Her face was round and her eyes hazel. Her heavy lips parted in a big smile at the sight of Hood.

"I'm Missus Hargrave. Come in! Come in!" she said. There was a hint of laughter to her voice. She glanced down at Sam and frowned slightly. "Is he safe?"

"Yes," Hood answered.

"Then let him come in, too."

She threw the door wide and Hood called Sam and stepped inside. He found himself in a small hallway. At the end of the hallway a staircase led to the top floor. To his left, a small sitting room with heavy, dark furniture that gleamed from fresh polish. To his right, a dining room. The table gleamed.

Sam walked through both rooms, sniffing suspiciously. Then, he found the rag rug leading to the sitting room. He scuffed the rug with his paws, turned around three times, and settled down with an air of contentment.

"What can I do for you?" she asked.

"I heard you might have a room for rent," he said.

"Lucky you came when you did. I just finished packing up the former renter's trunk to send to his folks back East. I can have the room cleaned in a couple of hours." She looked him over shrewdly, noticing the absence of a pistol on his hip. "You're no gunman and you sure do not look like a hard-rock miner."

Hood shook his head. "I'm a minister."

Her eyes widened. "Well, I'll be. Maybe this is a sign that Gold Town is getting civilized. The room is normally five dollars a day, but since you're a minister — you are planning on opening a church here, aren't you?" she asked, pausing. He nodded. "Then I'll make it five dollars a week on account of you setting up here. I've got a real nice room in the back where it's quiet. It's a little bigger than normal, and I've got a few old rugs you can throw down in the corner for your friend." She nodded at Sam. "Price includes dinner. And a bone for your wolf. Out back, we have a tub house where you can bathe. You'll have to pump the water in from the cistern. Hot water, you'll have to make yourself, but you can use the stove in the kitchen."

"I'll take it and thanks," Hood said gratefully. He reached into a pocket and took out a five-dollar gold piece. "Here's for the first week."

"Thank you," she said.

"Is there a livery stable near?" Hood asked.

She nodded. "There is. But Skeeter charges an arm and a leg and then some to stable your horse. I've got a barn that you can use if you want. It's solid and clean and there's good hay that my husband put up before he went and got himself killed in the mines. I won't charge a penny for it."

"I'm grateful," Hood said.

"Well, we're settled then," she said. "If you come back in a couple of hours, your room will be ready."

"Appreciate that," Hood said. "Come on, Sam."

Sam opened an eye and looked at Hood. He whined in protest.

"He can stay. I don't mind," she said. Slowly, she reached down to ruffle Sam's fur on his neck. Sam watched her movement suspiciously, but when her fingers began to scratch his ears, he seemed to sigh with contentment.

"You've made a new friend," Hood said. "Then go ahead and stay, lazybones," he said to Sam.

Hood stepped outside into the morning sun and felt the promised heat of the day warm upon his shoulders. He straightened his back with a grimace and his back popped like tiny firecrackers with the movement. Two men were walking anxiously toward the house. They walked faster and faster, each trying to outdistance the other. When they turned toward the house, Hood held up his hands and said, "Sorry, boys. I got here first."

They looked at him and the one on the left said, "Ahhh," and spat a long stream of tobacco juice to the side. He shook his head disgustedly. "Seems like I'm always a day late and a dollar short."

"Don't suppose you'd be willing to share on shift changes," the other said.

Hood shook his head. "Sorry. But I'm not a miner."

"Then what are you doing here?" the first asked, his brow furrowing in thought.

"I'm a minister," Hood said quietly.

Both laughed and the first man said, "Well, you surely came to hell. I'm Hank Wooten and this here" — he jerked his thumb at the other — "is Cacklejack. He's not a bad sort when he remembers to take a bath."

"Pleased to meet you," Hood said and shook hands.

"Would you let us buy you a drink?" Hank asked.

Cacklejack slapped him on the shoulder. "Dummy. He's a minister. You don't expect him to drink, let alone drink with the likes of us."

"Why not?" Hank demanded. "He puts his pants on the same as us."

Hood laughed and said, "Some other time. Right now, I want to get a few things and clean up."

"That's a deal," Hank said. He looked at Cacklejack. "Come on, bonehead."

They walked away arguing with each other every step. Hood laughed quietly and crossed to Sheba. He took her reins.

"Come on, girl," he said and reached to rub her nose, but she jerked away from him. He laughed. "Always the temptress, aren't you? Well, we have a place for you to stay and if it meets up with its owner's opinion, then it will be quite a royal place to stay."

He led Sheba around behind the house and nodded in satisfaction when he saw the barn, painted as white as the house. The rails of the corral next to the barn were neatly notched into posts set firmly in the ground. At the back of the corral, a shelter had been built off the side of the barn for horses to get under into the shade when the sun rose hot in the sky. A trough with a pump stood near the overhang.

"What do you think?" Hood asked Sheba.

Sheba grumbled deep in her throat and moved toward the barn, walking beside Hood.

The barn was cool without the sharpness of the sunlight. Hood took Sheba to a stall and stripped his saddle from her back, swinging it over a side of the stall with his saddlebags. He removed her bridle and draped it over the saddle horn, then used an empty hemp gunnysack to rub her down.

Her skin trembled with pleasure and Hood laughed aloud.

"You're easy to please. Now, let's get you some fresh bedding and I'll see if I can round up some oats for you."

He climbed into the loft and forked down some hay and spread it in her stall. But there were no oats, and he promised her that he'd buy some from the feed and grain store — if he could find one — then he patted her rump and left, heading down into town.

The store was empty of customers when he returned, and the storekeeper greeted him with a welcoming grin.

"Did you get the room? If you did, you've the luck of a New Orleans gambler."

"I don't know about that," Hood said easily. Before becoming a minister, he had been a fair hand with cards. But that was far behind him now. As far behind as the marshal's star he once wore at Walker. "I understand that their luck depends on their skill with the cards. Mine depends on someone else."

The storekeeper raised an eyebrow questioningly and Hood continued.

"I'm a minister."

"A *minister?*"

Hood smiled and held out his hand.

"Amos Hood."

The storekeeper took his hand and shook it vigorously. "I'm right glad to meet you. We've been needing a preacher ever since the town sprung up and that's been 'bout three years now. I'm Howard Bledsoe. But everyone calls me Howie." He leaned closer to Hood and whispered conspiratorially, "Everyone but my wife. She insists that people call me Howard. She means well, but it sort of puts some people off their feed."

Hood smiled. "We'll see. Meanwhile, I need a few things."

"Name them," Howard said and straightened, placing his thumbs under his red and yellow suspenders, snapping them. He wore a clean collar and a starched white shirt. His hair was oiled and combed straight back. Around his waist he had tied an apron.

A woman came from the back of the store. She wore a dark blue dress, severely cut, and sleeve protectors pulled up to her elbows. Her hair had been pulled back in a hard bun. A pair of bifocals was perched on her snub nose. But there was a severity to her black eyes, a hard look that stared out suspiciously upon the world, and her lips were drawn tightly against each other as if she had been sucking a lemon.

"This is Amos Hood, dear. He's a minister," Howie said. "Mr. Hood, this is my wife Hazel." There was a slight tremor to his voice, and Hood caught it as he nodded at the wife.

"How do you do, ma'am?" he asked.

She sniffed and raised her head to look down her nose and through her bifocals at him. It was an affectation, Hood knew, as he could seem only a blur to her through the bifocals.

"Another of those ruffians — a cowboy or a miner, I suppose," she sniffed. "Well, we don't give credit to that kind of people. We have been left holding credit slips too many times to warrant going out on the limb again."

"Mr. Hood is a minister," Howie explained again nervously. He eyed his wife warily, uncertain of how this was going to be received. And that, too, was a habit, Hood recognized.

"A minister? Here in Gold Town? That's good and bad," she said. "Good because we need a minister, and bad because we get our hopes up for a change for the better only to have them amount to nothing but fluff when he is driven out of town."

"I guess we'll have to see what happens," Hood said easily. "We'll just have to trust in

29

the Lord."

"Trust in Him all you want," she said peevishly, "but that doesn't mean that others trust in Him as well. Then, you have problems. I hope that isn't so, Mr. Hood."

"So do I," Hood answered. He turned back to Howie. "I could use some soap — something other than that lye soap — and a couple of white shirts. Mine are a bit threadbare. And are those cans of peaches I see?" He pointed to a neat row of cans on a shelf behind Howie.

"Yes, sir. The only ones in town. They're pretty expensive, though," he warned.

"Give me a can of them, please," Hood answered, grinning. "And open the can if you will. I haven't had peaches since I left Tennessee as a younker and that's been quite some time now. Oh, and would you have any boot black? Mine are fair scuffed."

"Yes, we do," Hazel put in. "And I wished more around here would take pride in their appearance other than those who work the saloons. That should be your first duty. Close them down, I say, so decent folks will have a good place to live."

"It is a mining town," Howie said, then almost cringed when his wife laid her hard eyes on him. "What I mean is that the town hasn't been here long enough for us to even get a marshal, let alone try to close the saloons down. We might have a riot if we do that."

Hazel said, disgruntled, "All that has to have a beginning sometime. Might as well be now. Those cowboys terrorize the town, Mr. Hood. Almost on a daily basis. And when they get started, the miners come right behind them. It's really bad when both take a disliking to each other and tear the town apart while fighting each other. And it all begins right there in those saloons, you ask me. That's the devil's workshop!"

"Do you have a church?" Hood asked.

"No, we sure don't," Howie said hurriedly. "Like I said, the town's too new. We don't even have a schoolhouse, or schoolmarm to teach even if we did have one. If we did have them, the cowboys would probably burn them down. Or the miners. Churches and schoolhouses change a town."

"We need law and order and God here and not necessarily in that order," Hazel said firmly. "Now, if you'll excuse me, Mr. Hood, I need to get to work. Come back when you're finished, Howard. I have some bills of lading that we need to go over."

"Yes, dear," Howie said, a bit of defeatism in his voice. He smiled sheepishly at Hood. "She means well. But" — his voice lowered

31

— "she *is* narrow-sighted. What's good for her is good for the town. You catch my drift?"

"Yes," Hood said. "One more thing: Is there a place where I can get some clothes cleaned? A laundry perhaps?"

"The Chinaman," Howie said, gesturing south. "He does a good job with shirts and things. And he cleans coats and pants as well. You can find him behind the Sampling House. That's a bar despite its fancy name," he added.

"Thanks," Hood said. "What do I owe you?"

Howie glanced quickly toward the back of the store, then shook his head. "Nothing. Let's just say it's a welcome to Gold Town."

"I appreciate that," Hood said, gathering the package Howie made. He took the can of peaches Howie had opened for him and slipped a knife from his pocket. He drank some of the juice from the can and walked out of the store, spearing the peaches one at a time with the knife blade.

He ambled down the street toward the feed and grain store at the edge of town. He stayed close to the buildings on the board-walk to avoid miners and cowboys staggering out of bars and into the street. The day was early, but those who had been on shift and just released had night and day switched around. The cowboys, however, seemed to ignore time as they slipped in and out of one of the saloons at will. Hood registered this, and watched the foot traffic and wagons and riders in the street carefully. He had, he realized, already committed himself to be the town preacher, and from the look of things, he had a long row to hoe.

A pair of bat-wing doors slammed open and a cowboy and a miner tumbled out, biting, kicking, slugging, and trying to knee each other in the groin. Dust billowed up like a miniature tornado as they landed in the street. People crowded out of the saloon and stood on the boardwalk and in a semi-circle around the fighting pair, glasses of beer in their fists, urging the fighters on.

One of the fighters, a big burly man, apparently a miner, with tangled black hair and beard and a long scar coming down from the corner of his left eye and disappearing into his beard, threw his lighter opponent, a cowboy with a blue work shirt, chaps, and spurred boots, away from him. The miner rose and ran to stomp the cowboy with feet the size of snowshoes, but the cowboy arched his back and struck out with his spurs like a fighting cock, tearing chunks of flesh and beard from the miner's face.

The miner let out a scream and reeled away. The cowboy rose and sank the narrow toe of his boot into the miner's groin. The miner screamed again and fell down into the dust, the cowboy moving around him, kicking viciously.

"Hold this," Hood said, thrusting his package into the arms of a watcher. He leaped off the boardwalk, elbowed his way through the crowd, and stepped between the cowboy and the miner. The cowboy glared at him.

"I think he's had enough," Hood said softly.

"Like hell!" the cowboy said thickly. He turned his head and spat a glob of blood onto the ground. "He blindsided me when I did nothing!"

"That isn't true," a voice said from the porch. The crowd parted to reveal a well-kept man in a black frock coat and brocade vest and with a well-trimmed mustache. His black hair was combed straight back. His slate gray eyes stared at the cowboy, lifeless and hard.

"You shoved between him and his friend and spilt his beer," the man said softly.

The cowboy looked uneasy. "This ain't none of your affair, Ellis."

"It is when you interrupt my game." He

reached deliberately inside his coat and removed a long black cigar. Carefully, he cut the end with a penknife attached to a gold watch chain crossing his vest and lit the cigar.

"Now, go away like a good boy," Ellis said, nonchalantly waving his hand in dismissal.

"As soon as I deal with him," the cowboy said, jerking his chin at Hood.

Ellis looked at Hood and smiled faintly. "I think that would be a big mistake. Now, I don't want to have to tell you again to move on."

An edge came into his voice, and the cowboy shuffled his feet nervously in the dust. He looked at Hood and sneered.

"This ain't over, mister. You 'n me have a reckoning to come," he said, wiping blood from his face with the sleeve of his hand.

"I sincerely hope not," Hood said softly. "It would really go against my ways."

"What are you? A preacher man?" the cowboy asked scornfully.

"Yes. I am a minister."

The cowboy stared a minute, then glanced at Ellis and turned abruptly on his heel and left, stalking down the street. A few cowboys glanced at Ellis and Hood and trailed after him.

Hood looked at Ellis. "Thanks. That might

have turned ugly."

"I expect you could handle it," Ellis said. He saluted Hood mockingly with his cigar and turned to reenter the saloon. He limped heavily, and Hood glanced down and noticed the built-up boot on Ellis's left foot.

Slowly, the crowd drifted away. Hood reclaimed his package and hesitated, studying the bat-wing doors, then shook his head slightly and turned to make his way back down the street to the feed and grain store, where he purchased a bait of oats for Sheba. Ellis looked familiar. But in the West, all men tended to look familiar after a time. It wasn't the man, though; it was what the man had become that made the memory keep the image.

2.

Gold Town appeared to be a town that never slept, Hood thought as he tossed and turned in his bed, trying to sleep. Sam kept raising his head to study Hood to see if he was going to get up, then resting his head back on his paws and closing his eyes. Wagons rattled by constantly in the street, and there were the sounds of bullwhackers popping their whips, shots and curses, a pair of pianos banging away on unrecognizable songs, and bottles crashing through windows.

At last, Hood fell into a troubled sleep. The nightmare returned, and again he saw as he had seen a thousand times his fiancée jerking from the shot and falling into his arms, a look of surprise on her face, and the man who shot her firing again at Hood when Hood was Tom Cade, and himself walking toward the man, shooting deliberately, tearing him to pieces with well-spaced shots from his Schofield .45.

Then Hood awoke, his bedclothes wet with sweat and light pouring through the open window. He lay on his bed for a minute, the dream still with him, then rose and walked to where a ewer and basin rested invitingly on a small table beneath a mirror. He poured cool water into the basin and bathed his face, trying to wash away the dream that could not be washed away, only covered by the morning and, if he was lucky, the night. But now, he didn't think about the night, and was concerned only with the day.

He dried his face and drew a deep breath. He looked into the mirror. His black hair, the color of a raven's wing, had night twists in it. Bristles showed along a long jaw, and his blue eyes looked haunted and pained in his thin face. He glanced down at Sam watching him from his place on a rag rug. He smiled wanly.

"Bad night, boy," he said. "How was your night?"

Sam whined and rose to a sitting position, ears cocked forward. His tongue lolled out the side of his muzzle. He raised one paw and waved it at Hood as if concerned about Hood's dream.

Hood crossed to the brownish black Hitchcock chair by the window and sat. An oil lamp, white with tiny roses on its shade, rested on a small reading table next to him. Sam crossed to him and rested his head on Hood's lap.

"Good boy," Hood said, ruffling Sam's ears. He drew a deep breath and glanced down into the street through his window. Sam moved his head under Hood's hand and nudged it, hoping for more attention. Absently, Hood's fingers moved, digging into the thick ruff around Sam's neck.

The day was overcast with faint shadows showing on the dirt street. An old dog lay on the damp ground beside a horse trough across the street. Two women walked down the boardwalk, talking animatedly between themselves, wicker baskets hanging from their elbows. A drunk leaned against a post, and even from across the street Hood could tell he had wet himself. Riders passed by on horses, sometimes three abreast, looking hard left and right as if searching for trouble. Hood had seen this before countless times when he had been marshal in Walker. Down the street, a wagon had been pulled up to Howie's store. A solidly built man in worn shirt and trousers and dusty boots with mule ears flapping carried a sack of flour over his shoulder to the bed of the wagon and carefully placed it inside. The wagon was already loaded with spools of barb wire and Hood winced, remembering times in the past when barb wire had nearly caused range wars between ranchers used to running stock on open range and farmers wanting to pen off their land to keep their crops from being ruined by roaming cattle.

He sighed and turned away from the window. He rubbed his jaw and stood, crossing to the washbasin. Sam watched him alertly until Hood picked up the bar of soap and carefully began to make a lather. Then, Sam dropped to the floor to wait.

Hood took his ivory-handled razor and stropped it on a strap hanging from a hook at the side of the table, then shaved with quick, confident strokes. He washed the excess soap from his face, touched up a few spots with the razor, then cleaned the razor and emptied the water from the basin into a pail.

He selected a clean shirt and collar and took his time dressing, tying his string tie so the ends fell evenly against the white of his shirt. He put on black trousers and a black frock coat. He used the towel to buff the shine he had placed upon his boots before going to bed, and stepped into them, working his feet until they fit comfortably against his arches, then stood.

"All right, Sam," he said. "Let's see to breakfast."

Sam leaped to his feet and trotted to the door, waiting impatiently for Hood to open it. Then, he fell in beside Hood as they walked down the short hall to the dining room. They were alone in the room, and Hood pulled back a chair and sat while Sam dropped to his haunches beside him.

Mrs. Hargrave came into the room, beaming at them, wiping her hands on a dish towel.

"Morning," she said cheerfully. "Hope you rested finely. I normally don't offer but I will for you. I can make eggs and bacon or even throw a steak on if you want. And," she added, looking at Sam, "I have a plate of scraps for him if you don't mind."

"I'm grateful and I'm certain Sam is as well," Hood said. "I appreciate your hospitality. Eggs and bacon would be fine."

"Coming right up," she said, and bent to give Sam a pat before hustling back into the kitchen. Hood heard a pan clatter on the stove and bacon began to sizzle in the hot pan. Mrs. Hargrave reappeared, bearing a large mug of steaming coffee and a plate of corn muffins, and placed them in front of Hood.

"That's to keep you occupied until your

41

eggs are ready," she said. "Butter's in front of you."

She scurried back into the kitchen before Hood could thank her. She called for Sam and he rose, casting an apologetic look at Hood, and trotted into the kitchen.

Hood smiled and tension slipped from his shoulders. This was the closest feeling he had had to being home in a long time.

The day was still overcast as Hood and Sam stepped from the door of the boardinghouse and hesitated for a minute on the porch. The town was noisy and busy, wagons creaking as they rolled through the town, loud music coming from the Texas Saloon and the Sampling House. The bat-wing doors on both seemed to never stop swinging as cowboys and miners hurried in and strolled out, contented with the drink they had taken on.

"Well, boy," Hood said softly, "let's give the town a good looking over. We'll need to find someplace to hold meetings until we can get a church built. That is," he amended, "*if* we can get one built."

Sam sneezed from the dust and Hood grinned.

"Gesundheit," he said, and together they stepped down from the porch into the street and strolled toward the center of town.

There wasn't much to see: five saloons, feed store, general store, a couple of lawyers offering their services, a bank with bullet holes in the planks from someone trying to rob it. A hard-eyed man armed with a pistol and scattergun stood just inside the door of the bank, closely watching the folks inside as well as what was happening on the streets. Hood nodded pleasantly and continued on, but he felt the man's eyes steady on his back as he passed. A livery stable and a pair of corrals were at one end of town, and across from them was another boarding-house, but there was an evil look to this boardinghouse. One end of the porch sagged and broken planks formed the porch floor. A shutter hung on one hinge half across a dirty window, and the door appeared to be held shut by a wooden arm latch.

Along the other side of the street from where Hood stood were three hotels, spaced two buildings apart, and a two-story flop-house with a red light still burning in the window. A balcony had been built above the boardwalk and three women, dressed in thin night robes, sat on spindle chairs idly combing their hair — two brunettes and one blonde. The face of one of the brown-haired women had the hard planes of an Indian.

Down the street were three eating places, one earning the name of restaurant, while the other two served customers on plank tables with kegs for chairs. The restaurant, Frenchy's, had a brief menu, while the other two, each with a sign spelling EATS, had a never-changing menu of steak and eggs. A barbershop separated the two. Next to one was a blacksmith shop and then a Butterfield Stage station.

Behind the livery stable corrals was Tent Town — dirty canvas dwellings spread in a haphazard fashion. Some of the tents were doing business as cheap saloons with planks laid across empty beer barrels. The beer, Hood knew, would be green yet and the whiskey cheap for what it was — alcohol, lye, a few handfuls of parched corn, maybe a jar or two of molasses, and a couple of rattlesnake heads tossed in for kick. Beyond the tent saloons were several tents with makeshift signs offering various services. Slatterns walked among the tents, their dresses torn and dirty and the flesh of their faces sagging from defeat. Still other tents were shared by miners, and Hood knew that the trouble with the miners must come from Tent Town, as many of them would be too young and inexperienced to know how they had already been defeated by life, relegated to toiling far below the surface of the earth in dark and dank tunnels owned by others who lived in fancy houses as far away as Denver.

The bat-wing doors of the Nugget Saloon opened and closed regularly. Hood turned and found Ellis leaning against the side of the building, in the process of lighting a long black cigar. A faint whiff of bay rum came from him. His black hair was carefully combed, and his cheeks glowed from a meticulous shaving. His face was white and thin. He wore a black coat and pants and a black vest with a discreet pattern woven into the fabric. A watch chain was looped evenly over the front of his vest. A black gun belt was belted around his waist, the ivory-handled Colt holstered on his left side, butt forward. Another pistol was in a shoulder holster beneath his left arm. It was with an effort that Hood kept his eyes from glancing down at Ellis's feet and carefully polished boots, the left one built up.

"Good morning," Hood said.

Ellis smiled faintly and blew a stream of cigar smoke away from them.

"Is it?" Ellis asked. He smiled sourly. "I suppose it is. Every day I awake is a good day for me. I think I'm long overdue for a hike to the pearly gates, or," he said reflectively, "to the other place. Which is more likely."

"We don't have control of that. At least it isn't something we should be worrying about, although most do a time or two."

"What is that, homespun philosophy?" Ellis asked teasingly. From the mouth of someone else the question would have been an insult, but not from him.

"Could be," Hood said. "I'm from the hills of Tennessee. My father was a preacher before me and my grandfather as well. I had a lot of philosophy growing up there."

"Did you?"

"And you?" Hood asked.

Ellis shook his head and said, "All over. I can call one place a home as well as another." He shifted his cigar to the other hand and held out his right. "I think we should know each other as I expect we'll be having a lot of times together. I'm Ellis."

Hood took his hand. Ellis's grip was firm but not challenging. "Amos Hood. Just Ellis?"

"That'll do," Ellis said mockingly.

"All right. So, do you own this saloon?"

Ellis turned around as if seeing the saloon for the first time. "No. In fact, I really don't want to own one. Just another responsibility that I don't want. This place is owned by Ed Starkman, although he's seldom around. Snoopy, the bartender, handles most questions that seem to come up. You'll know him when you see him. Looks like he could pick up the saloon and carry it to where you want it. His nose's been broken and sort of leans to the right.

"Me? Well, I just play cards and try to mind my own business. Except for a few times when someone irritates me."

"Like that cowboy yesterday?" Hood asked.

"I don't like liars," Ellis said softly. "That is what I call an 'irritation.' "

Hood studied him for a long moment while Ellis smiled patiently at him.

"I have a clubfoot," Ellis said.

"I beg your pardon?" Hood said, feeling his cheeks redden, knowing that Ellis had read his deliberate attempt not to look down at the gambler's boots.

"I was born with a clubfoot," Ellis said. "You've been making an effort not to look. That is what you wanted to know, isn't it?"

"I'm sorry."

"Don't be. I'm used to curious people."

Hood cleared his throat. "Actually, I was wondering what kind of law there is in Gold Town."

Ellis took a long pull on his cigar and let it out in tiny O's before answering.

"There isn't any law here," he said at last. "The miners rule the town until the cowboys come in — Frank Gannon owns the Circle G north of town on the only grass and water there is that far north. Up by Wolf Creek. It is a battle between the cowboys and miners, and the town waits to see if it's going to get torn apart or not."

"I see," Hood said. He turned and looked at the town. "And no law."

"Nearest law is the county sheriff, and he doesn't get down here very often. San Juan County's large," Ellis explained when he noticed Hood's frown. "He only has four deputies. But he has offered to put another one in here. Only trouble is that anyone who takes the badge is soon killed by the cowboys."

"So the cowboys are the main trouble," Hood said.

"Yes and no," Ellis answered. "When the miners come off shift on payday, there's usually enough fights and glass breakage to force rebuilding. And when the mining payroll and cowboy payroll hits on the same day, hell's to pay.

"There is a lot of question about how Gannon gets so many cattle to run on his

48

spread, though. The answer is easy, although no one will bring it to Gannon's face. He takes some of his boys down into Mexico and brings a herd back."

"Stolen?"

"Yes. And quite a few of his cowboys aren't as good with cattle as they are with their pistols."

"Ah," Hood said. "I see what's happening here."

"Do you?" Ellis asked. He gave a curt laugh. "Well, you'll see more of the 'happenings' pretty soon. There's been whispers of bringing in a town tamer. A special marshal, you see. Although," he added, "there is no provision for a marshal in this town. But" — he gestured with his cigar — "there's not a provision for a judge but we have one, although he stays drunk most of the time. There isn't much else for him to do."

"Has anyone talked with this Gannon and the mine owners about keeping a rein on their boys?"

"The last deputy tried that. Gannon called him out in the street and killed him. Of course, Gannon already had an edge before the deputy left the jail. Some of his cowboys were posted around with rifles and scatterguns."

49

"What happened?"

"Gannon shot him while the deputy was figuring on what to do. You'll be able to meet Gannon. Today's payday out at the Circle G and he and his boys will be coming into town. That's when the saloons — especially the Texas, the Nugget, and the Sampling House — will do most of the business that allows them to stay open for the rest of the month. And" — he deliberately knocked the ash off his cigar — "you'll see what the rest of the townfolk do as well."

"Any idea of where we could hold church services?" Hood asked, changing the subject.

Ellis frowned for a moment, thinking. Then he gestured down the street toward the livery stable. "You could ask Skeeter. He has an old barn that he doesn't use anymore. It'll take a bit of work to fix up."

"Idle hands need something to do," Hood said, smiling.

Ellis laughed. "That they do, preacher man. That they do."

He nodded and walked back through the bat-wing doors. Hood stood for a moment thinking, then turned and walked back down to the livery to beg the barn from Skeeter if he had to, hoping that Skeeter

would have a cautious Christianity within
him and would donate it.

3.

Hood found Skeeter drowsing in a chair outside his livery stable in the warm morning sun. He wore denim jeans tucked into mule-eared boots and a faded red union top beneath wide, worn brown suspenders. A dirty tan hat, creased with sweat stains, had been pulled low over his forehead. He needed a shave unless he was growing a gray beard. Hood cleared his throat and Skeeter opened one brown eye.

"Yeah?" he grumbled irritably. "You want sumthin'?"

He turned his head and spat a long brown stream of tobacco juice into the dust.

Hood smiled disarmingly. "I understand you might have a stable to rent?"

Skeeter eyed him suspiciously. "I ain't renting to another stable man. No sense in cutting my own throat for business."

"I don't wish to open another stable," Hood said. "I am looking for a place to hold

Sunday services."

"You a preacher man?"

Hood nodded. "Yes. Yes, I am."

Skeeter reached a dirty forefinger under his hat and scratched. He removed the finger and studied the nail, then resettled his hat and studied Hood.

"Well, sonny, I don't think Gold Town is ready for a preacher," he said. "Not that I'm against one comin' in and tryin' to set up shop. But Gold Town is just a little too young for that to be a good idea. You might be bitin' off more than you can chew."

"Probably," Hood said easily. "But I'd like to try."

Skeeter sighed and rubbed the stubble on his chin with a calloused hand. "Being a preacher man, I suppose you don't have any money anyway to rent that place. So, I reckon you can use it. It needs fixin' up," he said hastily. "I ain't footin' the bill for that. No sense throwin' good money at a poor investment." He pointed toward the south. "It's right down there. Built it 'fore the town grew and found I was a little out of town. So, I built this 'un. That 'un has been settin' empty for a year now." He frowned. "Maybe a little more. Can't seem to keep track of the time. Not that there's any use for knowin' anything but sunup and sundown."

"I appreciate it," Hood said, offering his hand.

Skeeter studied it suspiciously for a second or two, then took it.

"You got your work cut out for you, sonny. I wish you well, but I doubt if you're gonna have much luck. Folks around here don't care much for Sunday obligations. What time they got off from work they prefer to spend down at one of the saloons. Or raisin' hell," he added.

"Well, maybe I can convince them of the error of their ways," Hood said.

"Uh-huh," Skeeter said, and pulled his hat back over his eyes.

Hood waited for a moment, then turned and walked back down the street in the direction Skeeter had pointed. He could see the stable about a half mile distant, and decided against fetching Sheba. It would be good to stretch his legs. Sam fell in beside him.

He kept to the side of the road. A small group of cowboys came galloping by, raising a cloud of dust behind them. Hood held his hand over his nose and mouth to keep from breathing the dust. Sam sneezed twice. The last rider turned and looked back at

Hood. He pulled his horse in, then apparently decided that he didn't want to confront Hood, and slapped his spurs against the sides of his horse and galloped after the others, heading into town.

Rebel yells came from the cowboys, punctuated by gunfire as the cowboys hit the town limits and galloped down the main street.

Hood sighed and walked on, enjoying the heat of the day upon his shoulders.

Tumbleweeds were stacked against one side of the stable and some shingles were missing from the roof. Dried manure was on the floor, and swallows swooped nervously above his head when he walked inside. Old musty straw covered the floor of the stalls. But the ladder to the loft was sturdy and the floorboards were sound. Still, he reflected, it was going to take a heap of fixing up to get it ready for services. The first thing to be done would be to clean out the manure and straw and scrape the floor. Then cobble some benches together in place of pews. He could get by without a lectern, and nobody said a piano or organ was needed for services.

He drew a deep breath and let it out slowly before walking back to town. Best get at it, he thought. Rome wasn't built by standing around and wishing shingles on the roofs of houses.

Howie was stacking bolts of cloth when Hood walked through the door. Howie smiled and came down the small ladder to shake hands.

"You getting settled in?" he asked.

Hood nodded. "Been looking around. Met a man called Ellis who put me onto Skeeter's old stable to convert into a church. I reckon I'll need a few building materials to get that job done."

"Ellis?" Howie frowned. "I'm surprised he'd pass a hello to you as you walked by. He's killed three men here. God knows how many before he came. He's quick with a gun. But" — he shook his head — "I've never heard of him starting a fight and drawing without trying to talk the other fellow into letting bygones be bygones. Still, I wouldn't call him a good man who would go out of his way to help a preacher."

"Oh?" Hood raised his eyebrows. "He struck me as the friendly sort. But then again, first appearances are often deceiving."

"They are that," Howie said fervently. "You'd do well to remember that."

Hood smiled and said, "All are welcome

in God's house if they enter it. And like Jesus said, would you expect to find me in the presence of good men or sinners? Which has the greatest need?"

Howie shook his head and sighed. "You're right about that, Amos. Well, what can I do for you today? Building materials, you said?"

"Yes. I need some new shingles, hammer and saw, nails, and some lumber. There's a sight of fixing up to be done at that old stable before we can hold church."

"Well," Howie mused, "I can help with the shingles and hammer and saw and nails, but I don't handle lumber. You'll have to go to Jed Turnbull for that. He has a place over in the next valley. He shares water with the ranchers below Gannon. Not far, maybe twenty miles if you don't mind riding up and over the hills to the north. He runs cattle and cuts lumber and has his own mill for plank making. But fact is, I saw him come into town just a little while ago. He usually stops at the Texas Saloon for a drink or two and a visit with his friends before he comes over here and buys his supplies."

"Over by Gannon's place?" Hood asked.

"No. No, not near Gannon. Gannon's place is farther north. He just runs cattle." Howie's voice lowered. "People say any-body's cattle. And he's got the cowboys to do it, although," he added bitterly, "I'd say most of those cowboys haven't punched cattle in quite a few years."

"Uh-huh," Hood said, turning. "I'd better get over to the saloon and have a talk with Mr. Turnbull while he's in a good mood. All right if I come back later?"

Howie nodded. "Yes. I'll have your order waiting for you out back. I haven't a wagon. You probably should try Skeeter again. Or maybe Turnbull will help out. He's a hard man, but you won't find a more honest man around. And tough. He has a lot of riders on the payroll. That's why Gannon and his riders swing a wide berth around Turnbull's land."

"Thanks," Hood said. "I'll see you later."

Hood pushed the bat-wing doors open and stepped inside, moving to one side and waiting for his eyes to adjust to the change in light although several lamps were burning. Black smoke covered the chimneys allowing little light to escape. Five poker tables stood between him and the back, the last one occupied by Ellis and four others playing poker. To his left were a roulette wheel and a faro table, both unoccupied. Seven men stood at the bar, and there was a large and garish nude hung on the wall behind the bar. Four of the men were clustered around a fifth. All had the look of ranchers and they were laughing at some joke one of them had told. To his right, Hood noted two gunnies, carelessly dressed in blue work shirts that needed washing, but with pistols belted low. The gun belts and pistols looked well cared for.

The two eyed him suspiciously as Hood walked across the room and stopped by the five ranchers.

"Mr. Turnbull?" he asked.

A broad-shouldered man turned and studied Hood warily with sharp blue eyes. He wore a red shirt neatly pressed, denims tucked into high boots, and a leather vest. His hair was salt and pepper and his face lined with many sun creases. His gun belt was cinched high as a cowboy would carry it, and the walnut handle was rubbed and scarred from much use. But it was the type of wear a cowman would make upon the weapon, and Hood imagined that it had been used many times for opening cans of beans and twisting rawhide tight around a fence post.

"I'm Turnbull," he said. He held a half-full glass of whiskey in his right hand.

Hood extended his hand. "I'm Amos Hood. I just arrived in town yesterday."

"Well, I can use an extra hand," Turnbull said. "I need a fence rider. You ain't too good to ride fence, are you? Most cowboys won't do it. Beneath their dignity."

"No, thanks," Hood said. "I have enough work laid out ahead of me. I'm a preacher."

Turnbull's eyes widened. He placed the glass upon the bar and held out his hand.

"We've been needing a preacher here in Gold Town. Ain't never had one before so we ain't got a church to offer to you. There's a lot of ranchers, good folk, who will be pleased to hear one came."

Hood shook his hand. Turnbull's grip was firm and the deep calluses in the palm of his hand rasped against Hood's own. This was a man who ran his ranch from the back of a horse and didn't stay in the ranch house while his riders did all the work.

"Thank you," Hood said. "Skeeter said we could use his old stable outside of town as a meeting place, but it has to be fixed up some. I could use some help."

"What kind of help?" Turnbull said, a frown pinching the skin between his eyes.

Hood smiled and said, "Well, just about any that you can give. I need lumber and a couple of hands to help me fix it up for services. I can't pay you right now, but once we get going, I hope to get some parishioners working to help build a new church. But I'm afraid that's down the line. I will pay you as soon as I can."

One of the two men down at the other end of the bar laughed. "Ain't that pretty! A man comes in here to have a drink in peace and quiet, and beggars come holding their hands out and whining."

The other with him laughed and said, "Reckon you hit the nail on the head, Wade."

Wade stood and straightened his shoulders, his hand dropping down toward his pistol. "And reckon the town really don't need no preacher, right, Wilson?"

"Right," the other said, stepping away from the bar. "Now, why don't you just go back out and leave the men to drink in peace?"

His voice carried an undercurrent of threat, and his eyes grew shiny in anticipation of a fight.

"Leave it alone," Turnbull told him from beside Hood.

"I'll betcha he ain't even carrying a gun," Wade said, ignoring Turnbull. "What you say, Mr. Preacher Man? You carrying a gun?"

Tiny muscles worked at the corners of Hood's jaw. His eyes hardened and slowly he pulled his coat aside to show he was unarmed.

"No," he said softly. "I've never felt the need for one before."

Wilson laughed, hard and mean. "Ain't that something? He comes into a saloon without carrying a gun and thinks that he can be with the men."

The other four men moved away from the bar and Turnbull and stood quietly, spread apart, facing the two gunmen.

"I reckon," one said softly, "that he can come and go where and when he pleases."

The smile slipped from Wilson's face. "Five against two. You scared, Wade?"

"Nope. Seems like things are probably even now, given they're cowboys."

"Six," a soft voice said from Hood's elbow. He turned and noted Ellis standing by him. His eyes had changed color and looked silver even in the dim light of the saloon. A mocking half smile clung to his lips, and his coat had been drawn back to free the handle of his pistol set butt-forward on his left side.

"This ain't your show, Ellis," Wade said uneasily. "It's him we want. We ain't got no use for a preacher in Gold Town. Gold Town don't need no preacher. We're getting along fine without one. Let him in and the next thing is folks are gonna want a deputy sheriff. Of course," he added smiling slyly, "the last one and the others before him didn't last long, did they?"

"All things change," Ellis said mildly. "Maybe it's time for Gold Town to change."

"I think you all better just get on with your own business," Turnbull said. The others nodded in agreement.

"Ain't that something?" Wade said. "What do you think, Wilson?"

"Depends," Wilson said. "Where you stand, Ellis?"

Ellis smiled faintly. "Why, right in front of you, Wilson. Your eyes going bad?"

"Five would be even enough," Wade said. "Six is a fool's game, Wilson."

"Drink your drinks and go," Turnbull said. His voice had the ring of command to it, and hatred blazed from Wilson's eyes.

"We got a right to be here just as much as the preacher," Wilson said.

"I think you've worn out your welcome, Wilson," Turnbull said. "Be on your way."

"Don't make yourself too comfortable, preacher," Wade warned as the pair began backing toward the door. "This ain't over yet."

"We'll be seeing you without your keepers around," Wilson said, baring yellow teeth in a smile.

Anger rushed through Hood's veins as his eyes held Wilson's. He knew instinctively that he had to deal with one of the cowboys or he would lose the respect of the others and be fair game for any cowboy or miner once word got around that he had backed away from a fight. His new friends wouldn't always be around to back him.

Hood sighed and removed his hat and coat, folding the coat neatly and placing it on the bar.

"Take off your gun and put it on the bar," he said to Wilson. He glanced at the others. "Mind keeping his friend from interfering?"

"You don't have to do this, Reverend," Turnbull said.

"Yes, I do," Hood said quietly, his gaze intense on Wilson.

"All right then," Turnbull said. "You heard him, Wade."

Wade spread his hands. "All right with me."

"By God!" Wilson swore. He unbuckled his gun belt and slammed it on the bar. "Let's dance, preacher!"

He lowered his head and charged Hood, fists swinging wildly.

Hood stepped aside, tripping Wilson as the cowboy stumbled by. Wilson fell, skidded across the floor, and hit a spittoon with his head. The spittoon spilled over his head. He came up, sputtering.

"Damn you!" he yelled and came at Hood, swinging both fists, murder in his eye.

Hood backed away and hit Wilson on his ear. Wilson stumbled and nearly fell. Again Hood hit him, a swift left-right combination that landed full on Wilson's chin.

Wilson's eyes crossed and he stood for a moment, weaving on his feet. Then, he fell forward, his face smacking the floor, his nose breaking with an audible *crack.*

As quickly as the fight began, it was over.

Calmly, Hood shrugged back into his coat and replaced his hat. "Care for your friend. He's had a time of it," he said to Wade.

The bartender silently placed a basin of soapy water on the bar. Wade took it and dumped it over Wilson's head. He looped Wilson's gun belt over a shoulder and helped Wilson to his feet. Wilson was shaking his head as they left the saloon.

Ellis smiled and shook his head.

"Afternoon, gentlemen," he said, walking back toward his game.

"Don't that beat all," one of the ranchers said. "Ellis taking the preacher's side."

"I wouldn't put too much stock in that he'll keep doing so," Turnbull said. "We get any law in town, he'll come under watch."

He turned toward Hood and smiled and said, "Well, I reckon you'd better meet the rest of your saviors." He clapped the one next to him on the shoulder and said, "This here's Ira Hayes, has the I-Bar-H."

"Glad to meet you, preacher," Hayes said, extending his hand. "That sure wasn't much of a fight."

Hood shook his hand. "Enough for me."

"And this here is J. R. McKellon, Josh Campbell, and Jess Harris. They got the Lazy M, Circle C, and J-Bar-H. Respectively," he added. "I own the Rafter T."

Hood shook hands all around. "I appreciate what you all did for me."

"Think nothing of it," Campbell said. "We appreciate you coming to Gold Town. Makes a sign that we're growing up into something other than a mining town."

"I hope you ain't one of them fire-and-brimstone preachers," Harris said. "They usually cause trouble with their rantin' and ravin' from the pulpit. Gets folks all narrow-minded, it does."

Hood laughed and shook his head. "No. Afraid that isn't my style. I don't think folks need to be reminded of what they are, but of what they can become."

"There's a different one," McKellon

grunted. "And I'm one that appreciates that."

"Well, I've got branding almost done," Hayes said. "I can send in a couple of boys to help you with your church."

Harris and Campbell shook their heads.

"Afraid I can't. Just yet," Campbell said. "I'm just in the middle of bringing in spring calves. When I'm done, though, I can give you some help."

"Same with me," Harris said.

"I can give you a couple now," McKellon said. "We're just riding fence and putting up hay. I can spare a boy or two from the haying crew."

"And I'll bring in a load of lumber for you," Turnbull said. "I've got some that has the green aged out of it."

"I appreciate that," Hood said. "Before you go, though, could you take a load of stuff out to the stable? I have some things Howie's holding for me."

"Sure can," Turnbull said. "Come on then. Let's get to it!"

They finished their drinks and headed toward the door. Hood followed, pausing to look back at Ellis. Ellis lifted a glass of whiskey and smiled faintly at Hood.

Hood nodded and followed the ranchers out of the saloon. He wasn't certain, but a little nagging thought suggested he had seen Ellis before. But where?

And then the thought slipped from his mind as gunshots sounded from the street and a rebel yell erupted as horses galloped out of town.

Hood hurried through the bat-wing doors. Campbell lay in the street, his gun at his hand. Hood leaped down from the boardwalk and kneeled at Campbell's side. A crowd began to gather around him.

"Thought . . . they was . . . gone," he whispered. Then his eyes closed and he slumped back in Hood's arms.

"He dead?" Turnbull asked harshly.

Hood placed his fingers against Campbell's neck and felt the faint pulse there. He shook his head.

"No, but he needs a doctor almighty fast."

McKellon ran down the street toward the doctor's office.

"They called him a name and pulled on him," a loafer said. "He didn't have a chance, although he took it just the same."

"And there ain't a damned thing we can do about it," Harris said. "Ain't no law here anymore and the sheriff don't come here except once or twice a year."

"That's the truth. But we do need law," Turnbull said.

Harris shook his head. "Good luck finding one to take the badge. 'Sides, Campbell pulled his gun. Gannon will have those boys plead self-defense and there ain't no way we can argue otherwise."

"We still need law," Turnbull said.

"Yes," McKellon said, coming back with Doc Martin. "But who's to do it?"

4.

Campbell didn't die, but in the excitement of the shooting, both Turnbull and Hood forgot about taking building supplies out to Skeeter's old barn. The day after the shooting, somewhat frustrated, Hood sought out Skeeter to see if the livery man had a wagon and team he could borrow. Reluctantly, Skeeter let him use a broken-down wagon with parts of the planks that formed the bed of the wagon missing and the seat springs worn so the seat sagged to one side.

Skeeter was a little perplexed when Hood asked if he could also borrow one of Skeeter's shovels, but Skeeter let him have one, more to get Hood away before he asked for something else.

"Drive a man into the poorhouse what with this thing and that," Skeeter mumbled as he helped Hood harness the team.

Hood grinned. "Yes, but think how your kindness will be received. Folks around here may stop thinking you're an ornery old cuss."

"That ain't what I want," Skeeter shot back. "A man's got his reputation to uphold. 'Sides, if it gets out that I'm a soft touch, won't be gettin' no peace around here at all what with one person after another wantin' something."

"I promise I won't tell a soul," Hood said solemnly as he climbed onto the wagon and gathered the reins.

"Yeah, that's what people say. Then one way or t'other they get to forgettin' their promise, and the next thing you know a man's reputation is gone. Now you bring that team back in good condition. I don't need no wind-broke horses around here. And I need that wagon to haul hay and feed down here."

"I'll take care," Hood said, and clucked to the team.

Hood's order was waiting for him at Howie's store, and the merchant helped Hood load the order in the wagon, casting frequent looks over his shoulder to see if his wife was coming after him.

"I appreciate this," Hood said.

Howie shook his head. "A man has to do something sometimes to get something good in return. I just hope you get through the first Sunday preaching."

"Well, we might have to hold services outside for a couple of Sundays, but the Lord willing, I should be able to hammer together something by the third."

"You get anybody to help?"

"I thought I did," Hood said slowly. "But what with the shooting and everything, I expect the help is forgotten. I don't blame them."

"Folks don't like running afoul of Gannon either," Howie said in a soft voice, casting a look up and down the street as if he expected a band of cowboys to come racing down the street after him. "He's a mean one. And I'll bet you get to meet him before long. He's always on the prod for something or the other. And a preacher is right up his alley."

"Why would he be angry that I'm in town?" Hood asked. "Seems to me that folks have a right to come or not come to church."

"You don't understand," Howie said. "You come and the next thing you know, law comes, and then folks get to wanting another thing after another, and Gannon doesn't want that. That's why —"

He broke off abruptly, pressing his lips together in a thin line as he looked away.

"That's why . . ." Hood prodded.

"That's why we don't have any deputy," Howie said bitterly. "Gannon finds one reason after another to gun them down as soon as they're appointed."

"He's pretty good with a gun then?" Hood asked, climbing onto the wagon seat.

"He doesn't have to be the way the fights come about. But he does have a couple of men out there who have a reputation with a gun. A man named Bodie — little more than eighteen and meaner than a hydrophobic dog — and I hear he's sent for a man from Tennessee called Reb Johnson."

A coldness settled in Hood's stomach and his shoulders tightened.

"Reb Johnson?" he asked.

The storekeeper looked at him in surprise. "You've heard of him?"

"Yes, I've heard of him. Or at least Johnsons from Tennessee. They're bad and long on memory when they figure someone's stirred up against them."

"You run into them?"

Hood smiled thinly. "A time or two. Well, the day's wasting and I want to get some work done before eventide."

"You take care, preacher," Howie said, and stood back as Hood slapped the reins and the horses lurched forward.

The day was bright and clear and Hood relaxed, enjoying the sun making the mountaintops look purple and deep green from the forest that had been pushed back by miners over the past year or so. The thick grass smelled sweet to him, and he caught patches of yellow and blue flowers where they appeared to be shaking themselves free of the earth. He heard a meadowlark sing. Sam trotted near the wagon, occasionally swinging out to investigate a different smell, but always coming back to the wagon in case Hood needed him. Sometimes, a bird would jump and Sam would follow its flight with his eyes, but he seldom moved away to chase it. Once, a rabbit jumped, and Sam gave a halfhearted chase before giving up.

"Something bothering you, boy?" Hood asked.

Sam looked up at him, then turned his attention back to the road and the land.

Hood laughed and pulled the wagon off the road and halted near the building. He studied it for a long moment, then sighed and climbed down. He attached a flatiron to a lead and dropped it on the ground in front of the off horse.

"Well, nothing but to get to work," he said. "The work isn't going to get done by itself."

He took the shovel from the bed of the wagon, and moved resolutely into the stable and began scraping the dried manure and moldy straw from the floor, steadily working his way from back to front.

He was about halfway done when a voice helloed him from outside.

He leaned the shovel against one of the weathered-wood stalls and stepped outside to meet three men sitting their saddles easily. The middle one pushed his hat off his sunburnt forehead as Hood emerged, and gave him a friendly smile, blue eyes dancing beneath long blond hair. He wore jeans and a brown and white checkered shirt that had seen better days. The man on his left had red hair and blue eyes and wore jeans and a gray shirt, while the third wore jeans and a faded red shirt. Wisps of brown hair poked out from under his Stetson and brown eyes regarded Hood carefully.

"Howdy," the middle one said. "I'm Vince Packer and this" — he jerked his thumb to his left — "is Johnny Tyler. This other one with the sour puss is Crease Williams. McKellon sent us in to help you. And" — he cast a critical look at the stable — "it sure looks like you're needing a couple of hands or even three or four to make this thing into a church."

"I'm Amos Hood," Hood said, stepping up to the horses to shake each man's hand. "And you're right, it does need a few hands to make it somewhat presentable."

"Well, none of us is too good with building," said Packer, "but I can set shingles and I expect the others can tear out the old stalls, if you want them out."

He climbed down from his horse and tied it off to the wagon. He took a pair of worn leather gloves from a back pocket and pulled them on. He grinned at Hood, took a bundle of shingles from the back of the wagon, and headed toward the stable.

"Reckon we'd better get to it as well," Tyler said cheerfully as he tied his horse next to Packer's.

Soundlessly, Williams took the shovel from Hood's hands and headed toward the barn, while Tyler grinned at Hood and grabbed a crowbar and followed Williams into the barn.

Hood looked down at Sam and said, "Well, what's left for me to do?"

Sam ignored him and went under the wagon and into the shade, settling himself with a sigh.

■ ■ ■ ■

Gunshots came from the town along with shrill yells. Hood looked up from planing the furze off some of the stall boards that Tyler had hauled out. Wood shavings curled around the sawhorses that Williams had hammered together. Hood wiped the sweat from his forehead with the sleeve of his shirt, and watched as five cowboys galloped by, firing their pistols into the air, spurs goading their horses.

A couple of riders grinned drunkenly when they saw Hood standing by the saw-horses, and fired a couple of shots at his feet. Sam came hurtling out from under the wagon and in one leap, pulled one of the cowboys from his horse. Threatening growls came from his throat as he clamped his jaws upon the wrist of the cowboy's gun hand and shook it savagely back and forth.

"Help! Jesus! Help! Get him off! Get him off!" the cowboy yelled, his face going pasty white as he tried to push Sam away with his free hand.

The band of cowboys reined around and headed back toward Hood.

"Sam," Hood said quietly, "that's enough."

Sam dropped the cowboy's arm and went to Hood's side, crouching, a low growl rumbling from him.

The cowboys reined in and looked at the cowboy lying on the ground, cradling his wrist with his left hand. The leader turned hard eyes toward Sam and raised his pistol. Hood calmly stepped in front of Sam and said, "I don't think so. He was only protecting me."

"A wolf!" one of the other riders exclaimed. "Kill 'im!"

"Now why would you want to do that?" a voice said from behind Hood.

He turned and saw his three helpers walk to their horses and pull Winchesters from their saddle sheaths.

"Packer!" the leader exclaimed. "What are you doing here?"

"Helping the preacher," Packer said easily. He indicated Tyler and Williams. "So are they."

"The preacher? I heard you were in town," the leader said.

"This ill-mannered fellow is Croak Stone," Packer said. "He rides for Gannon. As do the others."

"You stay out of this, Packer," Stone said. He gestured toward Sam. "That wolf took after Johnny Crane. Damn near tore his

78

hand off."

"Well," Packer drawled, levering a round into his Winchester. "I don't think we're gonna do that. You see, we ride for the I-Bar-H. Not Gannon. It'd be better now if you all would just turn your horses and ride on."

"I want that wolf's ears," Stone said thickly. "Be damned if I will until I collect them!"

"Be dead if you try," Williams said. He turned his head and spat.

"What the hell —" Stone said.

"I don't like you," Williams said. "Simple as that."

"Fact is none of us do," Tyler added.

"You see," Packer said conversationally, the bore of his Winchester wandering aimlessly back and forth over the cowboys, "we get kinda tired always having to ride Gannon's range to find I-Bar-H cattle. Last time we did, it looked like some of those steers had a different brand burnt over the original. 'Course we can't prove anything unless we kill the steer and look under the hide, but it sure looks suspicious."

"You callin' us rustlers?" Stone asked, his eyes narrowing.

"Nope. Just saying things look suspicious," Packer answered. "Now, you and your boys just ride on out. And take that Crane with you," he added, pointing the Winchester at the cowboy still on the ground. "Fact is, I'd take him to Doc Martin. That wrist don't look none too good."

"Slim! You and Billy help Crane onto his horse," Stone ordered. He placed his pistol back in its holster. "This ain't over, Packer. I'll remember this!"

"Sure hope you do," Packer drawled.

Silently, the cowboys turned their horses and trotted off. Crane rode slumped over the saddle, his right hand cradled against his chest. One of the cowboys took the reins from Crane and started back toward town.

"Guess it's all over," Williams said. He hawked and spat again. "Too bad. It woulda done the valley good if we could've read the Good Book to a couple of those boys."

"Reckon it would," Tyler said. He lowered the hammer of his Winchester and slid it back into its sheath. "But maybe we'll get the chance again."

Packer hooked his arm under his rifle and gave Hood a grin. "And you better watch yourself, preacher. Those boys don't forget. Some of them rode with the Broken Arrow outfit down Mogollon way. Croak was one of 'em. Fancies himself a gunman. Word is that he killed two men. But I ain't seen any of his cemeteries. Some say Gannon was, too. Since he came up here, ranchers have been missing a lot of cattle."

"I see," Hood said thoughtfully. He had heard of the Broken Arrow. That outfit had tried to keep the range free from Glidden wire when some of the ranchers went together to build drift fences to keep stock from wandering too far. A range war was threatening before Matt Brennan, the Mora gunfighter, rode into the country. The Broken Arrow thought it could drive Brennan away, but the gunfighter proved to be a harder case than they expected. After he killed the top gun on the Broken Arrow, the ranchers banded behind Brennan and drove the gunmen away from the Broken Arrow.

"You think there's going to be trouble?" Hood asked.

Tyler grinned. "No doubt about it. There always is."

Williams pointed toward town. "Looks like we're gonna be busier than before. Unless I miss my guess, that's Turnbull in that wagon with a load of lumber. And ain't those two riding with him from the J-Bar-H?"

Tyler took his hat off and held it high to shield his eyes from the sun. "Think you're right, Crease. That looks like Harry Owens and Junior Manning. He's the one on the left. Think they're comin' to help us?"

"Mr. Harris said he would send a couple men in to help us," Hood said, watching the riders. Sam rose, slipped back under the wagon, and sat on his haunches, red tongue lolling out of his mouth. His yellow eyes carefully watched the wagon and the two men as they came near the others.

Owens had salt-and-pepper hair with wrinkles running across his face. He wore jeans and a blue work shirt. Manning had gray hair and brown eyes, his clothes a copy of Owens's.

Turnbull looked grim as he pulled up beside Hood.

"Here's the lumber I promised, preacher," Turnbull said. "There's been trouble in town. A bunch of cowboys rode through, a-shooting off their irons. One bullet chanced to hit Bledsoe's wife as she was crossing the street."

"Is she all right?" Hood asked, frowning.

"Looks to be. But I don't know. Ol' Doc's with her now." He looked into the distance beyond them. "You have trouble, too?"

"A bit," Hood said.

"Gannon riders," Packer said. "One of them was Croak Stone."

"Croak! Well, it looks like you got off

easy," Manning said. "I'm Junior Manning and this 'un here is Harry Owens. Mr. Harris sent us and said you need a little carpenter work done."

"Croak didn't want to go up against three Winchesters," Parker said. "And you are a sight for sore eyes. We hope to get this building ready for Sunday services. Although," he added, turning and looking at the stable critically, "I think it's gonna take at least two weeks 'fore this thing is ready."

"Then we'd better get to work," Owens said, swinging down from his sorrel. "And am I glad you needed help. Rather do carpenter work than put up hay."

"I've done a bit of carpentering," Manning said, following Owens to the ground. "I can build pews, if'n you like."

"I'll work the sides with Williams," Owens said. He pulled a pair of worn leather work gloves from a back pocket. "That is, if that's all right with you, preacher?"

"It certainly is," Hood said gratefully. He indicated the stable boards. "I've been working on building a pulpit."

"Why don't you boys unload the wagon first," Turnbull said, climbing down from the seat. "I've gotta get back to the ranch. Sorry, but I can't help today," he added, looking at Hood.

"You've done enough," Hood said, shaking his hand. "I sure welcome your help."

"More if you need it," Turnbull said. "Just let me know."

"Thanks. I'll take advantage of that."

Turnbull stepped closer to Hood and dropped his voice. "I can let you have Panhandle Smith if you want. He's my ramrod, but he's mighty handy with a sidearm. You hear of him?"

"I've heard of him," Hood said. "Killed a few over in Texas, didn't he?"

"A few," Turnbull admitted. "But he don't go looking for trouble. He don't back away either. If he's around, I don't think the Circle G will give you much of a headache."

"I'll let you know," Hood said. "Right now, getting this stable ready is my main concern. That and what happened to Missus Bledsoe."

"Let me know," Turnbull said. He swiveled his head and looked out at the cowboys in the distance. "But I'd walk careful if I was you. Leastways, for a while."

Hood followed Turnbull's gaze silently, considering the cowboys, who were now little more than dots in the distance. His right hand slipped along his thigh as if seeking his pistol. He took a deep breath and let it out slowly. The past was still too close to

84

be forgotten. But maybe this town would set the past into deep memory. He could only hope.

He turned to Crease and said, "I'd better get into town. All right if I borrow your horse?"

Crease waved his hand. "You go right ahead. We'll stay here."

"Appreciate it," Hood said, taking the dun's reins.

"This ain't good at all, preacher," Turnbull said, shaking his head. "Not good at all. Shooting a man might have been a little easier with some folks, but a woman . . ."

"Yes," Hood said quietly. "I know. Tempers are probably flying right now."

He clapped his heels to the dun's sides and galloped away.

5.

Blood stained the front of Mrs. Bledsoe's dress. Howie was holding her hand in Doc Martin's office while he rocked to and fro, tears streaming down his face.

"How bad is it?" he asked Martin.

"All right from what I can tell," Martin grunted. "The bullet didn't go through so I'm going to have to go after it and hope that it's not in a hard place. Three inches higher and it would have torn her face all to hell."

"They shot my wife!" Howie blubbered.

"And that's not the worst of it," Martin said in a low voice while he packed a bandage around the wound. He glanced at Hood. "I don't mean this isn't bad enough, but folks have been upset for quite a while with the happenings around here. There's been talk of forming a vigilante committee. And you know what that means. Mark my words. This is a bad one."

Hood nodded. A vigilante committee would start out with all good intentions, but after they took care of the real bad men, they'd start looking around for others to hang. Soon, members of the committee would start focusing on those they had a grudge against, and innocents would soon be swinging from the nearest tree or sign.

"We gotta do something for law around here!" a loud voice proclaimed from the bottom of the stairs leading to Martin's office. "Now the cowboys are shooting at our womenfolk and who knows who's next? We need some men who aren't afraid of bringing law and order to Gold Town."

"That's Tom Howard. He owns the Homestead Mine — the largest around. The last two gold shipments he tried to make were held up near Road Agent's Rock, about ten miles south. He's been a hothead ever since the first shipment was stolen," Doc Martin said.

Hood sighed and walked out on the landing of the stairwell.

"Folks!" he called out, raising his hands. "Listen! Listen!"

The voices died away and the onlookers turned questioningly toward him.

"Taking the law into your own hands isn't the answer to your problems. Nothing good comes out of forming a vigilante committee."

"We need to do something!" a voice shouted from the back of the crowd.

"I know that, but there must be regulated law. Not a group of men hanging folks on a whim."

"Law's two days' ride from here!"

Several words of agreement came from the crowd.

"Who are you?" a voice asked.

Hood noticed the speaker, a grizzled mucker in a red shirt and tan pants that showed time spent underground.

"My name is Amos Hood. I'm a minister," Hood answered.

"A preacher? Well, I wish you luck but ain't no God here, preacher. This here is the devil's doings and will stay that way until we get something done!"

"Please. Go about your business," Hood pleaded. "No good is going to come from you standing here, jabbing your fingers in the air, and shouting threats. Go about your business and think about what can be done before you act rashly!"

Slowly, the crowd dissipated, men going off in twos and threes, still speaking angrily in low voices, and Hood sighed, removing his hat and wiping his head with a bandanna he took from a hip pocket as he walked down the stairs.

"You got lucky," a soft voice drawled from the boardwalk.

Hood turned and recognized Ellis, lounging against a post, smoking a long, thin cigar. He was dressed immaculately in gray trousers and dovetail coat with a matching vest. A blue dress shirt was under the vest, with a gray satin cravat tied around his neck. The ivory handles of a pair of pistols peeked from beneath his coat. His hair was neatly combed and his gray eyes shone with amusement.

"I agree," Hood said. "But it's only temporary. And probably only because I'm a minister. I'm afraid the next time that won't matter anymore. Then, I don't know what I'll be able to do."

"Don't you?" Ellis asked mockingly.

"No," Hood said.

"I think you do," Ellis said with a small laugh.

"I don't suppose —" Hood began, but Ellis cut him short.

"I'm one of those men that a vigilante committee would eventually get around to," Ellis said. "I'm afraid I wouldn't be much use to you even if I was so inclined."

"I'm sorry to hear that," Hood said quietly.

Ellis waved his cigar and declaimed, "Save me, and deliver me from the hand of strange children: whose mouth talketh of vanity, and their right hand is a right hand of iniquity."

Hood smiled sourly. "The Bible is a handy instrument for everyone. Even those who are disparaging. But you are surprising, Ellis."

"Really?" His lips twisted in an ironic grimace. "I suppose the Ellis you see is that. But there once was another Ellis . . ." His voice trailed off.

Then he shook himself and laughed and pointed his cigar at Hood. "You do bring a person to confess, don't you? One would think you were familiar with the mysteries of the Church of Rome."

"And you? Are you familiar with the mysteries?"

The smile disappeared from Ellis's face and the skin tightened over his high cheekbones. "There are no mysteries."

Abruptly, he turned and made his way down the street to the Sampling House, opened the door, and entered.

Hood watched him go, frowning to himself. Ellis was an enigma, there was no doubt about that. But Hood sensed a dark and terrible secret within Ellis that he fought constantly, and Hood wondered how long it would be before that secret made itself known despite all Ellis did to keep it buried in the recesses of his mind.

Hood shook his head and walked to his horse and mounted. He turned the horse's head back toward the soon-to-be church and lifted the horse into a trot. He hoped that when Ellis finally confronted his demons he would be able to help him.

"How she doing?" Packer asked as Hood rode up on Crease's horse.

"She took a bullet just below her collarbone," Hood said, handing Crease his horse's reins. "Things aren't setting well with the town right now."

"Uh-huh," Crease said. "I suppose there was some talk about vigilantes."

"Yes, there was," Hood answered.

"There's always talk of vigilantes every time something happens. A knife fight with someone cut to ribbons, cowboys shootin' out windows, someone down in the tents gettin' hisself shot, stage robbery — the worst is Tom Howard. Whenever one of his gold shipments gets stolen, he wants a vigilante committee to clean out Gold Town."

"Yeah," Tyler said, making a face. "And this might just be what he's needin' to get it formed. Then, everyone's gonna have to walk on eggshells around here. I heard about vigilantes up in Virginia City, Montana. They even hung the sheriff, Henry Plummer. Ain't saying he didn't need hanging, but way I heard it, they cracked a few necks of folks who didn't do no wrong. Just made someone mad and words flew back and forth, and the next thing is someone's neck got stretched."

"Hope you're wrong," Hood said.

"Uh-huh, but I ain't," Tyler said firmly.

"I'd say we done a pretty good day's work," Packer declared, changing the subject. He eyed the old stable critically. "Got the roof reshingled, the stalls broken down, and the wood toted out, floor scraped so some lady's nose don't get offended at the smell of manure, a lot of siding replaced. I'd say it's time that we quit for the day."

Hood nodded. "I agree. Let's fold it up. I'll buy you each a drink."

Packer shook his head. "Well, if that don't beat all. A preacher buying drinks. I thought all you folk were dead set against John Barleycorn."

"A lot of us are, but I'm not too sanctimonious to admit enjoying a glass of whiskey

92

now and then myself. We're only human. Long as you don't pull on a jug too long, I don't see what the problem is."

"The problem," Crease said, "is that I don't think this would be a good time to be in town. I don't think folks would take kindly to cowboys elbowing up to a bar. I think it's best if we have that drink another time, Hood. Best if we head back to the ranch roundabouts."

"I'm almighty thirsty," Tyler said. "But right now, given what happened and all, I don't think I wanna press my luck none."

Packer shrugged. "I 'spect that there's still a couple of cowboys in town. I don't think another couple would make much difference. But I'll abide with you two and take that drink when folks' tempers cool off some."

"It's yours whenever you want it," Hood said.

The cowboys helped Hood carry the tools and lumber inside the stable, then mounted their horses and with a wave of hands, rode at a trot in a wide loop that would take them around Gold Town.

"You know, Sam," Hood said quietly, "I think bad things are coming."

Sam whined, and Hood paused to ruffle his fur and scratch behind his ears before climbing into the wagon and driving back to town.

6.

The summons came just after Hood had finished supper and was taking a walk around town with Sam. All at once, Howie stepped beside him. Hood smiled at him and asked, "How is your wife?"

"She'll live," Howie said quickly. He glanced around furtively and lowered his voice. "We're having a town meeting at my store at eight. We'd like you to be there."

Hood eyed him curiously. An uneasy feeling began to spread over him. "What kind of town meeting?"

"To decide what we are going to do," Howie answered.

Vigilante justice, Hood thought, disheartened. *Why is it that people always want to rush to vigilante law to solve their problems? Why?*

"Yes," he said slowly. "I'll be there."

Howie looked at him sharply. "You don't sound too enthused about it, Reverend."

"I guess I'm not," Hood said. "I don't believe in vigilante law. But I'll come."

"Good," Howie said, and stepped away from Hood and walked back to his store.

Hood shook his head and looked down at Sam. "Well, boy, it looks like we are going to have our work cut out for us. I just hope I can convince them not to resort to vigilante law. I don't know how, but I'm going to try."

Sam stepped in front of Hood and nudged his head against Hood's leg, stopping him.

At the same time, a crowd boiled out of the Nugget and surrounded two men who were warily waving knives at each other. Hood tried to push through the crowd, but couldn't. He watched helplessly as the older one sliced at the other's belly, but the miner skipped nimbly away. Again, the older one tried to gut the younger one, and again caught only air with his knife. The third time he tried, the younger one glided to the older's side and stabbed him in the belly, then ripped out and stepped back. For a moment, the older one stood, looking stupidly down at himself as his intestines began to roll out. He tried to push them back in. His knees buckled and he fell to the ground, still trying to stop what was happening to him, but the gash was too large and he fell forward on his face in the dust.

A victory yell went up from the miners and the few cowboys that were in the crowd. The young man smiled triumphantly, and accepted the glad hands that patted him on the back as the crowd moved back into the Nugget. Hood knelt by the miner and rolled him over. The miner tried to speak. Then his body spasmed, his eyes rolled back into his head, and a slow sigh slipped from him and he was dead.

"He dead, Reverend?"

Hood nodded. "Yes. Yes, he's dead."

Four men appeared around the miner and lifted him up.

"We'll take him to the undertaker," one said.

"Thank you," Hood answered and rose, dusting his knees off with his hands. He took out his watch. It was almost eight now. He sighed heavily and turned his way back toward the store. It would be better if he was on time or even a little early, before the insurrectionists took control of the meeting.

Howie looked around the room, counting heads. Satisfied with his count, he nodded and directed his attention to Hood.

"The doc says Hazel is going to be all

right. But her being shot should just be a warning of the need we have. Most of you know Amos Hood here. He's the new preacher in town. I asked him here tonight to try and keep things in order. We don't want to fly off the handle and do something rash that will cause us grief down the line," he said. He pointed to the people one at a time.

"This is Tom Howard, mine owner, and Mr. Turnbull, who is one of the biggest ranchers around. You know Skeeter, and the others are John Wright, our undertaker, Bill Langford, Charlie Russell, Keith Turner, and Jeff Albright. All of them are business-men who form the heart of Gold Town. Mr. Howard is here to represent the miners while Mr. Turnbull represents the ranchers. We want everyone to have a say in what's going to happen with our town."

Hood nodded at each and leaned back against a counter. Sam dropped to his haunches and carefully watched the group of men.

"All right. We're meeting to see if we can't resolve the problem of the miners and the cowboys who have a habit of, well, perhaps 'terrorizing' is a strong word, but it all amounts to the same, I guess."

"I'll be the first to admit that the miners

have a tendency of getting out of hand occasionally," Howard said. "It's hard to hold them in on payday after they've spent a month underground. They have a right to be able to celebrate."

"We ain't arguing that," Russell piped up. "All we're saying is that they just shouldn't carry things so far as they have in the past. Their celebrations often spill out into the street. Yet we, at least I do, understand wanting to celebrate. But when other people are endangered, then a line has to be drawn."

"I say the same for the cowboys and ranchers," Turnbull said. "My boys know that they cause too much trouble, I'll fire them. 'Course, I know it's easier to find cowboys than good hard-rock miners, but maybe you could make an example of one or two, Howard, and that might send a message to the others."

Howard shook his head. "We're having trouble right now with the miners. They want to form a union and it would take just something like that to set them off. And you know what that would mean to the rest of you if the miners get organized. You think you have trouble now. You haven't the slightest idea of what kind of trouble can come your way if you decide on that action. I do.

I saw it happen up around Cripple Creek when the miners organized. The whole town of Red Rock up in Colorado was practically done in by the miners because a few were fired to make an example."

He glanced at Turnbull. "I know we could tell them that the cowboys are being treated the same, but that won't cut much of a tunnel with them. They may leave the town alone for a while, but there will be a lot of fighting between the cowboys and the miners because each will blame the other for what happens."

"We all know what happened up in Virginia City," Russell said. "Maybe that's the way to go. We would at least have a court and could try the troublemakers."

"No," Hood said. "No, kangaroo courts are not the way to go. Not at all. The problem with that — vigilante justice — is that sometimes the innocent get swept up along with those who are considered to be troublemakers. Once you establish vigilante control, those who are involved in it become tyrants. I've seen and heard of it happening before. I don't know of one example where vigilante justice solved such a problem."

"Well, what we gonna do?" Langford asked curtly. " 'Pears to me that the only hope we got, or at least the only way open to us, is to form a vigilante committee."

"I don't know," Skeeter put in. "Now, I've been around towns like this longer than any of you. And I know at least one occasion when the town fathers brought in a town tamer because the sheriff was reluctant to send a deputy to it. We could get a town tamer and appoint him marshal and let him take over. But," he warned, "town tamers don't come cheap. You all are gonna have to dip deep into your pockets to pay him."

"There's a problem there," Hood said. "You have to find the right sort of man for that job. You get the wrong man and you end up with a dictator."

"But there are some out there who are good men," Russell said.

Hood nodded. "Yes, there are some out there who are good men. But like I said, the problem is in finding the right man. How many of you are familiar enough with town tamers that you can pick the right one and know you have done so?"

He paused and looked around the room. No hands were raised. He nodded. "I thought so. I don't have an answer, but I do know that vigilantes and town tamers are risky business. I'd suggest going to the governor and laying the problem out at his feet. He might have the type of man you need who'd make a good deputy sheriff or, if we're lucky, maybe even a deputy U.S. marshal."

"I know of a man who has a pretty good reputation," Turner said slowly. "Ben Thompson did a good job over in Hayes. It took him about six months, but he put that town right."

"Thompson?" Langford asked, aghast at Turner's suggestion. "He comes and his partner, Bowdine, comes as well. And we all know what Bowdine's like. They say he's killed forty men."

"I think Thompson can keep him in line," Turner said. "Leastways, I never heard otherwise. As far as Bowdine goes" — he shrugged — "he sets up a saloon wherever he and Thompson land. He wouldn't be any different a man than the others who own saloons here."

"The hell he wouldn't," Langford protested. "People back East even write dime novels about him. Art Bowdine. The Widowmaker."

"Dime novels don't mean nothing," Turner said. "You know how things are exaggerated in them."

"Yeah, but the exaggeration has to begin somewhere, have something to hook on to. Bowdine's a killer. Ain't no two ways about it. And I ain't too sure about Thompson either. What do you say, Reverend?" Langford asked.

Hood sighed and spread his fingers open in front of him. "I can only tell you that those who live by the sword die by it and those who hire the sword regret it."

"I put it to a vote," Turner said. "Otherwise, we can stay here all night arguing back and forth and settling nothing. Who's in favor of hiring Thompson?"

Five hands went up. Turner looked around the room in satisfaction. "Then it's settled. I'll get word off to him tomorrow."

"Somehow," Hood murmured, "I think we have just reaped the whirlwind."

Hood left, making his way back to Mrs. Hargrave's boardinghouse, troubled about what had just occurred with the town fathers in Bledsoe's General Store. He remembered the time he had spent as a lawman back in Walker, Kansas, before giving up his badge to become a minister. Lawman? He laughed grimly. Just a badge for what amounted to a legal town tamer, which in all reality was what Ben Thompson seemed to be. A terrible time, and Hood had come close to being little more than a murderer protected by the law.

Despairing, he shook his head, trying to think, to come up with an alternative plan that would be acceptable to those who now had the blood bit between their teeth and were willing to ride with it on pale horses. The Four Horsemen of the Apocalypse were coming nearer and nearer to Gold Town, and those who had just voted for Thompson did not foresee that the Horsemen meant the end of time.

"Nice evening, preacher," a voice said from the boardwalk.

Hood turned and recognized Ellis standing next to a post. The hot coal of Ellis's cigar glowed as he drew on it again and blew out a stream of smoke. Hood hesitated, then stepped up onto the boardwalk. Two chairs stood under the overhang. He took one. Ellis dropped into the other.

"Yes," he sighed, "I suppose it is in one way, but not the other."

Ellis raised his eyebrows and said, "The meeting at Howie's place?"

Hood looked at him in the growing dark. "You know about that?"

"Everyone knows about that," Ellis said, gently knocking the ash from his cigar. "And word around is that they plan on bringing in someone who can make law and order stick in Gold Town."

Hood shook his head and said, "That's a bad idea. A very bad idea."

"Incidis in Scyllam cupiens vitare Charybdim," Ellis said. "People fall into Scylla while trying to avoid Charybdis. And you, right now, find yourself between the monster and the whirlpool. You can't stop the whirlwind unless you sell your soul to the devil. And that would defeat your purpose in life, wouldn't it?"

"Is that what you'd do, Ellis?" Hood asked.

"I already have," Ellis said mockingly. "They come up with a name?"

Hood nodded. "Ben Thompson."

"Which means Bowdine will come as well," Ellis mused. "They are one and inseparable. You ever see them work?"

Hood shook his head. "I heard about them once."

"I saw them a couple of years ago in Hayes. Bowdine watches Thompson's back when Thompson has to face someone he's put out of town. The funny thing is, Bowdine is really faster than Thompson. But he seems willing to be Thompson's friend and let Thompson have the glory." His lips twisted. "If, that is, you can find glory in shooting down someone who has no chance against you."

105

"It looks like we are going to have to put up with them, though," Hood said regretfully.

"Then you'd better have more coffins made. A bloodbath is coming. Gannon's cowboys won't take too kindly being told to stay out of town. I've heard talk about the miners forming a union if they are not allowed to come into town when they wish." Ellis laughed briefly. "Maybe it's Thompson who'll find himself between Scylla and Charybdis. Now, that would be something to see."

"You think that will happen?"

"No."

"Then, what do you think we should do?"

"*We?* I hope that's the royal 'we' you're using. Do? The only thing you can do; sit by and let happen what happens until the townfolk get fed up with Thompson and Bowdine. The savior has been appointed and he already has a good start on his apostles."

They remained silent for a while in the dark. Then Hood suddenly said, "You know, Ellis, every time I run into you, I think I've seen you before."

"Maybe you have, Reverend. If not in this life, then maybe in a previous one."

He threw his cigar into the street, touched

the brim of his hat, and strolled down to the Sampling House and entered.

Hood rubbed the pads of his fingers against his eyes. He was certain now that he had seen Ellis before, but where?

The sun shone brightly when Hood awoke. For a minute he lay in bed, enjoying the comfort before reluctantly giving up. He rose, went to the washstand, and splashed water in his face and dried it with the towel on the rack beside the washstand. He took soap and built a lather and shaved, thinking over the previous night's happenings.

Well, he thought finally, *Ellis was right. There's not a thing that I can do but stand against them and hope others follow my lead.*

He glanced over at Sam sitting patiently by the door.

"Ready for breakfast, boy?" he asked.

Sam turned and scratched determinedly at the door.

Laughing, Hood took his hat, opened the door, and walked down the hall to breakfast. Mrs. Hargrave came out of the kitchen, placed a mug in front of him, and said, "You look like you could use a dozen eggs and a rasher of bacon."

"Half a dozen eggs," Hood said, smiling. "And half the bacon."

"Comin' up," she said. "Coffee's in front of you." She looked down at Sam. "Come on, your breakfast is ready."

Sam followed her into the kitchen, while Hood poured a cup of coffee and sat back in the chair, enjoying the first cup of the day. He half-closed his eyes and listened to her bustling around in the kitchen.

The sound of a woman fixing breakfast is a good sound, he thought. *Strange that others don't take pleasure in easy sounds like that.*

Then the thought of what had transpired in the night came to him, and he became agitated and fretful. The others had not seen what happened when men like Thompson and his friend came into a town. They just followed the exploits of those men by reading about them in newspapers and dime novels. There, Thompson and Bowdine appeared like knights in shining armor, battling the dragons for the innocent.

But there could never be innocence as long as those two were in a town. Such men drew trouble like iron to a magnet. They thrived on trouble and when trouble was not there, often made trouble themselves to justify being alive.

"Here you are," Mrs. Hargrave said, placing a hot plate in front of Hood. She stood back and hesitated, hands on hips.

"That meeting last night, Mr. Hood, what was it all about?"

Hood shook his head. "They decided to bring in Ben Thompson to put things right in town."

"Lord have mercy!" Mrs. Hargrave said. "That is not going to go well with Gannon and the miners. They give a thought about that?"

"It didn't make any difference. They had already made up their minds about what to do: vigilantes or a town tamer. There was a lot of talk about vigilantes, but I really don't think many there had the heart for setting themselves up as judge, jury, and executioner. It takes a certain type of man to cold-bloodedly hang a man and stand by and watch him die. Much better to bring in Thompson and wash their hands free like Pontius Pilate, letting the blood soak Thompson's hands. The only thing is that men like Thompson don't worry about killing. It is as natural to them as breathing."

Mrs. Hargrave pursed her lips disapprovingly and said, "Well, I reckon they're gonna have to learn that they are just as guilty as Thompson. Some people just have to learn the hard way despite being told."

She changed the subject. "How you coming along with Skeeter's old stable?"

"Making progress. Slow but certain. I figure another week or two and we'll have a church. Meanwhile, I need to find somewhere to hold church until we finish."

"The only place I can think of would be one of the saloons. Of course, you can use my stable if you wish, but that would be just as bad as what you have now. At least with a saloon, you'd have chairs."

"I'll have to give some thought to that," Hood said, smiling. "There'll be some who will object because a saloon will never be anything else but a saloon. Maybe we can sort of sweep things up and hold meetings in the stable until it's finished and the pews are in place."

"Either way," Mrs. Hargrave said. "But the sooner you get church started here, the better off you'll be if you want to give voice to your thoughts. And to get support from those who have been waiting for someone like you to come along."

She nodded at Hood and went back into the kitchen. Hood finished his breakfast and rose, calling for Sam.

They left, Sam holding the bone in his mouth as he trotted beside Hood to the wagon. Sam leaped into the back of the wagon and settled down to gnaw at the bone while Hood hooked up the team.

Soon, they were heading out east of town toward the stable. Hood looked forward to the day. Honest labor gave a man a certain feeling of accomplishment and well-being. He could use all that he could get.

The three cowboys were waiting for him when he arrived at the old stable. Packer greeted him cheerfully, while Crease and Tyler nodded somberly.

"We heard that there was a meetin' last night," Crease said. "You know what happened? Was it vigilantes?"

Hood shrugged. "No. They voted to bring in Ben Thompson."

Tyler swore and looked at Packer and Crease. "You know what that means. Our time in town is short-lived."

"Not necessarily," Hood said. "You step quietly when you come to town, I don't imagine he'll do anything against you."

"You know him?" Crease asked.

"I've heard about him," Hood said cautiously.

"And Bowdine?"

"And Bowdine," Hood answered. "He's good with a gun. Quick and very good."

"Well," Packer said, thumbing his hat back on his head, revealing a large white band where the sun hadn't touched. "If Bowdine

111

is coming, then I think we'll be all right. He's probably going to open a saloon and won't want us cowboys not coming in."

"Then again, maybe he don't care," Tyler said.

"I'd say just leave your guns at the ranch when you come into town."

"What!" the three asked, shocked.

"If you don't have any guns, then there's really nothing that Thompson can do, right? Neither one of you is a gunman, so you'd be safer if you're not carrying."

"Makes sense," Packer mused. He hawked and spat to the side. "No use giving him a way to call us out. Besides, we ain't the only cowboys that will be coming to town. There's gonna be others. I don't see him singling us out. We're just dodgin' shadows. Ain't no sense cryin' wolf until he's at your door."

Hood nodded his agreement.

"Well," Tyler said doubtfully. "I guess we'd be better off if we left our guns at the ranch. Makes sense what you say."

"Yep," Packer said. He took his leather work gloves from a back pocket. "In the meantime, let's see what we can do with this old place." He jerked a thumb at the stable.

By noon, they had finished repairing the walls and were rough-cobbling the pews together. Hood finished his pulpit and told the others that it was time to get lunch. The others agreed and followed Hood as he drove the wagon back to town. They pulled up in front of Frenchy's and tied off their horses. When they entered, Hood noticed Jess Harris sitting at the back, facing the door. He waved at them and motioned for them to come to the table next to him, which was set for four.

They made their way through the crowded tables until they came to the one next to Harris.

"Light and talk awhile," Harris said pleasantly. "I hear that you're coming along just fine on redoing Skeeter's old stable. Howdy, Packer, Crease, Tyler."

"It's taking shape," Hood said, shaking his hand. The others shook his hand also and settled in the table's chairs.

"How's the grass up at your place?" Packer asked.

Harris shook his head. "Well, it's been better, but we're able to put up some hay. I think we'll winter through just fine. How's

McKellon doing?"

"All right," Crease said. "Looks like the field alongside the sweet water is going to yield a lot. He's cut a lot of grass and has it drying in windrows. Should start putting that up pretty soon." He made a face. "We got the easy job, helping the reverend out."

"Shore beats putting up hay," Tyler said.

They all laughed, then Harris frowned.

"I hear Hayes has lost a few steers."

"Rustlers, I'll bet," Packer said. "They start mounting up this time of year. Reckon they're putting in for the winter themselves. I wouldn't put it past Gannon to have a finger or two in the pot."

Crease shook his head. "Way I heard it, Gannon's down in Mexico gathering another herd."

"Yeah," Tyler said dryly. "And I can imagine how he gathers them. He'd better be careful. I hear that Juan Ramirez is getting as mad as a rabid wolf about losing so many cattle. Put on a few more riders, the way I heard it. All good with a gun."

"Well, maybe we'll get lucky and Gannon will run into them," Packer said.

"Maybe he might," Tyler said.

"Boys, wishing another to come on hard times isn't right," Hood said.

"I know it goes against your grain, Reverend," Crease said. "But I believe God is looking elsewhere right now, given what's happening here and about to happen."

"What d'you mean?" Harris asked.

Crease lowered his voice. "You know the town boys got together last night and are bringing in Ben Thompson."

"Yeah," Packer said. "And you also know that they bring in Thompson, Bowdine comes along. Like Thompson's shadow. He watches Thompson's back."

"When'd this all come about?" Harris frowned.

"Last night," Hood said. "They had a town meeting over at Bledsoe's place."

"You there?" Harris asked, his eyes narrowing fractionally.

"Yes, I was there," Hood answered. "At least they didn't agree on forming vigilantes. For all of what he is, Thompson will be the law. And we need law here in Gold Town. Although," he added, "I don't agree with bringing in a shootist."

Harris gave a long sigh. "I reckon the first thing he'll do is post the cowboys out of town. Can't post the miners because they bring more money into town than the cowboys and the miners are already here."

"I guess we'll have to wait and see," Packer said.

Frenchy came to their table, carrying a pot of coffee, four cups hooked on the fingers of his other hand. Each man ordered steak and eggs. Frenchy took their order back to the kitchen.

"Well," Harris said, pushing himself away from the table. "I reckon the only thing for us is to wait and see."

"Seems like it," Packer said.

Harris said his good-byes and left. Crease looked skeptically at the others.

"Sure doesn't seem worried much," he said.

"He will be," Tyler said sourly.

"I hope not," Hood said.

After finishing their meal, Hood decided to stop by Bledsoe's and pick up some whitewash to take back to the soon-to-be church.

"Uh-huh," Packer said, eying the whitewash glumly. "I reckon I see what's in store for us now. I gave up whitewashing when I came out West. Seemed like every year Pa was having my brother and me putting a new coat of whitewash on our fence and once every two, three years on the house."

"Well, it's gotta be done sooner or later," Crease said with a wicked grin.

"Sooner's coming 'fore later," Tyler said. "But the only thing for it is to buckle up and get it done."

"You know," Crease said, "we got the inside pretty well scraped out, but you still can smell the old horse shit. I got an idea. Maybe if we burned a little sage inside, that might cover the smell up some."

"Won't hurt to try," Packer answered, then asked hopefully, "You want I should gather some sage while these boys get to white-washing?"

"Now wait a minute," Crease protested. "It was my idea. Reckon I should be the one to gather the sage."

"You can use the wagon while we get started," Hood said to Crease. "You can help us when you get back with the sage."

"And it better not take all day either," Tyler said.

"Now, boys, would I do that to you?" Crease asked innocently.

"You sure as hell would," Packer muttered.

And Hood laughed.

When they arrived back at the old stable, two riders were waiting for them, hunkered down in the shade. They stood when they saw Hood, and brushed themselves off before walking to the wagon.

"Hayes sent me and Slim in to give you a

hand. I'm Buck Holt. His other handle's Perkins."

"And two of the laziest boys who ever forked a horse." Packer grinned.

"Howdy, Packer. Crease. Johnny. Looks like you got a fair piece of work done," Slim said, eyeing the stable critically.

"We've been busy. I'm Amos Hood," Hood said, shaking hands with each. "And I sure appreciate your help."

"Well, when I draw a man's wages, I do the man's work. He wants us here, so here we are. What do you want us to do?" Buck asked.

"I'd like you to begin whitewashing," Hood said. "Johnny can help." Johnny made a face. The others laughed. "When Vince and I finish building pews, we'll come and give you a hand."

"I knew I shoulda volunteered to ride the range," Slim said. "But the sooner we start, the sooner we finish. What's Crease gonna do?"

"He's going to gather some sage," Hood answered. "He's got an idea that burning sage inside will cover up the smell of dried manure."

"And how did you talk yourself into that?" Buck said, looking at Crease.

"My idea," Crease said, adding loftily,

"Someone around here's gotta do the thinking besides the reverend."

Buck grunted, and grabbed a bucket of whitewash and a large brush and headed toward the church, Tyler and Slim following.

"Well, guess I'd better get going," Crease said.

"I'll give you two dollars to trade," Packer said hopefully.

Crease shook his head. "It's a mean job, but someone's gotta do it. After all, Vince, I'm doing you a favor by taking on the dirty work."

"Uh-huh," Packer answered glumly.

Crease laughed, and slapped the reins against the team and left.

"I guess building's better than whitewashing," Packer said sadly.

"Jesus was a carpenter, too," Hood said.

"Yeah, but I can't do miracles," Packer said. Resolutely, he went to the pile of lumber and began pulling out planks.

Hood laughed.

7.

Within three weeks, with extra help, the stable rapidly took shape as a church, makeshift perhaps, but a church nevertheless. Crease's idea had worked and the smell of manure had disappeared with the burning of the sage inside the stable. The wooden floor was nearly repaired, and the pulpit sat at the far end. Some pews had still to be added, but Hood was beginning to be hopeful.

At last they were finished, on Friday of the third week after Slim and Buck had joined them, and Hood decided, after stepping back and eyeing their work critically, that they would have the first service that Sunday. There still were a few things that were needed to tidy up, but they could wait and be finished at leisure.

"Boys," he said. "It looks like we have a church now."

"Hallelujah!" Packer said, wiping the

sweat from his brow. A spot of whitewash was dabbed on his nose and his clothes were spattered. "I was beginning to think that the Good Lord was set on making me a painter."

Tyler laughed. "You could do with a little blessing. It's the first time in four weeks that you haven't spent Saturday night in the Nugget, washing your gullet out with snake whiskey and whittling your bean with the girls. Especially that sweet, soft Hungarian devil with those dancing black eyes that you seem so sweet on."

Packer blushed and darted a glance at Hood.

"Now, Johnny, you know that a man has to let his hair down occasionally. But I ain't that wicked to be sniffing at girls like a hound dog following a bitch in heat." He reddened even more as he turned toward Hood. "I didn't mean that the way it sounded, preacher. It's . . . well . . . a man's gotta do some things to remind himself what he is. I mean . . ." he began again, getting flustered.

Hood laughed. "Better stop before you get your whole foot in your mouth, Vince. Habits are hard to break. I wasn't always a minister," he added.

Packer's eyes brightened and he nodded

his head vigorously. He looked at Tyler loftily. "Leastways, I ain't hitched to a deck of cards. And the Widow Hargrave," he added slyly.

"Now you just cut that out!" Tyler said, shaking a finger in Packer's face.

The others laughed, and Tyler turned red.

"Come on," Hood said, laugh lines crinkling at the corners of his eyes. "It's time for that drink. Fact, I just might join you for one."

Crease took his hat off reverently and raised his face to the heavens. "We give thanks, O Lord, for the bounty we are about to receive."

Holt followed suit, saying, "And thank you, Lord, for sending us this understanding preacher." He replaced his hat and squinted at Hood. "You're the strangest preacher I ever done see. Most of them would be shouting hellfire and brimstone and punching holes in the sky with their fingers. Man gets tired of hearing that everything he does is evil and gonna send him to hell or purgatory."

"Come on," Packer said hurriedly, afraid for the moment that Hood would withdraw his offer. "Time's a-wasting and I don't know about the rest of you fellers, but I'm fair parched."

He swung up on his horse, waiting impatiently for the others to follow suit. Then, he lifted his horse into a trot and turned toward town.

Ben Thompson and Bowdine rode into town in late afternoon, followed by two wagons loaded to the gills with gambling tables, a roulette wheel, and furniture. A sign painted white with the words CRYSTAL PALACE in black was roped to the side of one wagon. Dust covered everything, and Thompson and Bowdine looked out with red-rimmed eyes at the buildings and people as they led the wagons into town, stopping in front of the Nugget and dismounting.

Thompson and Bowdine used their hats to dust themselves off before straightening their shoulders and entering the saloon. Both paused on opposite sides of the door, surveying the room.

Cowboys, miners, and gamblers looked warily at them, noticing Thompson's black-handled gun belted on his thigh, halfway between his wrist and elbow. He wore black pants and a black shirt, with a red silk neckerchief tied around his throat. His eyes were startlingly blue beneath hooded red-rimmed eyebrows, and his lips were drawn thin under his hollowed cheeks covered with a salt-lined beard.

Bowdine was dressed in black with a black vest. His hair was silver and his eyes black and unblinking as a rattlesnake's. A pencil-thin mustache lay over his upper lip. He wore a belted ivory-handled Colt .45 at his hip, butt forward, and another peeking out from a shoulder holster. He was a head shorter than Thompson, but seemed more dangerous.

In the back of the room, Ellis sat, calmly playing solitaire, waiting for a game to make itself.

Hood and his workers sat at a table in the middle of the room, a bottle of Who-flung-John in the center.

Crease Williams looked up at Thompson and Bowdine's entrance and studied them for a moment before turning to Hood.

"You think that's them? Thompson and Bowdine?"

Hood nodded, his face seemingly calm, but the others could see a certain hardness come into his eyes and felt a chill pass over them. Sam lay lazily beside Hood's chair, his chin on his paws, eyes drooping, but aware of everything in the room.

"Yes, that's who they are," Hood said softly.

"You ever see them before?" Crease asked,

sipping his drink.

"No," Hood said, "but I still recognize them. There's a certain carry to people like them that sets them apart from other men. That's Thompson and Bowdine."

"Looks like trouble," Tyler murmured.

"You bet," Packer said firmly. "You just know by looking at them that you want to give them a wide berth."

"Man's just a man," Slim protested. "Every man is the same as all others."

"Tell them that," Crease said. "Some think that Colt made all men equal, but he didn't. He made some good with his Colt and others better, and others who more or less would probably shoot themselves in the foot if they ever tried to pull iron fast."

"Like I said before: Leave your guns at home and you won't get into trouble. Not even Thompson or Bowdine will go up against an unarmed man," Hood said.

"I dunno," Slim said doubtfully. "Leastways, about Bowdine. I got a hunch that he'd just as soon put a bullet between your eyes as look at you. There's just something about him that makes me think he's worse than Thompson."

"If you avoid them, you won't have trouble," Hood said. "Just walk away from anything. They might try to goad you into a

125

shooting, but you don't take the bait, you won't get yourself killed."

"Frankly," Tyler said, "I think I'd just as soon walk my own way and take a detour if our paths begin to cross. Don't make no difference to me what others might think. And if anything gets too unbearable, why, I can pack and just move on. I wasn't really looking for a job when I took this one. I can ride the grub line for a while until I find another ranch. Life's too short for tossing it up in the air in a shoot-out. I know I can't beat either one, so it's just plain stupid to go out looking for trouble with one or t'other."

Packer took a sip of his whiskey and looked toward the back of the room where Ellis sat calmly, dealing out solitaire.

"Wonder what he thinks about them," he mused.

The others glanced toward the back of the room, where Ellis appeared to ignore Thompson and Bowdine. But Hood knew he was watching them in his own way, and that he didn't give a damn if one of the two or both pulled their pistols and started shooting. There was a calmness to him that made him look disdainfully upon others.

"I think," Hood said softly, "that if I was to be afraid, I'd be more afraid of Ellis than either of the others."

The men at his table gave him a swift look, then looked away, considering his words, waiting for him to explain. But he didn't, and somehow, they knew that he didn't want to carry the conversation any further and that they needed to follow his lead.

Thompson made the first move, walking toward the bar. Bowdine fell in beside him, seemingly relaxed, but there was tension set in his shoulders, and Hood knew he had looked the room over and filed everything away. Thompson, however, moved easily, ignoring the others.

"Whiskey," Thompson said, ringing a silver dollar on the bar. He pointed to Bowdine as well. "For both of us."

"Yessir," the bartender said, knowingly bringing the good bottle from under the bar and pouring generous amounts in two glasses. He picked up the silver dollar, hesitated, then placed a quarter and nickel in front of Thompson.

Bowdine took his glass and turned so his back wasn't to the room. Thompson leaned a hip against the bar and raised his glass to Bowdine.

"Tomorrow," he said. He clinked glasses with Bowdine.

"Tomorrow," Bowdine said, and drank his

glass dry. Thompson followed suit.

They placed their glasses back on the bar and Thompson nodded to the bartender to refill them. He left the thirty cents and rang another silver dollar on the bar.

Bowdine studied the room idly. Then his gaze dropped to Sam lying next to Hood's chair.

"Take that wolf out of here," he ordered.

Hood looked over at him and gave a half smile.

"He's not hurting anyone," Hood said mildly.

Bowdine's face darkened. "I don't allow animals in my place," he said, the forefinger of one hand tapping the handle of his belted pistol.

"Your place!" Packer said. "I can't imagine Ed Starkman selling the Nugget."

"I bought this place from Starkman a month ago before we left," Bowdine said, his lips drawing down into a fine line. "I made him a firm offer that he found difficult to refuse."

Thompson looked over at Hood's group. "Art is the owner," he verified mildly. "It's his place now."

"All right," Hood said amiably. "All right if I finish my drink first?"

Bowdine gave a slight nod. "Finish your

128

drink, then take him outside. You're welcome, not the wolf."

"I appreciate that," Hood said.

"Ease up, Art," Thompson said. He raised his glass. "Tomorrow."

"Tomorrow," Bowdine answered. He looked back at the table. "You all cowboys?"

"Not him," Tyler said, nodding at Hood. "He's the new preacher."

"Preacher!" Bowdine exclaimed. His eyes crinkled at the corners. He turned back to Thompson. "Seems like the town figures it's all grown up, Ben."

He glanced to the back where Ellis sat, calmly playing solitaire.

"How about you?" Bowdine asked. "You a preacher, too?"

Ellis ignored him and continued with his game. Bowdine tossed off his drink and set the glass back on the bar. He started to walk to Ellis's table. Thompson nudged his shoulder.

"I think you need to get cleaned up," he said meaningfully, and gave a brief nod at Ellis. "You're getting a little cranky."

For a moment, Bowdine froze, his face ugly with intent; then he laughed harshly and turned to Thompson.

"You know," he said, "I think you're right."

He brushed more dirt away from his

clothes and turned to the bartender.

"Have someone haul hot water upstairs to the bath." He pointed back and forth between himself and Thompson. "Twice. Once for each of us."

"Yes, sir," Snoopy said. "I'll have someone right away, Mr. Bowdine."

Bowdine grinned at Thompson. "Doesn't it feel well, having the niceties of life?"

Thompson gave a slight smile. "Feels very good, Art. On the other hand, I think you could say we earned it."

He glanced back at Hood's group. A chill seemed to slip from his eyes. He locked on Hood's, and frowned slightly as Hood calmly held his eyes. For a moment, sudden tension gripped the room. Ellis placed the deck of cards gently on the table and leaned back in his chair, amusement evident upon his face as he slipped his coat aside, freeing his holstered pistol.

Thompson nodded slightly in Hood's direction and turned away, following Bowdine to the stairs.

"And have some men help ours unload our wagons. I want everything in place for the evening crowd," Bowdine said. A smile curled his lips sneeringly. "That is, if there are enough men around here to make a crowd."

Thompson and Bowdine climbed the wide stairs side by side and opened the doors upstairs, choosing their rooms in a manner known only to them. Then they disappeared into their rooms on the opposite side of the bathroom at the back of the hallway away from view of anyone below.

Tyler let out a long sigh.

"Man, did you feel that north wind settle in here?" he asked.

He drained his glass and set it on the table, pouring another shakily.

"What was that between the two of you?" Packer asked Hood.

Hood shrugged casually. "Who knows? People like them live by different philosophies and standards than other people. They have their own ways about them."

"Uh-huh," Crease said dryly. "But I got a feeling that he saw something in you that we ain't seen yet."

"Don't be so melodramatic." Hood laughed. "I told you that I haven't seen them before."

"Not them necessarily," Slim said. "But you did say you recognized the type."

"I think you been around more than one would think, Reverend," Crease said seriously. "You got something in your past that Thompson recognized. Don't know what it

131

is, but I think I don't want to know either."

"Let's have another drink," Packer said, reaching for the bottle. "One more to give us the courage to ride the long dusty trail back to the bunkhouse."

Hood covered his glass with his hand. "That's enough for me. A little taste and I've had enough. Besides, how many would come to services if they saw their minister staggering down the center of the street?"

"Here?" Tyler asked. He shook his head. "Not many, I reckon. Most townfolks have a bit of hypocrisy in them. I'm surprised that they brought in Thompson. Most town-folk would have formed a vigilante commit-tee. These people in Gold Town didn't want anything besmirching their lily-white hands."

Hood slapped his hands gently upon the table, rising. "Well, boys, I thank you for your help. Maybe later next week we can get together and finish out some of the little chores." He gestured toward the bottle. "You all finish that with my thanks."

"It's a hard job we got ahead of us," Packer said solemnly, picking up the bottle and shaking it. It was about a quarter full.

"All right." Hood laughed. "I'll spring for another. But after that, you're on your own, boys."

"You're the best of bosses," Crease drawled.

Hood nodded and went to the bar, payed for the second bottle, then headed for the door and stepped out into the hot afternoon. The sun was sinking fast toward the western mountains, and streaks of pink and purple were beginning to appear. He paused, taking a deep breath. He lifted his hands, studying them. Calluses had formed on the palms, and there was a stiffness to the joints that came from long hours working with the hands. But he felt satisfaction at what he had done over the past couple of weeks, and now he could prepare the first Sunday sermon to be delivered in Gold Town's first church. A melancholy gladness came upon him and he gave a deep sigh again, this time letting it out slowly.

The door behind him opened and he half-turned. Ellis stepped out and leaned against a post facing him. His eyes were half-hidden beneath the three-inch brim of his flat Stetson. He took a cigar from an inner pocket and carefully notched the end before striking a match and lighting it. He blew a small cloud of fragrant smoke toward Hood and smiled gently.

"That Bowdine fancies himself hell on wheels, doesn't he?" Ellis said pleasantly.

"For a moment there, I thought the place was going up."

"Appreciate what you did back there," Hood said.

Ellis shook his head. "Why, I did nothing."

"You made Bowdine reconsider what he wanted to do."

"Bowdine is one of those people who have looked into the big abyss and lost their souls. They can't shoot or kill enough to fill that abyss. And they don't care who is standing in front of their pistols when they do."

"You don't believe that this is over, do you?"

Ellis gave Hood a tiny smile and drew gently upon his cigar.

"No, I don't. Someday, Bowdine is going to remember what happened in there and decide that he had been insulted. Then he'll come gunning to wipe out the perceived insult."

"You or me?" Hood asked.

Ellis shrugged. "Both, more than likely."

"And Thompson?"

"It's only the marshal's star that makes him better than Bowdine. And a little more grip on his temper. He'll come along with Bowdine."

134

Hood gave a deep sigh and removed his hat, running his fingers through his hair. "Life sure can get complicated, can't it?"

Ellis nodded. "But I think you can handle it."

"I'm just a minister," Hood said.

Ellis grinned as he turned to walk back into the Nugget.

"Not always," he said mildly. He touched the rim of his hat before stepping through the swinging bat-wing doors.

Hood stood for a moment, staring at where Ellis had disappeared, wondering why Ellis was going out of his way to talk with him.

8.

Hood surveyed the packed church with satisfaction, noting that not everybody was related to the merchants. A few cowboys were there, as well as miners, even a few tired-looking women from the saloons who ignored the withering looks sent their way by the self-anointed good women of Gold Town. Some farmers and wives were there, wearing their Sunday clothes, and their children with shiny freshly washed faces and hair slicked back.

It is a good start, he thought, *and maybe will get even better.* A church sent a message to all that the town was growing up. Or at least, *trying* to grow up.

He walked up to the pulpit with Sam at his heels. When he turned to face the congregation, Sam dropped to the floor, resting his chin on his paws, alert to the people in front of Hood.

"I welcome you all here," Hood said

pleasantly. "And I thank you for coming to this service, which is the most important one, I believe, for the first service transforms a building into a church, the sacred from the profane. That, I believe, is a necessary beginning for a town to make its first step toward becoming a place for all and not a selected few."

Voices murmured and heads nodded at Hood's words.

"But there is another beginning that must be made as well. A town cannot grow without laws and people to make certain that those laws are equal for all and followed by all. In Second Samuel, we find that the sword is not enough to make a place to live. A council was held during a lull in the war so that Abner, the son of Ner, and Joab, the son of Zeruiah, could meet by the pool of Gibeon to try and negotiate a peace. But the peace talks fell apart and Abner and Joab sent their followers against each other. Twelve men a side drew their swords and tried to slay the others across from them. That place lost its serenity and became known as Helkath-hazzurim, the Field of Sword-Edges.

"Abner fled followed by some of Joab's men, who finally caught him at the Hill of Ammah in front of Giah next to the wilderness. There, Abner made a final entreaty to Joab, calling, 'Shall the sword devour forever? Do you not know that it will be bitter in the end? How long will you refrain from telling the people to turn back from following their brothers?'

"And Joab became ashamed of trying to enforce his will upon others and told his men to lay down their arms. That was the beginning of peace between the two and upon the land."

Hood paused, looking out over the congregation.

"We find the same thing happening here in Gold Town. Laws are not made for all, but only for a select few, and guns instead of swords are brought in to enforce the will of a few upon all. We cannot live by that, brothers and sisters, for that way is only death for many."

A rustling came from the congregation as men cast furtive glances at each other, uncomfortable with Hood's words.

Hood smiled gently and quietly explained what he thought should be done, finishing with a blessing upon all that bolstered the congregation's spirits, leaving all able to walk from the church with heads held high and feeling good about themselves.

The temptation had been to slip into a

hell-and-damnation sermon, but Hood had pulled himself back from the edge of the temptation and segued into a gentle talk about the goodness of man and how that goodness should be allowed to prevail and overcome evil by its passive presence.

Howie Bledsoe and Hazel, her arm in a white-on-white sling, stopped in front of Hood on their way out of the church. Bledsoe shook his head and said, "Reverend, I'm not saying you were right in your view of the trouble in Gold Town and the cure we all decided to take, but I do recognize your right to that stand. Can't say for the others, but I think a lot of them will feel the same as I do."

"You say 'all,' Mr. Bledsoe, but I didn't see many cowboys or miners there. Or farmers. Only townfolk," Hood said easily.

Bledsoe flushed and said, "Well, Turnbull represented the cowboys while Howard represented the miners. I'm sorry you feel the way you do. We must begin somewhere, Reverend. This is only a beginning. When things get right, we'll do something else. But if we are going to be a town, then we have to start somewhere. And none of us can tote a gun unless we figure on getting ourselves killed."

Hood shrugged. "You may well be right.

However, remember that he who lives by the sword shall die by the sword. And violence gives birth only to more violence. And," he added significantly, "Howard represented the owners of the mines, not the miners themselves. Turnbull represented ranchers and not the cowboys."

"We're going to be meeting with Thompson this afternoon," Bledsoe said uncomfortably, changing the subject. "We'd like you to be there since you were with us at the beginning of our town committee."

Hood hesitated, then said, "Of course. If that's what you want."

Bledsoe nodded, shook Hood's hand, and stepped aside as others came forward to greet Hood and compliment or thank him for bringing religion to Gold Town.

Hood automatically took their hands, murmuring his thanks, but his thoughts had slipped elsewhere, thinking that hiring Thompson was only a little less dangerous than forming a vigilante committee, though now, any blood spilled would not be on the committee's hands. An uneasiness settled upon him as he thought about the meeting. Would Thompson follow the committee's stipulations? He didn't think so, and he dreaded what would come.

The committee met with Thompson in the Nugget Saloon, which had changed its name to the Crystal Palace. The floor had been swept and the tables washed and re-varnished. Bottles were arranged neatly behind the bar, labels forward, and the men working the saloon all were dressed in stiff white shirts and string ties, lending an air of formality to the saloon. The piano player was working his fingers loose by playing a soft melody that Hood couldn't recognize at first; then the chorus of "Old Black Joe" came softly to his ear.

Thompson, wearing a stiffly starched white shirt with a string tie and a black suit with matching vest, his hair slicked back, his face freshly shaved, sat easily, facing the committee. His eyes regarded the members dreamily. Bledsoe was the first to speak.

"Welcome to Gold Town, Mr. Thompson," he began. Thompson inclined his head in thanks. "We thought we should get together and explain what we want."

"I'm willing to listen," Thompson said softly, "but I will make the laws as we go along in order to maintain the peace. Basically, it is simple: If anyone makes trouble, fighting, shooting their guns in the air, racing horses on Main Street, they will be given a warning. The next time they raise a ruckus, I will post them out of town. If they come back a third time, I will kill them."

A silence fell over the group, then Bledsoe spoke again. "Uh, Mr. Thompson, we hired you to do what we wanted."

"For which you are paying me five hundred dollars a month. You are hiring me to clean up the town to make way for other people to come in and settle. The only way I can accomplish that is to have a strict code that everyone must follow. The minute you start hemming and hawing with the law, adding this amendment and that amendment, you start lowering the quality or force of the law. There will be no middle ground, gentlemen. I intend on upholding the law strictly and being totally fair to everyone."

"Then you will allow the cowboys to come in?" Russell asked belligerently.

Thompson's eyes slid over to him and Russell squirmed slightly. Thompson smiled gently.

"Yes. Unless they make trouble. Then they'll be posted. In Virginia City, the vigilantes called it a 'white affidavit,' but when you get right down to it, one name is as good as another."

"And the miners?" Langford asked.

"The same," Thompson said. "They are welcome in Gold Town as long as they are mannerful."

"That's a lot of power for one man," Hood interjected.

Thompson's eyes focused on him, narrowing slightly. "I cannot work efficiently otherwise, Mister . . ."

"Reverend. Amos Hood."

"Strange," Thompson murmured, frowning. "I'm certain that I've seen you somewhere."

"Don't think so," Hood said. "I have that effect on a lot of people. I'm certain of that. I've heard about you, though. And your methods. If I heard right, you overstayed your welcome in a couple of towns that hired you."

"Which will probably happen here," Thompson said. "It usually does. A town hires me to clean it up, but once I do, I'm suddenly not wanted. Eventually, I have to move on."

"I'm not certain that we can abide by that," Albright said nervously.

"That's your choice," Thompson said. "But if you all feel that way, then you'll have to find someone else to do the job."

Dead silence filled the room except for

the faint notes coming from the piano. Then, one by one, the committee members nodded reluctantly.

"Fine," Thompson said. "Then we shall begin today. I'll have the newspaperman print up bills laying out the new rules and have someone post them throughout the town and at the edges of the town on both roads. The rules will go into effect immediately. Oh, I'll need somewhere to put those I arrest."

"I've got a storeroom I'm not using right now," Skeeter said. "You can use that if'n you like."

"Good. I appreciate it," Thompson said. "Now, if there isn't anything else, I'll get to work."

The committee filed slowly out of the Crystal Palace. Turnbull fell in beside Hood and cleared his throat.

"What do you think, Reverend?" he asked.

"I think there is a lot of trouble ahead," Hood said slowly. "I think it would have been better if someone had ridden to the county seat and asked the sheriff to appoint another deputy to maintain order in Gold Town. Folks are set in their ways, both cowboys and miners, and don't like to have their sense of order disrupted. You are going to have killings. Oh, they'll be within the law imposed by Thompson, but there will still be killings."

"And Bowdine will be there as well?"

"Yes," Hood said. "I've heard that he's killed at least forty men. Thompson isn't far behind. That's a lot of dead men who might not be dead if the town fathers hadn't decided Thompson was the only hope for their towns. No, Jed, I think all of you are using one problem to solve another. Robbing Peter to pay Paul, as it were. 'When the Lamb broke the fourth seal, I heard the voice of the Fourth Horseman and he came forth upon an ashen horse, and he who sat upon the horse was named Death and Hell came with him.'"

Hood gave Turnbull a sour smile. "I'm afraid that with Thompson you may have opened the pit and Death is riding forth."

"Yeah," Turnbull said disconsolately. "I have a funny feeling that you are right." He shook his head. "This isn't turning out the way I hoped."

Hood remained silent as Turnbull walked beside him. At last, Turnbull spoke again.

"What are we to do, Reverend?"

"Nothing," Hood said softly. "All you can do now is wait and see what happens."

"That's hard."

"I know."

"Would *you?*"

"All I can do is speak my mind. It is up to you folks to do what you want. But right now, I don't think it would be wise to try and push Thompson and Bowdine out of town. Others are going to want to wait and watch him do his job. It is when he is finished that all of you are going to have to take the reins from Thompson's hands. And I don't relish the idea of that happening."

"I don't like it," Turnbull said. "I know I voted to bring him in, but I still don't like it."

"The Fourth Horseman is here now," Hood said. "And I'm afraid Hell is already coming with him."

They walked the rest of the way in silence to Turnbull's buckboard, and Hood took his leave, making his way toward Mrs. Hargrave's boardinghouse. Sam trotted by his side, ears perked and head swinging slightly from side to side as if he scented trouble.

9.

The first killing came within five days of the committee meeting with Thompson. And it came with the cowboys Wade and Wilson, who rode into town and stepped down from their horses in front of the Crystal Palace. They hitched their guns in place and swaggered through the bat-wing doors and to the bar.

Snoopy, the bartender, dropped his eyes to their hips, then looked up to address the cowboys.

"You'll want to check your guns, boys," he said in a low voice. "I can check them here, if you want."

"Well, we don't want," Wade said insolently.

He leaned on the bar and jabbed a forefinger hard into Snoopy's chest.

"What we want is a glass of whiskey each."

Snoopy shook his head regretfully and said, "I can't serve you boys lessen you take

147

your guns off and check them. I do and I get into trouble with Mr. Bowdine."

Wade nodded at Snoopy's words, then suddenly reached over and grabbed Snoopy by the hair and slammed his face onto the top of the bar. Blood spurted everywhere and when Snoopy raised up and stepped back, his nose was flat against his cheek, blood flowing freely over his white shirt.

"Goddamn it, Wade! You broke my nose," Snoopy said, eyes watering as he grabbed a bar towel and tried to staunch the blood.

"We don't need no surly bartenders either," Wade said as Wilson walked around the bar and took a bottle of whiskey from beneath the bar. Old Hickory. Tennessee sipping whiskey.

He brought it back around the bar, grabbing two glasses as he came. He placed a glass in front of him and Wade and poured two generous drinks. They drank and wiped their lips on the back of their dirty sleeves.

"I guess we'll have a little respect here now," Wade said meaningfully. "All it takes is a pop on the ol' schnozzle to remedy things. Pour another," he added to Wilson.

Wilson dutifully topped off each glass and placed the bottle back on the bar between each of them. Snoopy, holding a bar towel to his nose, made his way toward a back

148

room and opened the door and went in.

"That'll stir things up," Wade said with satisfaction.

"Yeah," Wilson said, frowning. "But I wonder if we haven't knocked down the hornet's nest instead of wobbling it a little."

"Now, what the hell does that mean?" Wade demanded, frowning. He poured a glass of whiskey and placed the bottle back on the bar. Wilson had yet to drink his.

"It means that you've made certain that Thompson and Bowdine can't ignore us," Wilson said.

"You afraid?" Wade asked scornfully.

"Nope," Wilson said. "But when you poke a stick into a donkey's ass, you can expect to get kicked. Thompson and Bowdine have no choice but to brace us now."

Wade made a sound of disgust and said, "You're beginning to sound like you're still dragging on your mama's teat. You need a little backbone."

Wilson slammed his hand on the counter and gave Wade a dirty look.

"You ain't got no call to address me that way. Do it again and we won't be waiting for Thompson and Bowdine."

He dropped his hand significantly to the handle of his pistol, belted low.

"And you know I've always been quicker

than you."

"Then get a little backbone," Wade said, ignoring the threat.

The door to the back room opened and Bowdine stepped out, his coat off, his pistol close at hand. He grinned at the cowboys and stepped aside as Thompson followed him through the doorway.

Thompson noticed Wade and Wilson wearing their guns. He sighed and said, "Well, I guess it had to happen sometime, Art. Things were going too peacefully there."

"Foolish men," Bowdine murmured, bright lights appearing in his black eyes.

"I reckon I've got to warn you," Thompson said. "You boys are gonna have to leave town. You can come back when you're not carrying guns."

"Suppose we don't want to?" Wade said challengingly.

Thompson shook his head. "Why not just finish your drinks and go out and climb back on your horses and leave. That's much easier. And, like I said, you are always welcome back as long as you're not carrying."

"Reckon not," Wilson said, stepping away from Wade.

"I'll take the one on the left," Bowdine

said conversationally.

"This is really foolish, boys," Thompson said again, and his words sounded like he was genuinely sorry about what was about to erupt.

"It was foolish to put up those rules," Wade said.

"I guess the talking's over," Thompson said. "I truly regret this. But the law is the law."

"You ain't the law," Wade said hotly. "You've just taken it on yourself to be the judge and jury and executioner. If," he added, his lips curling into a sneer, "you can handle that."

Thompson remained silent, calmly studying them.

"Pull iron!" Wade shouted and dropped his hand to the butt of his gun. He managed to get it half out before Thompson's heavy gun roared and something struck him hard in the stomach, driving him backward.

Bowdine's gun spoke twice and Wilson flew back, landing on top of a table, slowly rolling off it to fall to the floor. His legs kicked twice, then drew up tight. He coughed once, then died. His gun had fallen from his holster.

Wade stared curiously at the dark stain slowly spreading over his shirt. He tried to bring his pistol up, but his arms wouldn't answer his demand. He looked puzzled at Thompson.

"I'll be damned," he said softly. "You've killed me."

"I didn't want this," Thompson said. "You left me no choice."

Wade fell to his knees. His pistol clattered to the floor. Then he bent forward and his forehead smacked the floor. He paused momentarily, then sighed and toppled to his side.

"And so it begins," Thompson said softly. He opened his Colt .45, ejected the spent bullet, and slipped a fresh one in.

Bowdine followed suit, then walked over to Wilson. He bent, studying Wilson's wounds. Then he shook his head mockingly.

"About two fingers apart instead of one," he said conversationally. "Must be losing my touch."

"You still needed two shots," Thompson said.

Bowdine grinned. "Mine twitched as I fired. I thought he might get away."

"How many does that make now, Art?"

Bowdine shrugged. "I don't know. I stopped counting a long time ago. Figured it just didn't mean anything to keep tally. You know your score?"

"Twenty-six," Thompson said.

"Figure you need to continue counting them?" Bowdine asked.

Thompson shrugged. "Seems like it's becoming harder and harder to remember them. But I figure the moment I stop, then all is lost and I cease to be a man."

The doors came open hesitantly and John Wright, the undertaker, peeked in.

"Heard the gunshots and thought there might be some business coming," he said.

Bowdine gestured carelessly at the two cowboys. "Right there."

He grinned and proclaimed:

Nothing became their lives so much as
    losing them.
Whether to waft toward heaven or hell
Was their journey marked by time,
And when time had ceased for them
And clearly tolled the bell,
Then closed heaven's doors
And opened the gates of hell.

Thompson sheathed his pistol and gave Bowdine a grin.

"Where did that come from? Shakespeare?"

Bowdine grinned back. "I think I just made it up," he said, his eyes laughing.

They turned toward the bar and crossed to it. Thompson reached over and nabbed two glasses. He glanced at the bottle, noting its label, and nodded. He poured two generous glasses and slid one to Bowdine.

"Tomorrow," he said.

"Tomorrow," Bowdine answered.

They drank and poured another.

Hood, followed by Sam, came through the bat-wing doors and looked first at Thompson and Bowdine, then at the bodies on the floor. He knelt and studied their wounds, then rose. He gestured toward Wade.

"Yours?" he asked Bowdine.

Bowdine laughed. "How did you know?"

"Two holes that close had to be yours," Hood said.

"And why not Ben's?" Bowdine asked.

"He doesn't feel the need for two shots. Yet," Hood answered. He looked at Thompson. "But that time is coming sooner than you think."

"Why, whatever do you mean, Reverend?" Bowdine asked, still holding the smile.

"You have a taste for it. Mr. Thompson doesn't. Yet."

Bowdine's eyes flashed dangerously and his gun hand quivered. Then he gave another laugh and relaxed back against the bar, his drink in hand.

"It's the first dozen or so that's hard," he said mockingly. "After that, the numbers don't matter much. Or aren't so important. We gave them their chance. They drew first. It was all self-defense."

"Maybe," Hood said quietly. "But they were cowboys. They didn't make their living by the gun. On that basis, it wasn't a fair fight."

"That's about enough," Bowdine said. His smile seemed stiff on his face and his eyes glittered dangerously.

"Art," Thompson said. "Let it alone."

"He called me a murderer," Bowdine objected.

"He's also not armed," Thompson pointed out. "You kill him in cold blood and we won't be able to hold back the tide. The town will become ruled by vigilantes."

Bowdine drank his drink, then poured another. "That's what you're good at, Ben: thinking. All right, preacher, I'll let you go. But come onto me like this again and there'll be an accounting."

Hood gave a small nod, keeping eye contact with Bowdine, then said to the men crowding into the saloon, "Four of you men help the undertaker to take these bodies down to his place."

"They're cowboys," a voice said from the crowd.

"They're also men," Hood said. "And they're entitled to a little dignity. Just like you," he added.

Feet shuffled, then four men stepped from the crowd. Three cowboys and a miner. They picked up Wade and Wilson and silently carried them from the saloon, Wright following close behind, nearly stepping on their heels in his anxiousness to be out of the saloon.

"It's all over," Thompson said quietly.

The crowd slowly broke up, some going to the bar, others back outside where they could spread the story of what had happened in the Crystal Palace as if they had been witnesses.

Snoopy stepped back behind the bar and began serving whiskey and beer as conversation rose rapidly in the room with excited stories and opinions flying through the air.

"Reckon that's it," Bowdine said.

"For now," Thompson agreed.

Bowdine poured each a drink and held his high.

"Tomorrow," he said.

"Tomorrow," Thompson answered.

10.

Long Johnson rode into town three weeks after the shooting of Wade and Wilson. He tied his horse, a tired, dusty dun, to the railing in front of the Sampling House, took a Henry rifle from the scabbard tied to his saddle, and walked inside, pausing for a moment, then to the bar. His clothes appeared almost colorless, but a bit of blue from his shirt slipped through the duster. He wore a tan vest and jeans. His boots were scuffed and the worse for wear, but the Smith & Wesson, hanging in the black holster belted lower than normal around his waist, gleamed, showing the care given to it.

He placed the rifle on the bar and slid a dollar across the bar to Tiny, the bartender, whose size repudiated his name, and said, "Whiskey. From the good bottle."

Tiny shrugged. "All whiskey's the same. We don't harbor local-grown red-eye. I'd recommend Old Overholt. It costs a little more, but worth it in my opinion."

Long nodded and tapped the bar in front of him. "Long as it's wet and you're quick about it."

Tiny placed a glass on the table in front of Long and filled the glass. He took the dollar and slid two dimes back. Johnson eyed him for a moment, then shrugged and took the glass, draining it.

"Good," he said, smacking his lips. He rang another dollar on the bar and tapped the rim of the glass. "Another. And leave the bottle."

"It's six dollars," Tiny said.

Johnson grinned and took the dollar back. He took a wallet from an inside pocket of his vest and removed six dollars and handed it to Tiny.

Johnson took the bottle and glass and his rifle and moved to a table at the back of the room. He stood the rifle on the wall next to his chair and settled down with a sigh. He took another drink and slipped his hat back from his forehead. A line of white showed beneath his blond hair where the sun had not hit. He scratched his scraggly beard, then poured another drink, sipping this one.

He looked around the room, noting the clean lamp chimneys, the polished oak bar, the bottles sparkling on a shelf below a large painting of a naked lady posing as Mazeppa. Twin mirrors bracketed the painting.

"Hear you got a reverend here named Hood," he said to the bartender.

Tiny nodded and began polishing bar glasses with a clean towel.

"He tall feller, about six foot, blue eyes, black hair, carrying solid meat on his shoulders?"

Tiny shifted his weight uneasily, pretending to rub at a spot on a glass that wouldn't come off. The question bothered him and he felt an uneasiness slipping like a dark curtain over him.

"Asked you a question, bartender," Johnson said quietly. He sipped from his drink, eyes black as twelve feet down steady on the bartender.

"Yes," he said reluctantly. "That's a good description of him."

"Got a wolf that trails him around?"

Tiny sighed and stacked the glass carefully on others at the end of the bar. He placed his hands on the bar and stared at Johnson.

"Mister," he said quietly, "I don't know what your beef is with the preacher and I don't care. He's mighty popular with folks around here and if something happens to him, folks are going to be mighty perturbed.

We got ourselves a marshal — Ben Thompson and his friend Art Bowdine, neither who seem to be reluctant to kill those who do not abide by the rules. You should have seen the rules riding in the way you did. Let me tell you: Those rules are strictly enforced by Thompson and I don't think you want to get contrawise with him. My advice is to leave the preacher alone. He does good around here. And if you want, you can check your guns here. Wouldn't be good to let the marshal see that you're still carrying."

Johnson gave a grim laugh and raised his glass, sipping. "Reckon I'll keep them. No Johnson ever gave up his gun willingly."

"What you got against the reverend?" Tiny asked.

"That's between him and the Johnsons," Long said darkly. "But seeing as how you're a nosy one, he was responsible for the insult of a Johnson back in Tennessee. We been hunting him ever since."

"You must be mistaken. Preacher ain't harmed anyone and the way he goes, I don't reckon he ever could."

"Uh-huh," Johnson grunted. He finished his glass and poured another.

The doors came open and Gannon walked in trailed by four of his rannies, Reb Johnson among them. Reb was halfway to the bar when he noticed Long and stopped. Gannon studied Reb for a moment, then walked on to the bar. His other three men slid up on either side of him. He tapped the bar in front of him with a stiff forefinger. Tiny slid a glass and bottle to him.

Reb and Long stared at each other, then grinned. Reb went over to Long's table.

"Well, how the hell are you?" Reb asked.

"Not bad. And you?"

Long went on. "I'm working. You know Cade's here? Calls himself a preacher now."

"I'll be damned!" Reb exclaimed.

Gannon poured a drink, tossed it off, and poured another before walking back to Long's table, leaving the bottle sitting on the bar. He stopped a few feet from the table.

"You're new here," Gannon said to Long. "Them guns is against the law if you carryin' in town."

"You're wearing them," Long said, nodding at Gannon's hips.

"We ain't staying long," Gannon said.

"Well, maybe I ain't staying long either," Long drawled. "Don't matter none to me what you think. But them guns stay with me."

"He's a Johnson, Frank," Reb said.

Gannon smiled thinly. "You're carrying a mighty big chip on your shoulder."

"Ain't found one to knock it off yet. Some tried, though."

Gannon remained silent for a moment, appraising him. Johnson stared back, then said, "You want something? Or just set on blocking my view?"

"My name's Gannon. I operate a spread up in the northern part of the valley. I'm always on the lookout for a good man. Might have a job for you."

Johnson leaned back coolly in his chair. "I thank ye. Maybe after I settle a little business."

Gannon shrugged. "Job is yours when you're ready."

Gannon walked back to the bar and poured another drink from the bottle.

"He pays good, Long," Reb said. He nodded at Long's rifle on the table. "You better plan on using that if'n you don't check it."

"I plan on using it," Long said. "And pretty damn soon."

The door opened again and Ellis stepped in. His eyes, like flat black ice, took in the room automatically. He noticed Gannon standing at the bar with his men. A tight smile came to his face and he touched the brim of his hat casually. Gannon nodded and turned back to the bar, studying his reflection in the mirror.

Ellis continued on to the back of the room, called for a bottle of Old Hickory, and took a deck of cards from the center of the table and began to deal solitaire.

The bartender came over with the bottle and a glass and placed them on the table before scurrying back behind the bar.

"You make me pay for my bottle and let this gambler drink free?" Long demanded.

"Leave it, Long," Reb said warningly, in a low voice.

"He runs a tab," Tiny said, taking a pad of paper and a pencil from a slot under the bar. He flipped through the pages and found what he was looking for. He licked the end of the pencil, made a notation, and returned the pad and pencil back under the bar.

"Maybe I wanna run a tab," Johnson said angrily.

"Don't know you," Tiny said curtly, and turned his attention back to Gannon and his boys.

"Goddamn," Johnson breathed. "I'll be a snake-crossed skunk if'n I let a bartender talk to me that way."

He rose and stepped free from the table as the doors opened again and Hood stepped in. He noticed the men at the bar, Ellis at the back and Long Johnson standing, facing Hood. He stopped and stood quietly, his hands loose at his sides.

Long grinned. "Yep, you the 'reverend' all right," he said with satisfaction. "Been hunting you for a spell."

"You're a Johnson," Hood said. "Long Johnson, I expect." He glanced at Reb. "You, too."

"You expected right," Reb said. "Reckon you know what we gotta do."

"You don't have to," Hood said unflinchingly.

"I'll give you first pull," Long said.

He crouched, his hand trembling above the handle of his pistol. Reb turned and took a small step to Long's right, his hand hovering over his pistol butt.

Hood slowly pulled his coat open and said, "I'm not carrying a gun, boys."

"Go get one," Long said, standing slowly.

"No," Hood said.

Long's brow furrowed. "I ain't never killed a man without a gun."

"I'm your huckleberry," Ellis said from behind Long. "I'm just the man you're looking for!"

His voice had a slight Louisiana drawl to it that Hood hadn't noticed before. Long turned to face him.

Ellis stood, the chair scraping over the floor. He stepped away from the table, standing easy, a small smile upon his lips.

"I'm just the one to dance with," he added, his eyes dancing.

A dark flush worked its way up through Long's gritty beard stubble and settled in his cheeks.

"You don't want to barge in to this affair," Long warned.

Ellis shrugged. "The reverend's my friend. I'd hate to see him inconvenienced."

Long rolled his shoulders uneasily, considering. Who was this man who stood so calmly, facing him and volunteering to fight with him? Most folk slipped away once they knew who he was. But this man seemed unworried. In fact, he seemed downright pleased with himself.

For the first time in a long time, Long felt a wariness work its way into his mind.

"Why, Long Johnson! You look as if someone just walked across your grave," Ellis said mockingly.

"Don't push it, gambler. This ain't your game," Long said thickly. His hand trembled above his pistol grip again and he slowly slipped into his crouch, unaware of doing so.

Ellis continued to smile as he pulled his coat back, revealing his ivory-handled pistols.

"Why, this is just my game," he said. "But as for you," he paused, shaking his head. *"Eventus stultorum magister."*

"What's that mean?" Johnson asked suspiciously.

"That's Latin. 'Fools must learn from experience.' Too bad your education didn't go far enough for you to learn the language."

"All right, cripple. You want it, you got it," Reb said. "From both of us."

"Say when," Ellis said. He grinned and softly stroked the handle of the Colt in a cross-draw by his left hip.

"Ellis," Hood began. "This isn't any of your business . . ."

"Why, I beg to differ," Ellis said, the accent growing thicker. "We've gone past you, pastor. Now, it's just between me and these poltroons."

Suddenly, Long's hand stabbed down to his pistol. He was bringing it up when a pistol roared and something slammed into his chest, knocking him to the floor. Ellis fired again, striking Reb in his forehead. Long looked up stupidly at the ceiling for a moment, then pulled his shirt away from his chest. Blood bubbled out in a froth from his chest. Bright blood, and he knew he'd been lung-shot.

Long tried to bring his pistol up, but it was too heavy for his hand and clattered to the floor.

"I'll be goddamned," he gasped.

"Probably," Ellis said, sheathing his pistol.

"Who are you?"

"Ellis."

"Never heard of you." The words were becoming harder to form. His tongue felt thick in his mouth and a darkness was slipping down over his eyes.

"It's foolish to pull on someone you do not know," Ellis said.

He touched the brim of his hat.

"Gentlemen," he said.

He walked across the floor and sat again at his table.

"Shit. I been killed," Long gasped. He coughed and a flood of blood spurted from his mouth. He tried to grin, but the darkness came fully over his eyes and he died.

"There's gonna be hell to pay for certain," one of Gannon's cowboys breathed. "All the same to you, Boss, I think we'd be better off leaving while the leaving's good."

"You may be right," Gannon said. He tossed off his drink and headed for the door. He stepped through it and onto the boardwalk, his cowboys crowding behind him. He glanced to his left and saw Thompson coming toward the saloon, Bowdine trailing just off his left shoulder.

Gannon gave them a slow smile and turned to show he had no weapons.

Thompson nodded at him as he slipped by and into the saloon.

"Boys, let's hit the leather," Gannon said. "This ain't the time for no confrontation."

He stepped into the saddle and, turning his sorrel's head, lifted the horse into a lope and headed out of town. His cowboys were hard upon his horse's heels.

Thompson stepped warily into the saloon and quickly took in everything. He looked at the bodies on the floor and nodded to himself.

"And they are?" asked Thompson.

"Said his name was Long Johnson," answered Tiny. "The other's Reb Johnson. They went after the reverend. Seems they had a beef to pick with him. Called the reverend out, but the reverend didn't have a gun. *He* shot them instead."

He pointed to the back where Ellis was playing solitaire.

Thompson nodded and walked back to Ellis's table.

Ellis ignored him and placed a red queen upon a black king, then dealt three cards faceup.

"You shoot those men?" Thompson demanded.

The ace of spades came up, and Ellis placed it carefully above the solitaire bank. He dealt three more cards. The ten of diamonds came up and he laid it on the jack of spades.

"Mister, I'm talking to you," Thompson said.

Bowdine moved to Thompson's left shoulder, his hand slowly swinging by his holstered pistol.

Ellis neatly folded the deck and placed it at his left hand. He leaned back in his chair, studying Thompson and Bowdine.

"And?" he asked politely.

Thompson's cheeks reddened slightly.

"You shoot those two?"

Ellis glanced at them.

"Had to. They were just too tightly strung," he said. "Didn't leave me much choice."

Thompson turned toward Hood and Tiny and asked, "That right? That how it happened?"

Both nodded, and Hood said, "Ellis gave them every warning and chance to leave.

They didn't take it."

"Uh-huh," Thompson said. He turned back to Ellis.

"Reckon you better take him in, Ben," Bowdine said conversationally from Thompson's side. His eyes remained fixed on Ellis.

Ellis gave a polite nod, his lips drawn slightly over white teeth.

"You are wearing guns against my rules," Thompson said, his words having a finality to them. "I'm afraid I'm going to have to post you out of town."

Ellis gave a small laugh and eyed Bowdine mockingly.

"You can try to take me in, Bowdine," he said. "But that would be a foolish bet."

"You saying you're better than me?" Bowdine challenged.

Ellis ignored him and turned back to Thompson.

"I'm willing to leave my pistols in my room if your friend does as well. Neither one of us is a lawman and, to my way of thinking, both of us are in the wrong if one of us is."

"We'll start with you," Thompson said, his eyes unblinking. "But I will give you the choice: Leave your guns in your room or get out of town."

"What? No warning?" Ellis taunted. "I

170

thought you promised a warning first."

"You killed those two. That's the difference. A big difference. They may have friends who'll come after you. That would cause me grief and I don't want grief. It's hard enough keeping the peace around here without having to worry about gunmen riding into town and shooting it up."

"And Mr. Bowdine?"

"He watches my back."

"Ah. Well, that certainly needs watching. All right. I'll take my pistols to my room. That all?"

"You'll be welcome in the Sampling House once your hips are bare. Meanwhile, take your guns out of here."

" 'My hips are bare,' " Ellis repeated with a smile. "Well, Mr. Bowdine, for the sake of law abiding, I guess I'll head over to my rooms right now."

"I thought you'd see things my way," Bowdine said sarcastically.

"Art, leave it alone. He said that he'd take his guns off. That's all I asked him. No reason to push the matter now."

Ellis smiled and stepped away from the table. He walked directly toward Bowdine, forcing him to step aside. Bowdine's face darkened, but Thompson stepped up and grabbed his arm.

Ellis nodded and leisurely walked from the saloon. The bat-wing doors swung to and fro behind him.

"You should have let me kill him, Ben," Bowdine said angrily. "He's going to mean trouble for us down the line. Big trouble if I don't miss my bet."

"We'll handle it then, Art," Thompson said. "Meanwhile, leave your Colts in your room as well. Carry that little thirty-two Manhattan in its shoulder holster and let your coat cover it. No sense in getting any other man angry enough to challenge us."

"You're the marshal," Bowdine said. He turned to leave. "Really, it doesn't matter one way or the other which I carry."

"I know that, Art," Thompson said quietly. "And I appreciate you doing what I ask."

"That's what friends are for, Ben," Bowdine said, and left.

Thompson watched the doors swing shut behind Bowdine. He pursed his lips as he contemplated again Ellis's words. Art was right, he mused. That man would cross him again somewhere down the line. He felt it and he had learned years ago to trust his feelings. He racked his brain trying to remember where he had seen Ellis before. Or heard about him. Yes, he thought, he *had* heard of him, now that he was thinking

172

about it. But where?

He sighed and walked to the bar and motioned for a drink. Within seconds, Tiny had a glass and his personal bottle in front of him. Thompson thanked him politely and poured a drink.

Yes, Art *was* right. He had an uncanny eye for the type a person was. He was seldom wrong. And Thompson knew Art was right this time for he felt the same uneasiness.

11.

Hood stood quietly in his pulpit, looking down at the caskets bearing the bodies of Long Johnson and Reb Johnson. A sadness filled him as he thought about the past Johnsons who had come after him in a feud that they had proclaimed after Eula Johnson went and got herself pregnant by someone and blamed it on him because he was the preacher's son and his future was pretty well formed at the time.

Unwillingly, he thought about what had happened when he had been young Tom Cade and had been sent by his father to reclaim the milch cow that had wandered off and was in Old Man Johnson's corn.

Tom walked on down to the lane leading up to the Johnson cabin. Johnson's oldest girl, Eula, was sitting on an old wicker rocker on the front porch, running a brush through her long yellow hair. When she saw Tom approaching, she raised her hand and drew it down her hair, arranging it to fall in large curls over her melon breasts. Tom always felt nervous around her as when he looked at her, her eyes seemed to become secretively all-knowing and he was pretty certain that eternal grace and salvation were not upon her — at least at that moment.

He stopped at the foot of the steps leading to the porch and touched the brim of his hat.

"Afternoon, Miss Eula," he said. "Your pa around?"

Eula stretched one long shapely leg out in front of her, pointing her toes so her homespun dress draped open and Tom could look up into the shadows.

"Now, what you be wantin' him for?" she asked huskily as if she had too much smoke in her voice.

"Reckon I've gotta beg his pardon again," Tom said. He looked away from the shadows beneath her dress. "Our milch cow's managed to get into his cornfield."

"Pa ain't gonna like that," Eula said. She leaned forward, and Tom could see the damp circles her breasts made against the front of her dress.

"Yes, ma'am, I know," Tom said. "But that cow sure has a liking for sweet corn and your pa's got the nearest field around."

"She sounds like a smart cow," Eula said.

She bit her lower lip, making it appear more bee-stung than normal.

"If'n she's so damn smart, she'd realize that your pa's ready to pepper her hide with buckshot," Tom answered. "He around? I reckon I'd better apologize and figure out some sort of restitution with him."

"Well, he ain't here," she said sullenly. "He went possum hunting last night with Old Hank and hasn't come home yet. Chances are he's holed up back in the swales with a jug or two. He dearly loves to top off a night's hunting with mash whiskey. Says it makes him feel foggy and cool inside. He'll be sleeping up right now, I reckon. Probably won't be home until eventide. You want to wait? I've got a goat fried up inside."

"I'd better get that cow out from the corn," Tom mumbled. "Pa'd have my hide stretched on the springhouse if I let anything happen to that cow."

She pouted. "Well, you can tie her up and then come on back up to the house."

"Yes, ma'am, I could do that. But if your pa came home and found that cow tied off, he'd figure out what had happened pretty quick. I think it better if I just take her on back home. Not that I don't appreciate the offer," he added quickly so as not to offend.

Eula ignored him. She tugged at her dress

until she pulled it down tight over her breasts.

"It shore is hot, ain't it?" she said. "Be nice to cool off down under the willows by the creek."

Her eyes changed expression and looked like two candles guttering down into the sockets of iron candlesticks.

"Want a drink of water?" she asked, rising lazily.

"If it's not too much trouble," Tom answered.

"Water's right here," she said, using her shapely toes to nudge a bucket by the porch post. She crossed to it and filled a gourd, handing it to him. "Water always tastes better when it's set a while in a cedar bucket, don't you think?"

He had to admit that the water had a warmish-cool taste to it like the smell of cedar trees in a hot July breeze. He handed the gourd back and she dropped it into the bucket.

"Tell you what," she said, stretching her arms and arching her back. "How about I help you with that old cow and we go on down to the creek for a swim to cool off? It'll be hot work getting that cow out of the cornfield when she won't want to go."

"That cow does have a mind of her own," Tom said, feeling foolish at having nothing more clever to say. But when Eula got to acting like this, it made him feel all hot and flustered inside like he was coming down with the fall fever and had to be dosed with castor oil.

Eula smiled lazily and stepped down off the porch. She stood so close to Tom that he could smell the soap on her skin and the faint sweat smell of the woman beneath. He became suddenly conscious of the stories he'd heard about her from his friends while sharing corn-silk cigarettes behind the church after Sunday services.

"Eula likes a sampling in her men," Billy Eston had said, coughing up the words from lungs filled with smoke. "And there's a lot of men who've enjoyed the sampling."

Knowing nods came from the others, but Tom kept quiet to not draw attention to himself.

"Maybe we'd better go get her out of that corn," Eula drawled. She turned and walked away, her backside switching under her thin dress like two raccoons wrestling in a gunnysack.

Swallowing hard, Tom followed her down the slight slope to where the cornfield began. They could hear the cow rustling among the tall stalks.

"You go down the left, and I'll come in from the right," Eula said. "We'll push her back to the end of the field. I reckon she came in where that corner railing don't fit so well?"

Tom nodded "Yeah. But she's a stubborn cuss. We'll have to keep her from doubling back and around on us. She knock down any more of your pa's corn and he'll know for certain that she's been in it. Fact, he'll probably know anyhow," he added gloomily.

"Cows don't move until they're pushed," Eula said, moving off to the right.

Tom slipped down the rows, jumping back and forth between them as he narrowed down on the milch cow. He could hear Eula slipping through the stalks on his right, the wrinkled leaves of the corn brushing against her dress like a gentle wind across sunburnt skin.

The cow saw them coming and tried to move around them, but they stepped in the cow's path, turning her with waving hands and shouts of "Whoo bossy." The cow flung a slather over her shoulders and turned and moved back the way she'd come, walking fast and stiff-legged along the path of downed stalks, her milk bag swinging from side to side.

When they came to the fence, she came to a scuttering halt and made one last try to get away, but Tom was waiting for her and stepped in her path and waved her through the fence.

"Now, let's see you get outta that one," he muttered at her once she was inside.

The cow ignored him and walked over to

the water trough and lowered her head, drinking.

"Come on," Eula whispered. "I'm hot. Let's go cool off down at the creek."

Tom cast a quick eye at the cabin, hesitated, then nodded. Boldly, he took her hand, feeling the calluses on her palms, and they ran lightly together down the slope strewn with bluebells and white clover. They slipped past the black raspberry bushes, and came to a halt under an old willow tree whose branches draped over the water like a lacy green curtain. Eula halted under the branches and backed against the trunk. Her eyes were shining now like sun-struck glass. He stood a few feet away, watching her breathe deeply like she couldn't suck enough air into her lungs. Then she laughed and in one motion, pulled her dress over her head and stood naked before him. He gasped as she laughed again and ran lightly past him, cleaving the creek water in a smooth dive that took her down deep into the water. She came up and used her palms to push her hair smoothly back from her forehead.

"The water's nice," she said. "Come on in."

Then, he was naked, and the water was cold upon him before he realized he'd stripped down, and Eula was up around him, her legs locked around his waist, her lips kissing him with a hunger that was both frightening and

filling. Above them, a jay shrieked and squirrels chattered warnings at the jay to stay away
from their nests in the boles of the oak trees.

Later, when they were dozing, wrapped in
each other's naked arms under the canopy of
willow, a deer came down to drink at the
creek. Tom moved slightly and the deer
paused, one foot lifted for quick flight. But he
heard no further noise that was strange to
him, and he bent his slender neck for a drink
as Tom slipped his lips close to Eula's neck
and drank the salty softness in the hollow
there.

Hood shook his head, trying to force the
memory away. But not all the memories
would slip away. He remembered that two
weeks later Old Man Johnson had come to
their cabin and demanded that Tom marry
his girl to make things right, as she was
pregnant. But he knew he had not been the
father and that Eula was easy with her
charms around other men and boys. His
father couldn't convince Johnson about that
and that night, his father explained that he
had to leave the hills of Tennessee and go
West. A great sorrow filled his heart at this,
for he loved the Tennessee hills and the
thought of leaving them made his heart
ache.

But he had taken his father's advice and

left that night, turning his steps toward the West. In time, a gunman taught him how to use the Schofield in his bag back in his room, and there had been too much killing before he became sickened at it all and left the town of Walker, Kansas, left his name, and became the Reverend Amos Hood.

But the Johnsons were not a forgiving lot. They began a feud in which his father had been killed, and then brought the feud west in search of Tom Cade. Those who found him were now dead. But there would be more; the Johnsons were a big family.

Firmly, Hood closed his mind against the past and raised his hands over the caskets.

"There is an evil under the sun and I have seen too much of it. Too many men have died for a worthless cause, seeing honor where none exists only because that has been the way of their people since the coming of man to this fair country."

The people in the congregation looked bewildered at each other, not knowing the meaning behind Hood's words. But he was their reverend and if he said it was so, then it was so. At least at the moment, some reminded themselves. Maybe the reverend would bear watching.

"There is a time for everything under the sun; a time to give birth and a time to die; a

182

time to plant and a time to bring forth from the root; a time to kill and a time to heal, although healing is hard and seldom done.

"A time to tear down and a time to build up; a time to weep and a time to laugh; a time to mourn and a time to dance; a time to throw stones and a time to gather them; a time to love and a time to hate.

"It is the hate that separates man from the other animals. And yet, there is no profit in hate.

"This man, Long Johnson, came to Gold Town, carrying his hate upon his shoulder, unforgiving, and bringing death with him. Here, he met his cousin Reb. It would be easy to forget their souls and the goodness that exists in all men although it may be hidden by some. Still, the Johnsons were two of God's creatures and although they were ready to commit the sin of Cain, they were still men. Although Cain had murdered, the Lord forgave him even when He sent Cain out from the Land of Eden to the Land of Nod.

"Long and Reb Johnson coveted sin and strove hardily after the wind.

"But should we do less than God? Jesus suffered the cross to show us the forgiveness that we must be ready to extend toward our fellow creatures. Can we be content to do less than Him?

"No. We must be ready to suffer the slings and arrows of outrageous fortune and fear not the terror that comes by night. In this manner, we can become free souls, forgiving souls, worthy souls of God's kingdom."

Hood paused, then said, "Therefore, I forgive these men who came out of the wilderness to slay me. I forgive them."

Hood stood for a moment, looking out over the congregation that had gathered to send Long and Reb Johnson on the path to wherever they had been sentenced by the Judges of Death. The congregation looked back at Hood. A few of the women sniffled into their handkerchiefs. The men, for the most part, seemed stoic, and with a sinking feeling, Hood knew he had not reached them, as it was not the time for them to be forgiving.

"Let us gather and take Long and Reb Johnson to their final resting place."

Silently, twelve men came forward and lifted the caskets on their shoulders and headed down the aisle and out the door, followed by Hood and those who felt the death of another human being.

Following the brief ceremony at Boot Hill, the crowd slowly dispersed. Hood waited until the last person had left, then stared down into the two graves where the casket had been placed. He heard a sparrow chirruping somewhere near, and the sound of meadowlarks and the sharp squeal of an animal caught in the talons of a hawk.

He raised his head and contemplated the hills stripped of trees on the bottom third and sodden with water from the various rockers that had been built to wash gold from gravel. Up near the top of the mountains were ugly holes carved in the mountainsides where men could descend into the blackness of the mountains in search of the mother lode buried deep in the earth.

He stared back down the hill to Gold Town, where people bustled back and forth, bent on their own ways, immersed in their own thoughts. It could be a good town someday, and probably would be after the scent of death was washed from it. He knew the smell of death; it smelled like bloody buffalo hides left too long in the sun and now in various stages of rotting. From the hill, he thought he caught a glimpse of Thompson walking the town, making folks behave by his mere presence. But when Hood stood next to Thompson or Bowdine, he smelled the same stench and knew that death had embraced both as partners.

He sighed and turned away from the grave, placing his hat correctly upon his head, pulling the brim down over his eyes.

Nothing could really be done for the town until it raised itself out of the darkness into which it had sunk when the gold boom started. It would take time for that. Time in which one generation would end in favor of another generation. But the earth would always be there and the sun would always rise despite the workings of man.

But that would be in the distant time, and Hood feared what would happen before that period was reached.

Back in town, Hood went to the stable and saddled Sheba, who snorted with annoyance that he hadn't come for her in a long time. To show her bad temper, she took Hood through a hard time, leaping high in the air with an arched back and coming down with a jolt that made Hood's teeth come together with a loud *snap*. Hood stayed with her until she had satisfactorily expressed herself to him. Then he rode out of town, turning Sheba toward the Upper Valley, Sam trotting patiently at Sheba's side, red tongue lolling out the side of his mouth. Occasionally, Sam would wander out, searching for an unwary rabbit, but appeared to be more interested in the land they were crossing.

The farther north Hood rode, the prettier the land became. Late-blooming wildflowers had taken root in patches of sweet grama grass and accented the green grass with colors of blue, white, pink, and yellow. He eased back in the saddle, content to let Sheba set the pace, enjoying the clean smell of earth and grass and pine that wafted down from mountains yet to be explored by miners.

Aspen stood in clumps near where water tumbled down a rocky creek, the white bark lending a freshness to the day. Meadowlarks and finches and partridges took wing at his approach to draw him away from their nests. A couple of squirrels hopped across the road, and once he thought he saw a golden eagle swoop down and catch a rabbit before soaring back in the air. Horses stood lazily in small groups, chest deep in the grass. Cattle walked slowly while they grazed the range.

Pretty country, he thought. *As long as man keeps his dirty hands off it. It all depends on the ranchers, though. Open range is difficult to control — especially when gold fever is still upon men who are looking for nearby pockets after their claims have petered out. They will eventually start to encroach upon the ranchers' land and the ranchers will keep that from happening with their guns.*

He shook his head, knowing that a range war would happen not too far down the line if peace could not be brought to the valley, a peace not brought by Thompson. There were more miners than cowboys, but few of the miners were good with guns. The valley could easily have bloody grass before reason settled in.

Depression set in as he rode and thought about the future. But the day was too nice for dark thoughts, and soon he lifted his head to once again enjoy the day.

As he neared the upper reaches of the valley, he could appreciate the ranchers' careful tending of the land. Hay had been cut and put up in stacks three times the height of an ordinary man. A few fences appeared, wooden now, but Glidden wire would be coming shortly, he knew.

The first gate he came to had a crossbar nailed to two wooden posts twelve feet high. A sign hung in the middle of the crossbar that marked the range as the Rafter T — Turnbull's spread — and impulsively, Hood turned into the hard-packed trail leading up to a house built of logs and stone near the far side of the valley. A large bunkhouse stood off to the left, and a well-tended corral was to the right, water troughs on two sides. A barn doubled as a smithy, and a solidly built man was working iron into steel. A couple of cowboys sat on the top rail of the corral, warily watching Hood's approach. A man dressed in a faded blue shirt and jeans with a pistol belted high on his right hip came forward on the porch and shaded his eyes while he considered Hood. The man was slim and gray-haired. His heavily tanned face showed a near lifetime working outdoors. Deep lines creased it.

Hood rode up to the main house and waited patiently to be invited down. At last, the man spoke. His eyes were green and appraising.

"Don't see no gun 'cept that Spencer. Light and sit awhile. Cookie's almost got lunch ready and you're welcome," he said. "Boss is in the northern pasture. We lost a few more cattle yesterday."

"Thanks," Hood said, stepping down from Sheba's saddle. "I could use some water from your pump for myself and my horse."

"And that wolf of yours, too, I expect," the man said dryly. "Well, there's a pan back of the pump we use for washing up before coming into the house. You can use that to give her a little water. I'm Abner Seldon.

Some folks call me Sparrowhawk. Me and Panhandle Smith keep things on an even keel."

Hood regarded Seldon for a moment, then said, "I've heard of you. From over in New Mexico. You were part of the Lincoln County War, I believe. Chisum's rider."

Seldon gave an easy laugh. "Yep. In my younger and foolish days. I'm older now."

"Sparrowhawk," Hood said, slowly turning the word over in his mouth. He nodded. "I've heard that name, too. Good with a gun, I understand. Up in Colorado at Bannon near the Divide. You killed a couple of men who came hunting you."

"Three," Seldon said softly, a change coming over his green eyes. "But that was a while back, too."

"The way I heard it, they came looking for you to build up their reputation."

"You heard right," Seldon said, his shoulders relaxing.

"I'm Amos Hood. I'm the new minister in Gold Town."

"Uh-huh," Seldon drawled. "I've heard about you. Swing a wide loop through the town, Ellis at your heels. A shadow, some say. But light and sit a spell. I judge a man even until he proves me wrong. Once. After that, matters seem to go the other way fast."

"Thanks," Hood said. He crossed to the pump and worked the handle until he had filled a trough for Sheba and the pan for Sam. Then, he washed his hands and face, cupping water in his hands. He shook his hands dry and started up the steps to the porch.

Seldon held out his hand and Hood took it, feeling the calluses and grip, hard, but not with a purpose. Seldon regarded him closely, then slowly nodded.

"Yep, I can see you're a man of the cloth. But not for long, I 'spect. You've had a hard past before you took up the Bible."

"Like you said, that was in the past. Gone now."

"Sit. Sit," Seldon said. He dropped into one of the chairs and balanced the chair on its back legs, one foot set against the porch railing.

Hood dropped gratefully into the other chair.

"Heard Ben Thompson and that Bowdine killed a couple of Gannon's men."

Hood nodded. "Yes. I'm afraid that they are the first of others to come."

"It a fair fight?"

"Wade and Wilson thought so," Hood answered.

"But —"

"They were wrong. Wade and Wilson overestimated themselves and got killed for their trouble. They thought they were the equals of Thompson and Bowdine, forgetting that they were mainly cowboys while Thompson and Bowdine made their living with their pistols. No, I don't think it was a fair fight. But I have to give Thompson credit. He gave them a chance to walk away from a gunning. If it would have been just Bowdine, though, Bowdine would have put out their lights in an instant. I don't think he's much for negotiating."

"Heard that," Seldon said, rocking slowly back and forth, his face sober with thought. He sighed. "Well, I reckon hard times are a-coming. Hope our boys stay clear. They're good boys, hardworking. I'd hate to lose any to foolishness."

"Tell them to leave their guns here when they go into town. That'll help a lot. And tell them to hold back on the Who-Hit-John. Some get belligerent after they get a couple under their belt. Fighting is viewed by Thompson the same as carrying a gun in town."

"I'll do that," Seldon promised.

A bell jangled furiously at the side of the cookshack behind the main house. Seldon grinned and rose.

"And now, you're in for some fine cooking. We got a cook that can rustle up any grub you might want."

"Strange that a man like that would be working a ranch," Hood said, falling next to Seldon as they made their way off the porch and around the house. "Most folk with a gift like that would find themselves in a fancy restaurant somewhere."

"Probably," Seldon said. "But Cookie had to take to the outlaw trail after killing a man up near Manitou Springs."

"How'd he kill him?"

"Poisoned him," Seldon said, and gave a dry laugh at the hesitant look on Hood's face.

Turnbull strode into the cookhouse just as Hood was enjoying a final cup of coffee after a plain meal that the cook had made seem elegant. Turnbull's face was purple like a thundercloud. He stopped in surprise at seeing Hood, then walked to him, extending his hand.

"Surprised to see you out this way, Reverend," he said, shaking hands. "You're a bit away from your church, aren't you?"

Hood shook his head, smiling. "Where would you find a minister? Around those who count themselves Christian while being a white sepulchre? Or out in the country where sinners are needing a bit of spiritual guidance?"

"You got me there." Turnbull laughed. "Cookie!"

The cook came out with a filled plate and a cup of coffee hooked on a forefinger.

"Gettin' so a man has to fix two meals around here, what with you gallivanting around the country," he said sourly.

"Get on with it, you old cuss," Turnbull said. He sipped some coffee while he addressed Seldon.

"Found where thirty head were taken, but lost their trail in the grass." He glanced at Hood. "That makes about sixty this month. At this rate, I'll be raising pigs come winter."

"You want me to ride out and see what I can find?" Seldon asked.

"Yeah, I think so. You're better at tracking than I am. Maybe you'll get lucky. Take some extra shells just in case."

"I always do," Seldon said, rising. "Pleased to meet you, Reverend." He touched the brim of his hat and walked out.

"So, what brings you out here?" Turnbull asked, shoveling food into his mouth.

Hood shrugged. "Just buried Wade and Wilson and thought I'd like to ride out in the country a spell to get the taste out of my mouth. Decided I'd go north as I haven't been up here yet."

"Don't think you've been south yet either, have you?" Turnbull asked.

"I hear most ranchers are up this way, so I thought I'd come on up and see where everyone lives."

"I can appreciate that," Turnbull said around a mouthful of bread and beans. He waved a fork toward the north. "McKellon is my neighbor and Campbell lives on the other side of him. Then, Hayes and Harris on the other side of him. Harris has the spread next to Gannon. He has his hands full with Gannon up there. Has to ride stock all the time." A dark cloud settled over his face. "That's why he picks riders who know stock and are handy with a gun. And that's what probably keeps him losing less stock than the rest of us. Especially Hayes. He's gone near broke a couple of times, but manages to bring herds over from Texas and up from Slaughter's ranch in the south. That Slaughter." He shook his head. "Hell on wheels with a gun. He don't let nothing go by and he tracks men down by hisself. Passes judgment on them on the spot. Not many want to go off with the Slaughter brand. He'll even loan a couple of his cowboys to help move bought cattle wherever the buyer wants them to go. Guarantees delivery. I expect that's why Gannon bypasses Slaughter's ranch when he goes down to Mexico to get a herd of cattle."

"What's Gannon's place like?"

Turnbull made a face. "A bit run-down but he has all gunmen on his brand — the Circle G. He's made runs at Hayes and Campbell's places because they sit back on the water and he'd like to have the water rights for the valley. Also has tried to buy them out, I hear. But Hayes and Campbell are stubborn. They've spent a lot of time building up their places and have no intention of selling."

He finished his plate and shoved it to the side, taking a fresh cup of coffee and blowing softly over the surface, sipping.

"Sounds like a fight's coming," Hood said. "Between ranchers and between ranchers and miners."

"Uh-huh. And I don't think it's far in coming." Turnbull's face darkened. "The townfolk bringing in Thompson and Bowdine may hurry up the fight. Folks around here don't like to tiptoe around another person, and they sure as hell don't like others giving them orders. So, I expect the town will probably find itself up the creek without a paddle, too. They'll be drawn in now, too. Right now, I don't think there's anyone who will be able to avoid what's coming. I sure hate that. This has all the marks of being worse than the Lincoln County War."

"I see you hired Sparrowhawk."

"Well, I have mostly cowboys here who use their pistols to open cans of beans and such. They might shoot a rattlesnake, but it'd probably take them three or four to hit it. Their guns are for range use only. Sparrowhawk is my — what do you call it — 'enforcer' will do. But he's more than that. Folks still eye him carefully when he goes to town, and I think he's the only reason why Gannon hasn't tried to take the Rafter T. Him and Panhandle Smith. Sparrowhawk and Smith take turns out on the range and no one wants to go up against either one. They're about equal with guns, but if push came to shove, I think I'd take Smith. There's just something about him that makes a person uneasy around him. Sparrowhawk is a bit more personable."

He slapped the table and stood up.

"I hate to cut this short, Reverend. But I've got some chores that need taking care of. Hope you don't feel badly of me for having to leave you," he added.

Hood laughed. "No, of course not. It's

still early enough for me to ride a little more up the canyon. So I'd better get going, too."

"Say, I just remembered. I'm taking a load of lumber into town in a couple of days. There's a new man who wants to start up another hotel. You need any more lumber? I can do two trips with one."

"I always need more lumber. We've used up all of yours and there's a few things more that I'd like to put out by the church."

"Oh?"

"Yes. I thought we might put up a school-house. I don't think it's going to be long before a teacher will be brought in for the children. I'd like to tie a house onto it, too. And maybe a fence as well."

"I reckon I can manage that," Turnbull said, taking Hood's hand.

"I can't pay you yet," Hood said cautiously.

Turnbull grinned. "Let's just say it's part of my yearly tithing. I'll get to it before winter blows in."

"I appreciate that," Hood answered.

They parted company with Turnbull walking Hood out to Sheba and Sam. They shook hands again, and Hood turned Sheba back down the lane leading to the road, Sam trotting next to them. When he reached the road, Hood turned Sheba toward the north and Sheba snorted happily, not wanting to be returned to the stable too early.

Hood rode past McKellon's and Campbell's places, noting that they were both in the middle of branding season, and on to Hayes's. He rode up to the main house, but discovered Hayes wasn't there. Then he rode to Harris's place. Like Turnbull, Harris had a sign hanging from a crosspiece over his gate, this one letting possible guests know that they would be crossing J-Bar-H range.

He hesitated for a moment, then decided not to ride up to Harris's house and instead rode on toward Gannon's place.

Gannon's spread was about six miles north of Harris's range, the ranch house and buildings tucked back up in a small side canyon. A spring bubbled up about halfway to the house. But no hay had been put up yet for the winter and as he neared the buildings, he could see where a couple of coats of whitewash were needed and some planks were in need of replacing where they had cracked, leaving wide openings. The bunkhouse looked like it could use a good shingling. But the horses that were in the corral had been well cared for and all looked like they had bottom. There wasn't a scrub pony on the place.

As Hood neared the house, built of stone and lodgepole pines, someone gave a shrill whistle and a man in worn clothes and scuffed mule-eared boots came out to stand on the porch to watch him as he rode up.

Hood pulled in Sheba when he was near the porch and looked over at the man, who remained silent, waiting on Hood. The man wore a gray shirt with jeans tucked into worn boot tops. He carried a pistol on his hip that showed use. His eyes were a sharp black, his nose humped from being broken a time or two. His hair was as black as a raven's wing in sunlight. His lips were thin, barely showing.

"Howdy," Hood said. "I'm Amos Hood. The new minister in town. Thought I'd ride out this way to say hello."

The man's face remained expressionless, regarding Hood.

Hood tried again. "I guess this spread is the one farthest north."

"It is," the man spoke harshly. "This is Gannon land and I'm Gannon. You're trespassing." He looked down at Sam, sitting beside Sheba's hoofs. "That's a wolf and we don't take kindly to wolves around here."

Hood felt a wash of annoyance and

stretched in the saddle, carefully keeping his hands folded over his saddle horn.

"Just trying to be neighborly," Hood said.

"That why you stood by and let Thompson and Bowdine kill two of my men?"

"They came looking for trouble and they found it. They pushed Thompson and Bowdine. Wasn't much I could do about that."

"Don't matter none to me," Gannon said. He nodded at the lane behind Hood. "But it's best if you get back. Wade and Wilson had good friends here. Most of the men are out tending cattle, but they get back and find you here, they ain't gonna take too kindly to that. Fact is, I feel the same way. You ain't welcome here, preacher. Leave and don't come back again. And take that wolf with you," he added.

Hood felt anger building up inside him and fought to keep it down. His hands twitched, wanting to feel pistol handles in them. But he forced himself to smile, thinly though it was, and raised a hand in farewell.

He turned Sheba and lifted her to a trot as he went back down the lane and the road. His mood darkened as he rode, the gloaming falling fast and bringing with it a chill. Gannon had something going, he thought, then chastised himself for not giving Gannon the benefit of the doubt.

Still, he mused, if he had ever come upon someone with a finger in the pot before, none was more evident than Gannon. He was cold — that was certain — but there was something behind the coldness, and Hood knew instinctively that sometime in the future he was going to have to deal with Gannon.

12.

Indian summer was upon them, the days sunny but with a smoky leaf taste to them. Light jackets and sweaters were brought out during the day, but at night, the temperature plummeted and heavier coats were needed for those willing to walk the town after dark. For those who frequented the saloons, there was enough heat from the cowboys and miners to remain comfortable, except for the stink of sweat that held like a rank fog over the rooms.

In the Crystal Palace, Ellis was hosting a game at the very back of the room where the stench was less noticeable. Five cowboys and one miner sat at the table covered with green felt. In front of Ellis was a large pile of chips ranging from whites worth a dollar to reds worth five dollars and blues ten. In the middle of the table, chips formed a small mountain. Ellis didn't look at his cards as the betting went around the table.

One quick glance and he remembered what they were and where he was standing in regard to the other players.

A slight, mocking smile traced his lips as he toyed with a silver dollar on the table. The silver dollar showed wear — it was his lucky piece and had been for years while he made a comfortable living from the poker tables, patiently riding out strings of bad luck, for he knew that it would change after a while. It always changed; luck was fickle and couldn't stay bad or good for any length of time.

Across from Ellis sat the miner — Hardrock, he called himself — who was frowning and staring at his cards with a fixed attention as if he could change the spots or numbers. Ellis wasn't worried; he had read the man already and knew the best he had would be three of a kind. Probably nines, Ellis thought. When Hardrock's face was clear and challenging, he would have three face cards.

Ellis had read the other tells that each man unconsciously used to telegraph his cards to one patient enough to wait for the signals. The men at this table were easier to read than most. And they were incapable of cheating. Ellis knew that if they tried, he would catch them immediately, and they knew Ellis did not tolerate anyone trying to cold-deck him. All knew that there was a cowboy in Boot Hill after fancying himself a match for Ellis in card manipulation, having learned the basics on trail drives when he cleaned out unwary riders. But professional gambling was different, and the cowboy hadn't had time to learn that. Ellis had planted him in Boot Hill when the cowboy made his second mistake by trying to pull iron when Ellis had confronted him.

"Come on," one of the cowboys now said impatiently. "You in or out?"

"Ain't decided yet," Hardrock answered. "You in a hurry?" His eyes kindled with fire as he stared at the cowboy.

"Say, there ain't no call for being that testy," the cowboy drawled. "But I would like to finish this hand before Christmas."

"Don't push it, cowboy," Hardrock warned, his attention drifting from his cards to the cowboy, and with that, Ellis knew that he had only a pair at most. He was out of the game for all intents and purposes, but was obviously considering whether to try and pull a bluff or not.

"You're out of your league, Hardrock," the cowboy said, the smile slipping away. His eyes flickered over the table. "You're a bit outnumbered here."

Hardrock glanced around the table, then laughed. "There ain't that many of you to make me break a sweat."

"Leave it," Ellis murmured. "Play or stand down. We've spent enough time with your fidgeting."

"I ain't a-scared of you, Ellis," Hardrock said harshly. "Without your guns, you ain't nothing but spit on the boardwalk. You got no more rights in here than I do. And I can snap you like a dried willow twig you get in my way."

Ellis tapped the silver dollar on the table-top and said, "You're out. Fold your hand and toss it in the deadwood. There's at least three, maybe four on the table who have you beat. Collect your chips and leave."

"Be damned if I will!" Hardrock blurted.

The cowboys glanced at each other nervously and slowly slid their chairs back in case the flame went up.

"I'm following up!" Hardrock said. He pushed all his chips in — about a hundred dollars, Ellis thought.

"Well," the cowboy drawled, shaking his head. "That be a bit too much for me."

"Well?" Hardrock sneered, looking at Ellis. "I reckon it's just me and you. You got the guts to go the whole way, Ellis?"

"You must have a sweet hand," Ellis said.

He counted a hundred dollars in chips and tossed them into the pot. "You're called."

Hardrock's face became a mottled red. He laid open his hand.

"Ace high," he said.

"Not much for all your grousing," Ellis said. He slowly turned over his hand, revealing a full house, eights over jacks.

"Why, you . . ." Hardrock sputtered, leaping to his feet, sending his chair crashing to the floor behind him.

"Think twice before you finish that sentence," Ellis said sharply.

Hardrock laughed. "I don't think you got the balls to pull that pot in. I'm a-taking it because you've won the last four hands in a row. Goddamnit! Ain't nobody that lucky."

"Now you're cross," Ellis said calmly, leaning back in his chair. He slid his hands down the front of his coat, smoothing the lapels. "You might want to think a bit before you take this any further."

Hardrock laughed arrogantly and reached for the pot, eyeing everyone at the table challengingly. The edge of his hand touched the pot to pull it to him when Ellis moved, slipping a small Spanish dagger with a silver handle from inside his jacket and stabbing it down into Hardrock's hand, pinning it to the table.

Hardrock howled and tried to pull his hand back instinctively, then howled again when he realized that his hand was truly pinned to the table.

"Jesus," one of the cowboys breathed. "That's gotta hurt like hell."

The others swallowed and stood, stepping away from the table, leaving Hardrock and Ellis to themselves.

Ellis twisted the knife, bringing the edge of the blade across the ring and little fingers of Hardrock's right hand. Hardrock howled with the movement as the knife circled in his hand.

"Move and I'll cut them off," Ellis said softly.

"No! No! No!" Hardrock babbled.

Fear struck home in Hardrock's eyes. Without full use of his hand, he would be fired. No one wanted to hire a powder man with only three fingers on one hand to handle explosives.

Sweat broke out heavily on his face and ran down his beard stubble.

"Please!" he begged. "Sweet Mary, have mercy!"

"Mary won't answer you," Ellis said calmly. "But I will."

With one movement, he jerked the knife free. The miner howled again, and bent over, clutching his wounded hand to his stomach.

Ellis reached into an inside pocket of his coat, withdrew a silk handkerchief, and tossed it across the table to the miner.

"Wrap your hand in this, then leave." He picked up a ten-dollar chip and tossed it on top of the handkerchief. "I never leave a man without eating money."

"I reckon that busts this game," one of the cowboys said.

"Reckon it does," another answered him.

Together they all sidled off, leaving Hardrock and Ellis alone at the table.

Ellis sighed. "Well, it was good while it lasted."

"You sumbitch," the miner growled, wrapping his hand with the handkerchief. He tucked the end of the handkerchief under the wrap on the back of his hand and came around the table after Ellis.

Ellis waited until Hardrock was close, then rose, the knife slipping back into his hand. He swept the knife across Hardrock's stomach, then stepped back.

Hardrock stopped and stared down stupidly as his intestines began to roll out. He reached for them and tried to stick them back inside, but they tumbled out over his hands.

He fell to the floor, then rolled to his side, staring up at Ellis, standing coolly over him.

"You . . . killed me!" he said.

"You killed yourself," Ellis said coldly. "You should've left when you were warned."

Hardrock tried to say something, but his eyes rolled back into his head. He shuddered twice, then lay still.

Ellis pulled the silk handkerchief from Hardrock's hand, wiped his dagger with it, then tossed the handkerchief disdainfully on Hardrock's body while his other hand slipped the dagger back inside his coat.

"Good Christ!" someone said.

In the back of the crowd, someone gagged and ran outside through the bat-wing doors. The sound of his retching sent two others outside.

Coolly, Ellis stacked his chips, then removed his hat, slid them inside, and carried them to the bar. The crowd parted for him, Moses parting the Red Sea. He emptied his hat on the end of the bar and motioned for Snoopy to count and pay him.

Snoopy came down, automatically grabbing a good bottle of whiskey and a clean glass. He placed both in front of Ellis, then methodically began to count.

Ellis poured a glass and sipped at it, his eyes watching the crowd carefully. The cowboys wouldn't be a problem, he knew, but the miners might figure they had good cause to rush him.

The crowd shifted nervously as Ellis moved his eyes slowly back and forth, warning them.

"We can take him," someone said from the back of the room, but he was quickly shushed by another miner.

"That's Ellis," a voice said. "At least three of us ain't going to make it if we rush him. You want to chance that you won't be one of the three?"

The bat-wing doors swung open and shut. Eyes shifted to the front of the saloon. Thompson stood, calmly surveying the room before crossing to Ellis. Everyone hurried to get out of his way.

Thompson looked at Ellis for a long moment, then used the toe of his boot to roll Hardrock onto his back. He studied the body for a moment, then raised his eyes to meet Ellis's.

"I reckon I should've put knives on that proclamation as well," he said.

Ellis shrugged and motioned for another glass. Snoopy brought one down and set it in front of Ellis.

Ellis took the bottle and poured two glasses full.

"Have a drink?" he asked politely.

"Still, I reckon I could take you in for disturbing the peace." He moved to the bar and took the glass Ellis offered. "But knowing you, you had reasons and damn good ones at that."

"Hardrock tried to take him on," a miner said from behind Thompson.

Thompson looked at Ellis's slim figure, then the bulk of Hardrock on the floor.

"I guess it's self-defense," he said mildly, sipping at his whiskey, his eyes steady on Ellis. "But I sure hope that this is the last case of self-defense for you, Ellis."

"So do I," Ellis said. But there was a mocking sound to his words, and all who heard them knew that it would make no difference one way or the other to Ellis if someone tried to repeat Hardrock's mistake.

"Somehow, you just don't make me feel good about it all," Thompson said amiably. "Good sense tells me I should run you out of town. But on the other hand, I really can't do that to a man who was just trying to defend himself. That miner'd got his hands on you, you'd be dead."

"He thought so, too," Ellis said softly. He clinked his glass against Thompson's glass. "To fools everywhere."

Thompson grinned. "I'll drink to that."

He raised his glass and emptied it.

"Another?" Ellis asked politely.

Thompson shook his head. "No. One's enough. The night's young yet, and I don't want to walk through it with a drink-bloated head. Thanks, though. I'll buy you one next time."

He pointed at the body and said, "Now some of you carry that poor ignorant fellow down to the undertaker's. I reckon the town's going to have to foot the bill. I don't suppose you left him with anything?"

Thompson looked questioningly at Ellis.

"Only ten dollars. I don't let a man go hungry away from the table."

"Nice of you," Thompson said. "Well, he has ten dollars. That should be more than enough to pay for his funeral. Get him out of here. And that ten dollars better end up in the undertaker's hand or there'll be an accounting for it."

Four men hastily lifted Hardrock and hurried out through the door. Thompson looked at Ellis, removed his hat, and sighed.

"You know, I probably should run you out of town. But I got a hunch that you wouldn't go peaceably."

Ellis smiled thinly. "You're probably right, Marshal. But" — he shrugged — "when you come right down to it, makes no difference to me one way or the other. I like things to be my decision. I made a promise long ago that I would come and go when I wanted, not when someone else wanted."

He pulled his coat open. The knife hung in its sheath from a shoulder strap.

"As you can see, I'm not wearing a pistol. I told you I wouldn't and I always keep my word. But on the other hand, as you can see, I would be fair game for anyone without a weapon of some sorts. Hence, the knife."

Thompson drew his lips in and thought a moment, shook his head.

"All right, Ellis," he said. "But you know that if I let you get away with it, others will follow your lead. Then I'll have a state of disruption . . ."

"Anarchy," Ellis said softly.

"Whatever. I'll have a state of it and others will take to carrying knives and there's something about a knife that will make a person more willing to carve another when, if he's carrying a pistol, he has to give a thought or two before shooting another. Any suggestions?"

"You're one step away from the pickle barrel," Ellis answered. "Choose wisely."

"Uh-huh. Well, I could make you a deputy. That way you could carry what you want."

"My hypocrisy goes only so far, Marshal,"

Ellis said.

"Then again, I could confiscate your knife and just give you a warning. You are entitled to that. What you do after that will be on your own head. But if word gets around, I don't think you'll have much trouble."

Ellis shrugged again indifferently. "That's up to you. Personally, though, I disagree. I think more people would be less hesitant about drawing on someone than facing another with a knife. There is something squeamish about getting in close with a knife. At least with a pistol, you have distance from another. But you do what you want and I'll do what I want."

Anger flashed for a moment in Thompson's eyes, then disappeared. A tightness remained to the flesh over his cheekbones.

"I reckon we'll let it stand at that, Mr. Ellis. You've been warned. The next time, you're posted out of town."

Ellis smiled faintly, almost mockingly. "Suppose we cover that possibility when the moment comes?"

"You've been warned," Thompson said firmly. "That's official."

"Fair enough," Ellis said carelessly.

Thompson looked like he wanted to say more, but touched the brim of his hat and walked from the saloon.

The saloon seemed to let out its breath in relief, and curious eyes turned toward Ellis. Some wondered why Thompson didn't shoot Ellis or post him out of town immediately. But these questions were asked of each other in low tones that wouldn't reach Ellis or another who might take word of their conversations to Thompson, or worse, some said, to Bowdine. The general opinion was that Thompson would listen patiently. But Bowdine?

They glanced back at Ellis, who was patiently pouring another drink.

Bowdine and Ellis seemed to be a pair with one a bare edge over the other. For some strange reason, it was agreed upon, Ellis would have the edge if it came down to a shooting.

And as Ellis placed his glass gently onto the bar and settled his coat before strolling out of the saloon, a few offered the opinion that that moment would not be long in coming.

13.

A week of uneasy peace followed, and some felt that Thompson had already brought law and order to Gold Town. But the naysayers were quick to dissolve this certainty by pointing out that a restlessness existed between the cowboys and miners when both came to town on payday. A smoldering fire seemed to exist between them, and it would take only a slight breeze to make it leap into flame.

That moment came on a Saturday when the stagecoach clattered into town with the driver shouting at the top of his lungs that they had been robbed at Parker's Pass, just as they had stopped to give the horses a blow after climbing to the summit. Beside him, the shotgun guard was slumped in his seat, his face ashen, blood seeping from a dirty rag he pressed against his wound to stop the bleeding.

"Robbery! Shooting! Robbery! Shooting!"

The driver pulled in the six-horse team and drew a couple of quick, deep breaths as a crowd gathered swiftly around him.

"Two men! They got the strongbox. Robbery! Shooting!"

Three men helped the shotgun guard down and gently carried him down the street toward Doc Martin's place.

"Inside!" the driver said. "They shot one of the passengers, too. Damn fool tried to get fresh with them and they shot him. Don't think he's gonna make it!"

Someone opened the door to the coach. A young woman, face pale, appeared.

"I did my best for him," she said. "But I don't think that he will survive."

Gently, men lifted the stranger from inside the coach.

A shock of black hair streaked with gray fell over his forehead. He wore a gray suit, dust-covered, and a matching vest. His face was thin and drawn, his eyes closed, lines of pain etched tightly around his mouth. He breathed shallowly, each breath seeming an agonized labor.

"Get him to Doc Martin!" a voice said needlessly as volunteers hurried off with the man between him.

The crowd suddenly parted and grew silent as Thompson made his way through it. He stopped and looked up at the driver.

"Did you get a look at them?"

The driver shook his head. "Nope. But one was on a paint. I'd recognize that soon enough. The other was on a Tennessee pacer. A sorrel."

"Just two?" Thompson asked.

The driver started to nod when the woman spoke up. "There were three. Another was up in the rocks."

Thompson's eyes swiveled to her. He reached up to hand her down from inside the coach.

She wore a small hat with a veil and a green traveling dress. Her eyes were emeralds and her hair a flaming red. Her face was oval and pale, her lips a faint red and full.

"And you are?" Thompson asked politely.

"I'm Miss Elizabeth Seton," she said calmly, brushing dust from her dress. "I saw the man ride away. He seemed to be wearing a gray suit. His horse was gray, too. But I didn't see his face. I think he did the shooting."

"Do you know the other passenger?" Thompson asked.

She shook her head. "No. He got on the stage at Tucson. He seemed friendly enough."

"Hello, Elizabeth," a voice said quietly from the crowd.

She looked swiftly around, then her eyes lighted on Hood. A smile tipped the corners of her mouth as she stepped forward, offering her hand.

"How good to see you —" she began, but Hood interrupted her as he bent to kiss her hand.

"Hood. Reverend Amos Hood," he said, briefly touching the back of her hand with his lips.

"I take it you know each other," Thompson said, eyeing the two speculatively.

"We met back in Kansas," Hood said. "Have you had a safe trip?"

A slight frown appeared between her eyes.

"Until the robbery," she said, taking her hand back. She touched her hair with the fingers of both hands to make certain it had not been disturbed.

The driver stepped stiffly down from the box. He pulled a red bandanna from a pocket and mopped his face.

"Lord! I need a drink!"

"I'll get the horses," a man said, climbing into the box to gather the reins. He clucked to the horses and slapped the reins gently across their backs.

Wearily, the horses moved forward, pulling the stagecoach down toward the Butterfield station. The driver slid his hat off his forehead. It lay on his back, held by the leather lace that was around his neck.

"All right, men," Thompson said loudly as he climbed up on the boardwalk and turned to address the crowd. "I need twelve volunteers to go with me and see if we can't pick up the robbers' trail."

There was a moment of hesitation; then men slipped their way through the crowd to stand in front of him.

"You men get your guns and horses. Meet me back here in twenty minutes. We don't want too much time to pass or the trail will get cold."

He looked down at Elizabeth. "We get the third man, do you think you might recognize him?"

"Maybe," she answered calmly.

"Good enough," Thompson said. "If you will excuse me, I must change."

He stepped down from the boardwalk and made his way through the crowd to the Crystal Palace.

Elizabeth turned to Hood and smiled.

"It's been a long time, 'Amos,' " she said, emphasizing the name.

"That it has, Elizabeth."

"Would you take me to a hotel?" she

asked. "I'm afraid that my luggage is at the top of the stage."

"I'll make certain that it is brought to you," Hood said, taking her arm.

"I'll take care of it, Reverend," someone said. Hood glanced at him and smiled.

"I'd appreciate it, Cacklejack."

"Not a problem."

Cacklejack tipped his hat to them, and turned to walk toward the stage.

"Let me get you settled," Hood said to her.

The crowd eyed them curiously as the two walked through it.

"As to the hotel," Hood continued, "I don't think you'll want to stay in any of them. But maybe Missus Hargrave has room for you in her boardinghouse. It's just down the end of the street. I stay there and can recommend it."

"Then, let's see if she can accommodate me," she said.

"It might be she is full with boarders," Hood said warningly. "Rooms are hard to come by in Gold Town."

"We'll only know after we get there," she answered.

"So, you changed your name, Tom," she said.

"I left Tom back in Walker," he said softly.

"I'm finished with him."

"I hope for good," she said. She gripped his arm tightly. "Amy's dead, Tom. You can't bring her back. I hate to remind you of my cousin, but you must let her go."

He smiled crookedly at her. "Yes, I know you're right. But she comes to me in the night, and sometimes I still feel her around me. It's very hard to get rid of memories."

"You must," she said firmly.

"I know." He changed the subject. "What are you doing here?"

She smiled. "I am a teacher. I heard about Gold Town through a friend who worked for a Mr. Turnbull. I wrote him and he wrote back, offering me a teaching position."

She glanced around the town and smiled.

"From what I can see, a teacher is needed here. They already have a minister."

"A lot of things are needed here," Hood said. "And I would like it if you would let Tom die. People know me as Amos Hood here."

"Of course," she said. "It's a good beginning. Amy would have approved."

"Thank you."

"That man who formed the posse. Is he the marshal?"

"On acceptance," Hood answered. "He's

a town tamer. Ben Thompson came when the town fathers decided they needed some law here."

"You don't sound happy about that," she said.

"I'm not. But it's out of my hands. You'll meet him. And his friend Bowdine. In time. Here we are."

He paused before Mrs. Hargrave's boardinghouse and opened the gate for her.

They walked up on the porch and Hood opened the door for her, ushering her in to the sitting room.

"Missus Hargrave?" he called.

"Be right there."

Mrs. Hargrave entered the sitting room and looked at Elizabeth. She beamed and held out her hand.

"Hello, my dear, and welcome," she said. "I'm Missus Hargrave."

"This is Elizabeth Seton," Hood said. "We were wondering if you have a place for her."

"This must be your lucky day," Mrs. Hargrave said. "I just had to kick a miner out for not paying his rent. The room is cleaned and airing right now. Would you like to see it?"

"I don't think that will be necessary," Elizabeth said, smiling at her. "If what Reverend Hood says is true, then I am lucky to have a

224

room available."

"That you are. That you are," Mrs. Hargrave said. "What brings you to Gold Town?"

"I'm a schoolteacher," Elizabeth said. "I heard you needed one."

"Well, now, that's just fine indeed!" Mrs. Hargrave said. "Anyone guarantee you a salary?"

"A Mr. Turnbull," she said.

"Ah. Well, you let me talk with Mr. Turnbull and see if I can't get your room and board for you," Mrs. Hargrave said. She glanced around the room. "Your luggage?"

"Cacklejack's bringing it," Hood answered.

"Good. Now, I expect you will want to freshen up some. You just follow me and I'll show you what all is available here. Ain't much, but it's better than any other place in town."

"I would appreciate that," Elizabeth said. She smiled at Hood. "Maybe later we can talk some more?"

Hood tipped his hat. "It would be a pleasure, Miss Seton."

"Come, come!" Mrs. Hargrave said, taking Elizabeth's arm. She waved at Hood. "You just go about your business, Reverend. I'll take it from here."

"I reckon I've been given my walking papers," he said jokingly.

The two women disappeared and Hood stared thoughtfully at the floor, hoping that Elizabeth would remember and not let the name Tom Cade slip unknowingly.

He heaved a sigh, then walked out of the house, Sam rising from his place on the porch and falling in beside him. Hood turned toward the stable. Sheba needed exercising and he was in the mood for a long ride away from Gold Town. A thinking ride.

14.

The posse returned the next day, two cowboys trussed with leather piggin strings and seeming the worse for wear. One looked sullenly at the ground while the second, much younger, stared defiantly at all concerned. Thompson dismounted in front of the storehouse they were using for a jail and slapped some of the dust from his clothes. His face looked a bit strained, but his eyes still appeared calm as a crowd began to gather in a half-moon around the jail.

"That's Jim Blake and young Kevin Gannon!" someone said, identifying the prisoners.

A miner stepped forward and looked at the holdup men.

"I see you've found them," he said, his voice rough as gravel. "Well, I reckon we can take them off your hands. Can't we, boys?"

The last was directed at the crowd behind

him. Shouts of approval came.

"Hang the sumbitches!"

"Give 'em what the others got!"

"Hang 'em!"

"Hang 'em!"

"Somebody get a rope!"

"There'll be none of that!" Thompson said sharply. "These men will stand trial over in Durango, the county seat."

"What kind of trial will that be?" a voice shouted from the back of the crowd. "A miners' court?"

Angry shouts were directed at the small group of cowboys at the back of the mob.

"I'm taking them to the county seat to stand trial. Now, break up and go about your own business."

"This is our business," the man in front said.

"You're Hughes, aren't you?" Thompson said. "Well, Hughes, I'm telling you all just once to break this gathering up."

"Or what?" Hughes asked belligerently.

"I'll kill the first man who tries to step up on the porch," he said.

"You can't kill us all!"

"No, but I can do enough. And none of you will know who I pick next."

"And when he gets done, I'll pitch in."

The crowd turned to see Bowdine standing behind them with a sawed-off shotgun. He smiled carelessly.

"This shotgun is loaded with double-ought buck. Both barrels. I reckon between Ben and me that we can take quite a few before you get close to the jail," he said conversationally. "Now, which one of you brave fellows wants to start this fandango?"

Nervous murmurings followed his words along with a nervous shuffling of feet as the crowd began to have second thoughts.

"Better break it up," Bowdine said.

"Let's do it!" a miner shouted.

Bowdine ambled up to him, smiling, and suddenly jammed the barrels of the shotgun under the miner's chin.

"All right," Bowdine said softly. "You're the first one. Now, listen carefully. I'm cocking this shotgun and holding the hammers back with my thumb. Anyone comes near to me or hits me or even comes up with enough oysters to shoot me, my thumbs come off the hammers and the shotgun blows your head clean off your shoulders. Now, you son of a bitch, fish or cut bait!"

The miner's face turned death white and he stood stock-still.

"Boys," he managed. "I'd sure appreciate it if you all would just back off for now."

"Break it up!" Thompson said again

harshly. "And while you're going, think about how a mob is as low as a person can go."

Sullenly, the crowd slowly dispersed, mumbling disconsolately and muttering dark threats.

Bowdine gave a push with the shotgun barrels, driving the miner back. The miner gagged.

"Now, you go along like a good boy," Bowdine said, lowering the shotgun's hammers. "And don't make me regret I didn't let the hammers fall."

Silently, the miner turned and walked hastily away.

Bowdine looked at Thompson.

"Well, Ben, that didn't take much. They're long on talk and short on nerve."

"That's true," Thompson said. He looked at the younger prisoner.

"You're Kevin Gannon?"

"Yeah. I am. And you ain't gonna like it when my brother comes in town to get me."

"Probably," Thompson said mildly. "But that happens and I think your brother ain't gonna like what happens either."

"He's got a lot of men working for him," Gannon sneered.

"Why, I expect he has," Thompson said, motioning for the two to enter the jail. "But what good will they do him if he's dead?"

It was evening the next day when Gannon led some of his riders into Gold Town. They tied their horses in front of the Sampling House and entered. There were several miners inside who hurriedly finished their drinks and left.

Gannon looked at the bartender. "Whiskey. All around," he said.

Dutifully, the bartender spun glasses on the counter and filled them.

The men took their drinks, sipping slowly.

Gannon left his on the bar in front of him and stared at the bartender. The bartender's face reddened nervously.

"My brother still in the hoosegow? He ain't been taken to the county seat?"

"Not that I've heard," the bartender said.

"All right," Gannon said. He took his drink, then addressed the others.

"I reckon we'll find Thompson down at the Crystal Palace. That's right, ain't it?" he added, directing the question to the bartender.

"Usually is," the bartender answered.

"Uh-huh," Gannon said. He hitched his gun belt, resettling the holster on his thigh. He thumbed off the rawhide loop holding the pistol in its holster. "Well, let's go down and have a little talk with this here marshal."

They left with the riders spreading out, some in the street, all swaggering after Gannon as he led his men down the street to the Crystal Palace. He pushed open the door and entered, his eyes snapping angrily around the room, hesitating on Ellis calmly playing poker with four others at the end of the room. Then he focused on Thompson sitting at the side, his back to the wall, calmly running a faro game.

Gannon stalked over to the table.

"You're Thompson," he snapped.

"Yes. Something I can do for you boys?" Thompson asked pleasantly. He raised his head and noticed that all were carrying iron.

"You can let my brother out of that jail. And the man with him," Gannon said.

"I see all of you are carrying guns," Thompson said. "Why don't you either climb back on your horses and leave or else check your guns with the bartender? Then we might be able to talk in a civilized manner."

"I ain't used to repeating myself," Gannon said irritably. "I want my kid brother and I want him now."

"You can't have him," Thompson said. He slipped a pistol from beneath the table and rested it on top, his hand remaining close to it. "Now, either leave or check your guns."

Gannon looked aghast at him. "We got you outnumbered twelve to one."

"Two," a voice said pleasantly from the stairs.

"We can include you in on this, too, Bowdine," Gannon snapped.

"It doesn't matter," Thompson said. "I'm giving you just ten seconds to comply. After that, I'm killing you, Gannon. I'm going to shoot you in the belly and watch you die."

He indicated the other riders with a nod of his head. "I don't think they'll be much help to you. You'll be dead. 'Course, they might get me, but then you'll never know, will you?"

"Oh, I expect more than one'll drop," Bowdine said. "I figure I'm good for three or four. And the table man" — he indicated a man perched on a tall stool with a shotgun in his hands — "will account for those that me and Ben miss."

"Move. Now. I'm counting," Thompson said. He began aloud.

Gannon hesitated for a moment, then shrugged. "All right. We're leaving. But it's a long way to the county seat."

"I know," Thompson said mildly.

Furiously, Gannon turned and stomped from the saloon, his boys right on his heels.

Thompson looked up at Bowdine. "That Gannon is beginning to be a nuisance."

"You want I should take care of him?" Bowdine asked.

Thompson shook his head. "Not yet. Let's see what happens next."

Bowdine laughed and came down the stairs, crossing to the bar and ordering a whiskey. His eyes fell on Ellis and narrowed slightly.

"You. Ellis. You sure remain uncommitted."

"Not my business," Ellis said.

"Just what is your business?"

"My own."

"I'm not sure I like that answer."

"Frankly, I don't give a damn what you like," Ellis said quietly.

Angrily, Bowdine turned from the bar, but was brought up short by a word from Thompson. Bowdine forced a smile and took his drink.

"Make certain that our businesses don't cross," he said. "Else, we just might have to dance a bit."

"You can lead," Ellis said. His eyes remained steadily on Bowdine, who hesitated a moment, then shrugged and tossed off his drink. He indicated another.

"Why, I guess we'll just have to wait for

the music, won't we?" Bowdine said.

Ellis smiled softly and dropped his attention to his cards. But everyone there knew that he was keeping Bowdine in sight, and a nervousness came over the crowd as they turned their attention back to their games and drinks.

15.

The first problem that Elizabeth had to overcome was to find a place where school could be held. Although Turnbull had offered to build a school, it would take time and finding carpenters would be difficult as most were working in the mines around Gold Town. But Hood solved that problem quickly by offering the use of the church on the outskirts of town. A few homesteaders got together and quickly roughed out plank benches and desks for the students. By the end of the week, Elizabeth held her first day of school.

That evening, Elizabeth appeared at Mrs. Hargrave's dinner table, her face aglow with excitement.

Hood grinned at her. "And how many students showed up today?"

"Twenty-eight," she said proudly. "And it doesn't look like there's a troublemaker in the bunch. I think most of them come from miner families, but that doesn't matter. There are rancher children, too, and so far, no trouble between them."

"Well, be careful," Hood warned. "There's a lot brewing in Gold Town right now and it isn't going to take much to set it off."

"Oh, surely things can't be that bad, Amos!" she said.

Hood nodded. "Yes, Elizabeth, they could be and are. There's a lot of tension between the miners and cowboys."

"I'll be careful," she promised.

Sam nudged her leg and she dropped her hand to pat him.

"How are you, Sam?" she said.

"You should always remember that Sam is a wolf, Elizabeth," Hood said.

"I know." Her hand hesitated for a moment, then she scratched behind his ears. Sam closed his eyes in contentment.

"He's friendly enough," she said.

"He is. Unless he's pushed or someone threatens me. But that is exactly what I'm talking about. The miners and cowboys seem friendly enough, but like Sam, it wouldn't take much for them to be at each others' throats. And to top it off, we have Ben Thompson and Bowdine, who aren't helping matters much, although some would say they are doing a pretty good job keeping the riffraff out of town. Personally, I don't think that will last. The merchants will be feeling the drop in customers and begin to whine soon. Who knows what will happen then?"

"You sound as if you've had experience in this before," she said.

"I have and you know I have," Hood said. He dropped his voice a notch and said, "Remember what happened in Walker."

Mrs. Hargrave appeared in the kitchen door, waving a large soup bone and calling Sam.

"You want your dinner, too, Sam?"

Sam left Elizabeth and trotted to Mrs. Hargrave, gently taking the bone from her hand and going into the kitchen.

"I saw what Mr. Bowdine and Mr. Thompson did when that crowd meant to hang those two cowboys," said Elizabeth. "That was one of the bravest things I've ever seen.

"I've met Mr. Bowdine since then," Elizabeth added. "I think he is a fine gentleman."

"Bowdine?" Mrs. Hargrave asked, her eyes narrowing with misgiving. "He is a dangerous man and as for gentleman, I don't think he even knows the meaning of the word for all his fancy talk and fancy dress. You'd be better off staying away from him. And that Thompson and Ellis as well. All three of them are like a magnet drawing trouble. Each one of them has planted men in Boot Hill."

Twin spots of color appeared high in Elizabeth's cheeks. "I find that hard to believe," she said. "Mr. Bowdine has treated me courteously."

"Uh-huh," Mrs. Hargrave said caustically. "But there's a snake inside him coiled and ready to strike. Anyone can seem genteel, but let one little thing happen wrongly for them and they strike without warning. At least a rattlesnake will buzz a warning."

"I appreciate your warnings," Elizabeth said. "But I don't agree with your opinion. I will be careful, though."

Hood remained silent, but he felt a certain dread in the pit of his stomach that Elizabeth would be overwhelmed by behavior she had no experience with. Only a more mature woman would be able to read behind the facades that covered such men as Bowdine and Thompson. Still, if he had to back anyone or needed anyone to back him, he would prefer Ellis every time.

He shook his head and attended to his meal. He hoped that she would not be hurt by either Bowdine or Thompson.

There followed a courtship of sorts between

Bowdine and Elizabeth as the saloon keeper took her on weekend buggy rides up in the northern part of the valley. They picnicked on the various creeks around town, finding spots shaded by willow trees along the banks. The weather held off raining, although the mornings and afternoons were cool.

Hood had misgivings about the courtship by Bowdine, but he was busy himself, trying to minister to those who needed it.

One evening, he met Ellis sauntering down the boardwalk. He stopped to visit with the gambler.

"Your friend is making a big mistake," Ellis said conversationally.

"Who?"

"The schoolmarm," Ellis said, smiling mockingly. "She's asking for trouble going around as she is with Bowdine."

"I know," Hood sighed. "But there's not much I can do about that. Not much at all. She's old enough to make up her own mind, and sometimes the young ones need to get burned before they learn."

Ellis nodded. "That's true. But it's the type of the burn that may be unsettling."

Hood leaned against a post and studied the gloaming as the sun dropped over the west cliff of the valley. He felt lonely and was grateful for Ellis's company. Sam sat beside him, and Hood took comfort in that as well.

"What do you think about Gold Town?" Hood asked.

"Concerning what?"

"Is it anything other than a momentary town? I'd like to think so, but lately I've been having some doubts. It seems to be a gold rush town and nothing more."

Ellis laughed. "The citizens are trying to establish Gold Town as something other than a gold rush town with their attempt at bringing law and order here. But the town is too young yet, and I think that if the gold peters out, then the town will go, too. Oh, a few may hang on to supply the ranchers in the Upper Valley. Bledsoe, for example, maybe Blackie, the smithy, but few others. There's no train through here and it is far enough off any trail leading to California. No, the whole town hinges on gold. But if you can believe Howard, the gold will never run out. Foolish, that. Everything has a beginning and everything has an end. Some just take longer than others to come about."

"And Bowdine and Thompson?"

"Now, there is a quandary," Ellis said, leaning against the opposite post from Hood. "In all reality, the town fathers brought them in for a halt to lawlessness. That means the miners, as they are always in town. The cowboys don't come in force except once a month or so. But the miners aren't the real problem. The answer is in the Upper Valley. A lot of ranchers are losing stock on a steady basis. If any trouble is going to come, it will come if the rustlers are ever identified. There will be a problem with the law when that happens whether Bowdine and Thompson are here or not."

"You paint a bleak picture."

Ellis shrugged. "My hypocrisy goes only so far. I believe I've told you that before."

Hood nodded. "Yes, you have."

"Well, then."

"What about Jim Blake and Kevin Gannon? Think Kevin's older brother will try and stop Thompson from taking them to Durango for trial?"

Ellis shook his head. "No. Oh, Gannon threatened to stop Thompson, but once he cools off, he won't. He really won't have to. The county sheriff, Nelson Futterman, sides with the cowboys. He's as worthless as teats on a bull. No nerve, but he is a great politician and manages to keep getting elected — thanks in part to Gannon's interest in the Durango courts. That will make some here angry and they will try to pressure Thompson to arrest Blake and Gannon again, but he has no jurisdiction outside of the town, and even here his jurisdiction is dubious. There is no town charter. Besides, if Thompson does arrest them for the same crime, that won't fly anywhere since they've already been found innocent."

Both stood in silence for a long moment, each taking comfort in the other's presence. At last, Ellis broke the silence.

"Do you think being a reverend is going to help out here?"

Hood turned toward him. "I can only hope."

"I think your former trade would be better suited for the town. But" — he shrugged — "the souls of men must be taken care of and for that, a shepherd is needed to guard the flock against the wolves. I wonder, though, if the Good Book is going to be enough."

He touched his hat and moved on into the coming night while Hood stood thoughtfully, pondering the parting words Ellis had left him with.

16.

Ellis's prediction proved to be truthful. Word trickled down from the county seat that Jim Blake and Kevin Gannon had been set free by a jury of their peers. Yet the people knew that had happened because Gannon had sent riders to the county seat to crowd themselves onto the jury. People were dismayed but, as Ellis had indicated, there was nothing that could be done about it.

As long as the pair stayed out of Gold Town. And Gannon made certain that they did not come into Gold Town, and the pair took their celebrating on over to Durango.

On the day word came down about the trial, Turnbull, McKellon, Hayes, Campbell, and Harris came to town for supplies, and went to the Sampling House for a drink and visit before heading back home. Hood heard that they were in town, and decided to go over to the saloon and visit with Turnbull.

He wanted to thank Turnbull for his kindness toward Elizabeth and to see if he'd be willing to donate a steer for the needy families down in Tent City.

Turnbull caught sight of Hood as he walked through the swinging doors and smiled.

"Hello, Reverend!" he said in a jolly manner. "Join us for a libation?"

"Thanks," Hood said. "I think I would like a whiskey."

The others looked in surprise at him.

"You drink whiskey?" McKellon blurted.

Hood smiled. "A little wine should be taken for the stomach's sake."

"That really ain't in the Bible, is it?" Hayes asked.

"Read Timothy," Hood responded, taking the proffered glass from Turnbull's hand.

"I agree," Harris said, raising his glass. "To happy days and sunny slopes."

They drank, Hood sipping his. The others refilled their glasses and lounged back comfortably against the bar.

"I wanted to thank you for what you are doing for Elizabeth," Hood said, addressing Turnbull.

"That's all right. No thanks needed," Turnbull said, but he was obviously pleased with Hood's compliment. "I understand that you have met her in the past?"

"She is a cousin to a woman I was planning on marrying. Unfortunately, Elizabeth's cousin was killed by a bullet."

"Sweet Lord!" Campbell said. "What happened to the shooter?"

"He was killed, too," Hood said grimly. He took another sip from his glass and changed the subject.

"So, what brings you to town?" he asked.

The air suddenly became filled with tension as the ranchers looked at each other.

"We've been losing cattle to rustlers," Turnbull said. "In fact, we have been losing so many steers that it is time we did something to stop it. We were just debating what should be done when you walked in."

"I see," Hood said slowly. "And what have you determined?"

"We've been thinking about starting a cattlemen's association," Hayes said. "I'm practically bankrupt from losing cattle. Much more and I'll be looking for a job as a rider myself."

"And what will the association do?" Hood asked.

The ranchers looked uncomfortable; then Turnbull said, "We'll bring in a range detective to set matters straight."

"Another shooter?" Hood asked.

"If it comes to that," Campbell said defensively. "I don't like it. Hell, none of us like doing that. Pardon me, Reverend. But I don't see where we got much choice. I've had my riders out day and night and still ain't having luck stopping it."

"Any ideas who's doing it?"

"Who else? Gannon, of course. However, we ain't been able to catch him. He's pretty clever. I figure he's moving the cattle as soon as he takes them to places down in New Mexico to sell them. Probably Tucson. Or maybe over in Kansas. It don't really matter. He's gotta be stopped all the same."

Hood sighed. "You know, this isn't any different than hiring a town tamer."

"Sometimes, you have to do things you don't want to," Harris said. "I guess what we're saying is that we're at the end of our rope." He shrugged. "Ain't much else we can do, as I see it. The marshal can't do nothing and the sheriff won't do nothing. That sort of leaves us between a rock and a hard place."

"You got someone in mind?" Hood asked. "I mean, someone other than a gunslinger?"

"We were thinking Charlie Siringo, but he went to Chicago to be a Pinkerton man. Now we're leaning toward Jack Craven."

"*Blackjack* Craven?" Hood said, placing

his unfinished drink on the bar. "The older brother of Ben Craven over in Blackwell?"

The ranchers looked uncomfortable; then McKellon spoke up defensively.

"Yes. That one. He's supposed to be good on the range."

"Yes," Hood said. "He is that. But he's nothing more than another Thompson or Bowdine. He doesn't bring many prisoners in."

"A good shot with a Winchester, I understand," Campbell said stubbornly. "I reckon that's what we need."

Hood shook his head and sighed. "Yes, I've heard he is. But I've also heard that he sometimes is a bit careless about who he kills."

"I reckon we need him," Hayes said stiffly. " 'Sides, I hear he uses a whip pretty well. Good enough to change a person's likelihood to latch on to steers that ain't his."

"The last man he did that to, he killed him. And the man was only sixteen."

"You seem to know an awful lot about such men, Reverend," Campbell said, eyes narrowing suspiciously.

"What do you expect?" Turnbull said, butting in. "Amos is a reverend. People come to him with their problems. It's only natural that sometime along his back trail he encountered folks who would speak of others."

"Uh-huh," Campbell said, unconvinced. "Well, reckon you're right, Jed."

"I hope this doesn't bring a spark to the powder keg we have now," Hood said. He pushed away from the bar. "Anyway, I wish you all luck. Although I don't agree with the method you all have chosen. It looks like the valley is going to be ruled by gunmen."

"You gotta do what you have to do," McKellon said. "I don't like it either, Reverend, but sometimes, you just have to grit your teeth and do what you think is necessary. It don't look like we have much choice."

Hood wanted to say they could have hired a Pinkerton man to investigate, but he knew that the ranchers were set on hiring someone who wasn't hesitant to be judge, jury, and executioner. In fact, he mused as he left the saloon, given what would happen in Durango with the sheriff, maybe they had a point.

17.

For the next month, Hood was kept busy with the church and helping Doc Martin to take care of the poor in Tent City. Typhus had been contracted, and was ranging indiscriminately over the backwash of Gold Town. But no one came from Gold Town itself to help, leaving Hood and Doc Martin making herculean efforts to try to curtail the epidemic.

At first, Elizabeth came to help as well, but her time was limited as she had to teach during the days and was exhausted at night — a condition that left a person open to typhus. Hood finally told her to stay home and leave the nursing to Doc Martin and himself.

At last, desperate to counter the disease's spread, Doc Martin took to handling the patients while Hood rampaged through Tent City with a torch in hand, burning the tents and half of the buildings where the disease had occurred. Some men tried to stop Hood, but Thompson, hearing about the threats made to Hood's life, came with Hood when he continued burning. The combined effort of a minister and a gunfighter was enough to keep the bitter people who lost their income with their gambling houses and houses of prostitution at bay.

Finally, on the twenty-seventh day, Hood and Doc Martin, both hollow-eyed and weary, saw the disease begin to fade away. Soon, it had run its course.

But in the meantime, over sixty people had been carted away to a separate cemetery, where they were laid to rest with quicklime thrown over them before dirt was shoveled to cover the graves. The cemetery was marked and quarantined by Doc Martin to keep any curious from digging up the dead to see what belongings had been buried with them.

During that time, Craven arrived in town, and took a room at the Deer Antler Hotel on a permanent basis while he roamed across the valley, searching for rustlers. Word began to trickle back about dead cowboys found on ranges that they were not hired to protect. Although several people gave voice to their doubts that all the cowboys were guilty, it was considered wise to hold one's tongue when in the presence of others.

But even Hood had to admit that rustling had trickled away some and the ranchers were, for the most part, satisfied with Craven's job. And all knew who had slain the cowboys, as a black jack of clubs or spades was left on the bodies.

Still, Hayes's cattle continued to disappear, as did Campbell's cattle.

One day, Hood entered Frenchy's Café along with Sam. The café smelled of coffee, browned biscuits, and thick slabs of beef cooking. He hesitated for a moment; then a stranger, wearing a clean black-and-white checked shirt and shotgun chaps, motioned him over to join his table.

Hood smiled and made his way over, pulling a chair out to sit. He studied the man for a moment. The stranger's cheeks were rosy red from a fresh shave and his hair was slicked back with lilac water. His eyes were brown and friendly, his face thin with high cheekbones. He held out his hand. Hood took it.

"I appreciate you sharing your table," Hood said. "I'm Amos Hood."

"Ah. The preacher," the man said. He glanced down at Sam, who sat alertly at Hood's side, his eyes watchful upon the man. "And this must be your wolf pet. I've heard a lot about you. I'm Jack Craven."

Tension set on Hood's shoulders, but he kept the smile friendly upon his face. Sam sensed the tension and growled softly, but Hood dropped his hand to Sam's head, silencing him.

Craven raised an eyebrow as he considered Sam.

"I don't think he likes me," he said conversationally.

"He's just nervous around strangers," Hood said, then asked casually, "I take it you have been riding the range a lot lately?"

Craven grinned cheerfully and shrugged. "Just doing my job. I'm having a little difficulty at the moment, but in time, I think I can correct the situation."

Frenchy came out from the kitchen with a cup of thick black coffee and placed it in front of Hood.

"We got stew, steak from a steer and not buffalo, fried potatoes, and fresh bread. Apple pie if you want it."

"I'll take the steak and potatoes," Hood said. He nodded slightly toward Sam. "Would you have something back there for him?"

Frenchy smiled. "Yep. Got some table scraps. That okay?"

"Perfect," Hood said.

Frenchy nodded and went back into the kitchen to fill Hood's order. Hood turned his attention back to Craven.

"I haven't seen you in church," Hood said.

"Oh, I'm a churchgoer." Craven chuckled. "But I've been just too busy to go to church. I'll be there when business tapers off more."

Hood nodded thoughtfully. "You consider what you do a business? Just curious," he hastened to add.

Craven smiled, but there was something about his smile that left prickling doubt on Hood.

"No offense taken. Yes, I consider it a business. I don't take a job unless the ranchers can convince me that I'm their last choice. I don't take pleasure in what I do."

"But you have killed a lot of men," Hood said.

"Only those that needed killing."

"And how many would that be?"

Craven shrugged and pushed his clean plate away from him, picking up his coffee.

"I really don't know. I used to, but the number's gotten away from me. Too many."

"I hear Hayes and Campbell are still having trouble," Hood said, leaning back as Frenchy brought out his dinner and a plate of scraps for Sam.

254

Craven frowned. "Yes. They are. I haven't been able to stop that from happening. The other ranchers seem to be happy with my work so far."

"What about Gannon?"

"What about him?"

"Is he happy with your work?"

Craven laughed. "No, I expect not. A couple of men were his riders."

"I see. Do you think the lost cattle are due to Gannon's involvement?"

Craven frowned. "I ain't got any proof about that. If I did . . ." He spread his fingers as answer.

Hood took a bite of steak and washed it down with coffee.

"I take it that you don't care much for my work," Craven said.

"No," Hood said. "I don't. I haven't found that killing solves all problems."

"But it does solve some of them, right?"

Hood nodded. "Unfortunately, yes."

"Well, that's what I do. Solve the necessary problems. If I can," he added.

Hood changed the subject and they made small talk until Hood was finished eating. He pushed himself back from the table and said, "I appreciate your thoughtfulness in inviting me to your table, Mr. Craven."

"You are quite welcome," Craven said.

"How about I buy you a glass to settle your meal?"

Hood hesitated for a moment, but the cheerfulness in Craven's face decided him.

"I would like that very much," Hood said.

Craven nodded and stood and for the first time, Hood noticed the heavy Colt strapped to Craven's thigh.

"I see you're carrying," Hood said. "The marshal has a rule about carrying guns in the town limits."

Craven gave a half smile. "Well, we'll have to cross that bridge when we come to it. In the meantime, how about the Crystal Palace? Is that all right with you?"

"It's all right with me," Hood said. He glanced down at Sam, who was still licking his muzzle from the table scraps. "Come on, you loafer."

Sam fell in beside Hood as they left Frenchy's and turned down the boardwalk toward the Crystal Palace. Craven paused in front of a black horse standing patiently at a hitching rail, a black saddle studded with silver conchos upon his back. Craven reached into his shirt pocket, pulled out some sugar cubes, and held them while the horse nibbled gently at them.

"This is a nice town," Craven said amiably. "It would be a good place to settle down once the riffraff are driven out."

He glanced at Hood.

"Don't you think so?"

Hood shook his head slightly. "I'm not certain yet who is the riffraff and who isn't. What makes one man riffraff and another not? It seems to me that God created all men equal."

He glanced down at the pistol swinging from Craven's gun belt and went on. "I'm troubled by the fact that men hire men to kill and other men accept money for doing the killing. How do we judge them? If we adhere to the Good Book, then all those men would be sinners of the first sort. Would that make them riffraff? And what about others who are the objects of the killings? If we accept that they are guilty of something that makes them the prey of gunmen, are they the riffraff?"

"That's something to ponder, Reverend," Craven said cheerfully. "But suppose the town is rid of all that. Including the gunmen. Would that make this a better place to live?"

"Yes. If, that is, once peace is brought to the valley, gunmen are willing to leave. But that, I think, will be very hard to have happen. Such men might have a tendency to establish kingdoms for themselves."

"I guess we'll just have to wait and see, won't we?" Craven said. He pushed open the swinging doors and stepped aside for Hood to enter.

Inside, the saloon air had trails of smoke hanging from pipes and hand-rolled cigarettes and cigars. The smoke slowly drifted around the tables. Hood noticed Ellis sitting at his usual place in the back. Bowdine stood at one end of the bar, watching the room alertly. Thompson sat at a faro table, manning the boot.

Craven led the way to the bar and motioned for the bartender.

"Whiskey for me," he said, and crooked an eyebrow at Hood.

"The same," Hood answered.

Snoopy slid a glass in front of each and placed a bottle between the glasses.

Craven eyed the bottle, then said, "Now, let's have a drink from a good bottle and not this Who-flung-John." He slid the bottle back toward Snoopy. "I believe you'll find such a bottle under the bar."

Snoopy hesitated, then glanced into Craven's eyes, now flat and expressionless, and hurriedly produced a bottle from under the bar, setting the first bottle on the bar shelf that ran under the mirror and a painting of the actress Adah Menken, seemingly naked, in her role as Mazeppa.

Craven studied the painting, then nodded approval.

"A great woman, her," he said, raising a glass. "The right painting to be placed in this den of iniquity."

Hood nodded and took a sip of his whiskey. "I suppose if your taste runs to such things."

"Yours doesn't?" Craven asked, bemused.

"No. But I can appreciate art."

"Then gaze upon the epitome of art," Craven said.

Hood shook his head. "No, that is a simple painting meant to appeal to men's appetites."

"You there!"

The voice came from behind them. Hood and Craven turned slowly. Thompson stood in front of them, his eyes flat, his hand relaxed by his pistol.

"Why, howdy, Marshal," Craven said easily. He held his glass with his left hand, his right close to his side in imitation of Thompson.

Hood looked down the bar and noticed Bowdine had moved away from the bar and now stood seemingly amused at what was happening. But his thumb caressed the hammer of his Colt.

"You're new here," Thompson said.

"In a manner of speaking," Craven said, turning slightly so Bowdine and Thompson were both in sight.

"Then I give you warning. The only one you'll receive." He nodded at Craven's pistol. "You'll have to check that at the bar or leave town."

Craven pursed his lips as if thinking, but Hood could see from the dancing lights in Craven's eyes that he had already made up his mind.

"Then I think I'll finish my drink and this brief visit with the reverend and ride on out."

"Just leave your gun with the bartender while you are here," Thompson said.

"I don't think so," Craven said, a slight edge to his voice. "But I would appreciate a bit of, shall we say, 'professional courtesy'?"

Thompson raised an eyebrow. "Professional courtesy?"

Craven nodded. "You keep the peace in town, I try to keep the peace out on the range. The way I see it, there's no difference between the two of us." He nodded at Bowdine. " 'Cept I don't have someone watching my back. I work alone."

Thompson gave a slight nod. "Maybe you should have someone."

"That's becoming rather apparent," Craven mused. "So I tell you what: You let me finish my drink and visit with the reverend here, as I said, and I'll ride from town. But I keep my pistol. If you want to take it, then go ahead, play frog and jump. But I'll take you first and you'll never know whether Bowdine gets me or not."

Thompson studied Craven a little, then gave a tiny smile and the air whooshed out of the room.

"Fifteen minutes," he said. "Professional courtesy."

"Fair enough," Craven said. He glanced down the bar at Bowdine. "Tell your dog to relax."

Bowdine flinched and his eyes glittered blackly, his face growing paler. His hand twitched over his gun.

"Art," Thompson said sharply. Bowdine looked at him. "Leave it. For now."

Bowdine nodded and relaxed, stepping once again to the end of the bar. But his eyes stayed on Craven while he turned away, leaving his back to the room. Hood could see Craven watching the room through the mirror behind the bar.

Craven lifted his glass. "Well, preacher, it looks as if we are gonna have to cut our meeting short. For now. I'm looking forward to having another little chat soon."

"Jack," Hood said warningly, but Craven went on.

"It's all right, Reverend. My business is finished in town."

"When you come back . . ." Hood left the rest unsaid.

Craven grinned. "I'll leave my pistol in my hotel room. I really don't mind that, but I surely do hate to have someone try to make me do something they want. Sticks in my craw."

He finished his whiskey. Poured another and sipped it away, all the time keeping an eye on Bowdine and on Thompson, who had stepped back to his faro game and laid his watch on the table, the face open, by his right hand.

Craven laughed, shook Hood's hand, and sauntered away from the bar, slipping through the swinging doors.

Hood took note of Bowdine and Thompson, then left, leaving his unfinished drink on the bar.

Outside, he took a deep breath, then reached down and rumpled Sam's fur. Sam grunted with pleasure.

"That was a little tense. I'm glad it's over without any more bloodshed. Let's call it a night, boy. Tomorrow, we'll take Sheba for a ride, okay?"

Sam seemed to shrug his shoulders. Hood laughed. "Sometimes, I think you can talk, boy."

He turned and walked down the street toward Mrs. Hargrave's boardinghouse, Sam trotting by his side.

18.

The morning was cool and dew still held on the grass and bushes. Bright colors shone forth from the dewdrops as Hood saddled Sheba, ignoring the filly's annoyance at being left in the stable and corral for such a long period. Some Apache plume and pink buckhorns were late blooming, and there was a hint of musk in the air that made Hood breathe deeply.

Sam stood at the door, waiting for Hood and Sheba to come to a settling of the ways, then trotted out in front as Hood gigged Sheba into a trot, heading out of town.

A cool breeze blew down from the north of the valley and Hood gave Sheba her head, resting back in the saddle, letting her pick her own gait. She moved up into a lope and tossed her head in enjoyment as she followed the light touch of her reins to turn onto the wagon road leading north.

Hood breathed deeply of the clean air,

enjoying the sharp tang of pine and the tannic of fallen autumn leaves.

In the distance, he saw three riders outlined on a small ridge for a second before disappearing on the far side of the ridge. Then, he saw another come over the ridge, riding slowly on the same trail the three riders had taken.

For a moment, Hood felt an impulse to ride after them, but then he shrugged and told himself that he was just out for a morning ride and it would be better to stay alone if he wanted to enjoy the ride.

Suddenly, he heard faint gunshots and reined in Sheba and sat, listening hard as Sheba danced around in a small circle, impatient at being held back.

"Maybe it's just someone shooting a leg-broken steer or horse," Hood said, but even as he said it, a hollow feeling came over him.

He dropped the reins and heeled Sheba back into a lope. Sam still ranged ahead, but more slowly than before, his head up, ears pricked forward. He glanced back at Hood as if to satisfy himself that Hood was still coming, then trotted forward toward the gunshot.

Hood topped the rise and studied the lay of the land, but could see only willows clustered along the stream, pine clinging to the sides of the valley along with bright yellowed leaves of birch and aspen.

Hood decided to follow the ridgeline and moved onto Campbell's land, noticing the Circle C brand on cattle calmly grazing. He glanced back, and could just make out the buildings and corrals tucked against the far side of the valley.

He frowned and turned his attention to the front, head swinging slowly from side to side as an uneasiness prickled the skin on his arms. He glanced down at the ground and saw fresh prints of four horses, three overlaying one, the first, he thought.

He followed the prints down a small gully and up the side. There, he saw two men lying dead on the ground.

He dismounted, dropping the reins before moving to their sides. He squatted and studied the big holes in their chests and two jack of spades cards lying on their bellies. He sighed and shoved his hat back away from his forehead.

"This isn't good, boy," he said to Sam. "Not good at all."

He stood and carefully studied the land. In the near distance, he saw a thin stream of smoke mounting lazily to the bright blue sky.

He walked to Sheba, swung up on her

back, and turned her head toward the smoke, riding carefully, studying the ground ahead of him.

Twenty minutes later, he rounded a small hillock and found the remains of a fire. Three branding irons lay in the middle of the coals. He stepped down from Sheba and knelt on one knee as he studied the branding irons. Circle G. Gannon's brand. But he was on Circle C land. He frowned and pursed his lips, thinking, then rose and stepped away from the fire.

Something struck him hard alongside the head and he had a brief sensation of pain as he fell forward into blackness.

A bright pain appeared behind his eyes, then disappeared into swirls of gray and black. He fought hard against the temptation to slip back into the darkness. He opened his eyes and looked curiously about him. He was in his own bed, Sam beside him on the rag rug spread over a well-waxed puncheon floor. Sitting in a spindle-backed rocking chair with cyma-curved arms and seat, Elizabeth dozed. The window was pushed wide open and a fresh breeze came softly into the room.

He tried to rise, but a hard pain slammed inside his head and he fell back on the bed, gasping.

Elizabeth came awake instantly and stood, coming over to the bed. She carefully placed a cold rag over his forehead.

"Don't move, Tom," she said softly, using a hand towel to wipe the perspiration from his face. "You'll need to take your time."

"What . . . happened?" he croaked. He licked his dry lips and she gave him a mouthful of water.

"You've been hit bad," she said. "A gunshot. A half-inch left and it would have killed you. As it is, you're in pretty bad shape. You need to stay down for a while. No," she said firmly, pushing his shoulders back to the bed when he tried to rise. "You'll only complicate things if you try to get up now."

He started to shake his head, but waves of pain washed over him. He gasped and closed his eyes against them. Sam pushed his head under Hood's hand and whined. Automatically, Hood scratched behind Sam's ears.

"Crease Williams found you, Tom," she continued. "He was riding into town and saw buzzards circling, then the smoke. He rode over to the campfire and found you lying on the ground as pale as a sheet. He rode over to Campbell's place and borrowed a buckboard to bring you into town. After he managed to convince Sam that he wasn't gonna hurt you. Doc Martin has been down. For a couple of hours, he didn't think you were going to make it. You've been lucky."

"I . . . two other men . . . by the fire . . ."

"They're dead."

"Branding irons . . ."

She shook her head. "Crease didn't say anything about any branding irons. But then, he was probably more concerned about you."

"Circle G irons . . . on Circle C land . . ."

The room suddenly swam into darkness and he slid gratefully into it, feeling the pain flood away from him.

And he slept.

He awoke again to sunlight streaming through the open window. Cautiously, he moved his head and felt only a dull ache. He glanced at the chair and saw Elizabeth rocking, reading a book.

"Elizabeth," he whispered.

Immediately, she marked her place and put the book on a small table next to her.

She felt his forehead and nodded to herself. She took a glass of water from the table next to the bed and cautiously raised

Hood's head so he could drink thirstily from the glass.

He sighed as she eased his head back against the pillow.

"How long have I been out?" he asked.

She grimaced. "The first time, five days. This time, another four. All in all, nine days."

"Church," he said, his voice a rasp.

"Mr. Bledsoe's making do until you can get back on your feet."

"Good."

"Do you feel like eating something, Tom?" she asked.

He nodded, then said, "Better go back to calling me Amos, Elizabeth. We don't want to start any bad habits."

She smiled brightly and nodded. "Of course. You're right. Amos."

She rose and left. Hood dropped his hand over the side of the bed, and Sam immediately nosed it up and over his own head.

"Good boy," Hood said.

Elizabeth appeared almost in an instant, carrying a tray upon which a bowl of beef soup and a cup of coffee rested.

She sat on the edge of the bed and waited while Hood worked his way up to half-sit and half-lie on the bed.

Carefully, she spooned the soup into Hood's mouth, following it after a few swallows with a bit of beef, which Hood chewed gratefully.

"Is Crease still in town?" he asked.

She shook her head. "Not that I know. I can send someone to get him, if you want. Cacklejack finally got a room here and he's off shift."

"Do that, please. I need to talk with him."

"After," she said sternly, "you finish your soup."

"Yes, ma'am," he said meekly, and dutifully ate.

"You wanted to see me?" Crease asked, walking into Hood's room with Cacklejack. "You're looking better than when I found you."

"I appreciate that," Hood said. "Did you see who shot me?"

Crease shook his head and said, "Nope. There wasn't anyone around when I arrived. Just those two dead cowboys and you."

"Nothing else?"

"No," Crease said, puzzled. "What else were you expecting?"

"Branding irons."

"No branding irons," Crease said.

"Strange," Hood said. "I'm positive there were branding irons on the coals. Circle G irons."

"You must've been mistaken."

"You know who the men were?"

"Rode for Harris," Crease answered. "At least one of 'em did. Jolly Driscall. I expect the other did, too, if he was killed along with Jolly."

Cacklejack nodded and said, "Word is that Craven killed them. I don't know why. He works for Harris and the others. Mayhap he shot you, too. By mistake."

"That's right," Crease said. "I found two jacks of spades on their bodies. That's his trademark."

"Anyone knowing why Craven would have killed them?"

"No," Crease said. "Not unless just because they were on Circle C land. That's all I can figure. But damn me if I can understand why they stopped to have coffee. They weren't all that far from Harris's place."

"I've got an idea, but we'll need Campbell's help and maybe Turnbull or McKellon or both. Is Campbell better?"

"Seems to be," Crease said.

"Would you see if Turnbull will let us have a little meeting at his place?"

"Uh-huh," Crease said. He took rollings

272

and tobacco from a shirt pocket and began to build a cigarette. "You want Turnbull's place 'cause he's a little more off the beaten path?"

"Yes," Hood said. "That plus he hasn't lost any cattle."

"What about the others? Harris and Hayes?"

"Guess it would be all right. But keep it quiet. I don't think Jack Craven needs to be there."

"He's the range detective for the Cattlemen's Association," Crease said, reminding Hood.

"I'd like to have this meeting just between the ranchers," Hood said. "If they want Craven to know afterward, then that's up to them."

"All right with me," Crease said, brushing his hands together to remove tiny shreds of tobacco. "When?"

Hood grimaced. "Give me five days. That should do it."

"What about me?" Cacklejack put in. "Anything I can do?"

"I'd appreciate it if you could find Ellis and ask him to come here."

"*Ellis?*" Crease and Cacklejack said together.

"Yes. And, Cacklejack, see what you can

pick up around town. Anything at all to do with rustlers and the miners, if any of them know anything."

Cacklejack nodded. "All right. But I still don't know what you want Ellis for. He ain't the man for casual calling, I 'spect."

"Maybe," Hood said. "Won't know until you try, though. One last thing. I need to see Vince Packer."

"I can get him," Crease allowed. "But what you want him for?"

"I have a hunch I'm going to need someone to watch my back," Hood said grimly. "I don't think this shooting was an accident."

"Gannon?"

"Maybe."

"Well, I'll put it to McKellon. I have a hunch he'll cut Vince free. Maybe me, too. I got a hunch watching you is gonna be a full-time job."

"I'd appreciate that," Hood answered.

Cacklejack was as good as his word. Ellis came to see Hood two days later. Mrs. Hargrave announced him suspiciously, but Hood told her that he wanted to see him. She left, muttering to herself about preachers seeing the devil when they didn't have to.

Ellis grinned as he took the spindle-backed chair and placed his hat on the table beside the chair. Sam rose stiff-legged and growling, hackles raised.

"Easy, Sam," Hood said, reaching down to smooth Sam's hackles.

"You look terrible," Ellis said.

"I'm getting back to my prime," Hood said.

"Uh-huh. I can see that. You asked me to come?"

"Yes," Hood said, levering himself up in the bed. "I need a favor."

Ellis's eyes narrowed fractionally. "What favor?"

"I'd like you to take care of Elizabeth. She's been seeing a lot of Bowdine and I don't like that. Bowdine isn't the type for her. Right now, she's fascinated with him. I'd appreciate it if you would try to take her on a drive, well . . ." He paused, embarrassed.

Ellis laughed. "You want me to court Elizabeth? What makes you think she'll have anything to do with me?"

"I don't know. But you're definitely a better choice than Bowdine. I have a hunch she'll be pleased that more than one man is paying attention to her. But," he added in warning, "that's all. Just an escort of sorts."

275

"That's it?"

"Yes. I have a feeling Bowdine isn't going to be satisfied with buggy rides and picnics for long. And there's no love lost between you and Bowdine. Is there?"

"Interesting," Ellis said, musing. "Very interesting. What's your interest in the woman?"

"I know her from a while back. She's the cousin of my former fiancée."

"I see. *Former* fiancée?"

"She was killed by a bullet meant for me."

Ellis nodded. "All right. No promises, though. She may not want anything to do with me."

"Let's hope you're wrong," Hood said.

"Yes," Ellis said, rising. He replaced his hat on his head and turned to go.

"Ellis?"

He turned back to Hood.

"Why is it I think we've met before?"

Ellis laughed. "You haven't figured that out yet?"

Hood shook his head.

"You've got a lot to come to you yet," Ellis said. "You'll figure it out."

Mockingly, he touched his hat and left Hood frowning, trying to drum up a picture from dim memory.

19.

Vince Packer came the next day to visit Hood, smiling cheerfully as he entered the room. He was covered with dust, and his heavy gun sheath bumped the arm of the chair when he sat. He removed his hat, exposing a white line on his forehead where the sun never touched. He crossed his legs. His spurs jingled on his down-at-the-heel boots.

"You look like hell," he said, smiling, rubbing the beard stubble on his jaw.

"Thanks," Hood said. "But I'm coming along. Figure I can be on my feet in a couple of days."

"Don't push it," Packer warned. "You might have a crack in the skull and them things take a long time to heal."

"You a doctor, too?" Hood asked.

"Nope. Been there, though. Horse kicked me in the head oncet and I was loopy for a couple of weeks after."

"Let's hope I'm right and you're wrong," Hood answered.

"Yessir, let's hope," Packer said.

"You've been working the range. You notice anything?"

Packer's face sobered instantly. "Yeah. I notice there are a lot more steers and cows with calves carrying the Circle G brand than before. Seems like Hayes and others are down quite a bit of cattle while Gannon is gaining. 'Course, you understand I ain't making any accusations. Word gets back to Gannon about that and I'll be dry-gulched some day when I'm out on the range. But there's been enough that the bosses are talking about fencing the ranges instead of using open range. That ain't gonna go well with those like Gannon who have been relying upon open range."

"I thought Craven was supposed to take care of that," Hood said mildly.

Packer's face flushed a dark red. "Yeah. So did the cowboys. But there don't seem to be much difference in cattle lost than before he came. A twelve-year-old boy was killed up by McKellon's line shack, too. I don't think you know his family — the Gordons down below on the Snake River. They're homesteaders. The boy was hunting when he caught it. The Gordons ain't taking it so well right now. 'Course, he was far away when it happened. Maybe someone thought he was paying too close attention to someone's cows."

"I don't doubt it," Hood said. "Was it Craven?"

Packer shrugged. "No card. And he always leaves a card when he kills someone. 'Course, that don't mean nothing. Maybe he found out that it was a boy he killed and decided not to leave one. Folks wouldn't take him killing a boy if'n he took credit for it."

He eyed Hood narrowly. "You got a hunch about something, don't you?"

Hood nodded. "It's just a hunch. Like you, however, I need to think on it some."

"McKellon cut me an' Crease loose with pay. Said we should do what you wanted."

"That's good of him," Hood said.

"Yeah. He likes the job you're doing churchifying and all. He says you bring something to Gold Town that ain't never been here before."

"What's that?"

"Hope."

That evening, when Elizabeth came to check on her patient, her face was rosy-cheeked, bright, and shining.

"You look like you've just had Christmas," Hood said, smiling.

"Maybe I have," she answered. "You know Mr. Ellis?"

Hood nodded.

"He took me for a drive this afternoon when school was out. Oh . . . Amos . . ." she stuttered, catching herself before she used his other name. "He is such a gentleman."

"Better than Bowdine?" Hood asked.

"Different," she said, hesitating. "Much different. I know he's a gambler and such, but I sense a goodness in him that I don't in Mr. Bowdine. Not," she added hastily, "that I'm saying anything against Mr. Bowdine . . ."

"But there's a difference," Hood finished. "And I suspect you like the idea of having two men come a-courting." He smiled mischievously.

She turned scarlet. "Amos!"

"It's the truth, though, isn't it?" Hood asked.

"Maybe," she said saucily. "There's something the same about both. Something dark. But with Mr. Ellis, there is a goodness there, too, that I don't feel about Mr. Bowdine. Although," she added, "he has been attentive as well."

"I'm happy for you, Elizabeth," Hood said.

"That isn't all," she said, blushing again. "A cowboy came to see me. A Mr. Williams. He sat and visited a long time with me after the children left and before Mr. Ellis arrived. He brought me some wildflowers. He called them Apache plume and pink buckthorns. They were beautiful."

"He ask you to ride with him, too?"

She shook her head. "No. But he was nice to visit with."

"So you have three men coming for you."

"Oh, you are bad!" she said, covering her cheeks with her hands.

"Well," Hood said teasingly, "I count three. Are there any more?"

She shook her head. "You stop that!"

"I hope you choose wisely," he said.

"Amos Hood! That's a long way off! And there's no certainty about that ever happening!"

She fluffed his pillow, then flounced from the room.

The smile slipped from Hood's face. It was good to see Elizabeth so happy, but there was also a problem. He was certain Ellis and Crease were all right with her. But how was Bowdine going to behave once he discovered that he wasn't the only one interested in Elizabeth?

A dark cloud settled over him as he

thought about Elizabeth's situation.

Within a couple of days, Hood was able to stand and walk a short distance from his bed before returning to it and lying down, panting from the effort. But it was progress, and he was determined to keep trying, concentrating on going a few steps beyond the previous walk.

By the end of the week, he was out of bed and able to make his way around town. He saw Packer strolling along on the opposite side of the street and waved at him. Packer waved back.

Hood stopped at Bledsoe's store to visit. Howie greeted him brightly.

"You look a little pale yet," Howie said. He pushed a jar of peppermint sticks forward, and Hood took one.

"I feel a little pale yet," he said. "But it's time that I started to get around instead of lying in bed like an invalid."

"Maybe you still are," Howie said. "You might be rushing things too soon."

"I'm okay," Hood said, sucking on the peppermint stick. "Just a little shaky. But I know I won't get better flat on my back. Besides, I have a flock to take care of, although I thank you for stepping in."

"That's all right," Howie said, waving the

compliment away. "I couldn't do it on a permanent basis. But I knew you'd be back soon attending to matters. The congregation feels the same way. We've had no loss in attendance and a little gain. So things are still looking up for us."

"Things seem pretty quiet around here," Hood observed.

"Yes," Howie said. Then, he frowned. "But business is falling off steadily. A little bit at a time, but falling nevertheless." He hesitated, then said, "It isn't just me. The other folk are saying the same thing. Except for the saloons. They seem to be doing all right. But they draw a different clientele, you know. A lot of folks are going up to Durango to get their supplies and things."

"Any idea why?"

Howie bit his lip. "I think it might be Bowdine and Thompson. Mind you," he added hastily, "I'm not saying it is them. But it's the only thing different that's happened with this town."

"Maybe it's time to let them go," Hood said, finishing the peppermint stick.

"Maybe. If they'll go."

Hood raised his eyebrows. "You don't think they will?"

Howie shook his head helplessly. "Bowdine has his saloon and is squiring around the schoolteacher. Thompson is making good money with his faro game and . . ." He paused.

"And," Hood prompted gently.

"He's been going around saying that the citizens need to have protection insurance so nothing will happen to them. That's the real reason that business is slumping off, I think. Tom Howard says that he's come out to the mine to sell the mine owners and placer miners insurance as well. I hear he's hitting the saloons and gambling establishments down in Tent City also."

"I thought that was the reason for him to be hired in the first place," Hood said quietly.

Howie nodded vigorously. "It was. Now, he's demanding more. But what can we do?"

"Fire him," Hood said.

"And have something happen to our places? All I own is tied up in this store."

Hood sighed and took a handkerchief from an inside pocket and mopped his face. He carefully folded the handkerchief and returned it to his pocket.

"You can always bring Nelson Futterman down from Durango to send Thompson and Bowdine packing."

Howie snorted. "You think Futterman will come down? He's no gunman and he knows it. He won't come. And the territory marshal is a week's ride from here."

"Well, at least you can try to fire him," Hood said.

"I suppose," Howie said worriedly. He tugged at his lower lip with thumb and forefinger. "Nothing to lose by trying."

"No, there isn't," Hood said. He patted Howie on the shoulder. "I'll see you later. Would you pass word that church services will be back on schedule next Sunday?"

Howie nodded vigorously. "At least that will be good news."

Hood met Crease as he walked down the street away from Howie's store. Crease smiled pleasantly.

"It's set," he said. "Turnbull said that the meeting will be Saturday out at his place. If," he added, "that's all right with you."

"All right with me," Hood said. "The sooner the better, I think."

"Craven hasn't been asked as far as I know," Crease said. "But he still might get wind of it."

"We can't help that. If he does, he does."

Packer came up and joined them. "What's up?"

"We're going out to Turnbull's Saturday for a meeting."

Packer smiled. "Okay. I'll just trail along a little back. What about you, Crease?"

"I'll pick him up at the ranch and follow him back to town."

"Well, preacher," Packer said. "It looks like we got you covered."

"I just hope there isn't another incident," Hood said.

The other two nodded.

"Me, too," Packer said. "But better safe than sorry."

"Ain't that the truth," Crease said.

"One thing more," Hood said. "You hear anything about Thompson and Bowdine selling 'insurance'?"

Both shook their heads.

"Protection money?" Crease asked.

Hood gave a short nod. "Way I hear it, Thompson's been calling on those in Tent City and the mine owners, telling them they need to pay insurance to keep things from happening to their places."

"Thought that was what the citizens hired them for," Packer said.

"That was my understanding."

Hood looked across the street at the Crystal Palace. "I guess it won't hurt to ask him," he said.

"Oh, no," Packer groaned. "Here he goes again, sticking his nose in where he shouldn't."

Crease sighed. "Reckon both of us better trail along on this stop," he said. "Sure hope none of them two takes things badly."

They hitched their gun belts up resolutely.

Hood grinned and walked across the street and through the doors. The smell of stale smoke and beer came to him. He paused, and noticed Thompson at his faro table and Bowdine standing watchfully at the bar. Snoopy was polishing glasses and arranging them in a pyramid.

Hood took a deep breath and walked over to Thompson's table.

Thompson looked up as Hood approached, and smiled.

"Well, Reverend, it's good to see you out of bed," he said pleasantly.

"Good to be out," Hood answered. "Could we have a little talk?"

Thompson raised his eyebrows, then said, "I reckon that could be arranged." He nodded at the two players at his table. "I'm closing down for a little, boys. Hope you don't mind."

The players shook their heads and gathered their money and sauntered back to the bar.

"Sit down, Reverend," Thompson said, nodding at the seat across from him.

287

Hood pulled out the chair and dropped gratefully into it.

"I really appreciate this, Mr. Thompson," he said.

"That's all right. Those two yahoos weren't betting enough to warrant much time. Now, what can I do for you?"

Hood leaned back in his chair and said, "Some folks have been saying that you've been offering them protection for their mines and claims. I understand you're doing the same down in Tent City."

Thompson's smile slipped a little and a hard watchfulness came into his eyes.

"That so? Well, I reckon it must be so then. You object?"

Hood nodded. "Why, yes, I do. Isn't that why you were brought to Gold Town and are being paid a salary?"

"In part," Thompson said. "But I reckon that was just for the businesses. The way I figure it, those others should cough up something, too."

The chair next to Thompson was pulled out and Bowdine settled into it, smiling at Hood.

"What's up, Ben?" he asked.

Thompson nodded at Hood. "The preacher thinks that I shouldn't be selling insurance to the citizens."

"And Tent City. And the mine owners," Hood said.

"And Tent City. And the mine owners," Thompson added mockingly.

Bowdine shook his head. "I don't know why it's any of his business. Seems to me that's between you and them."

"Not to me," Hood said softly.

"You seem to cut a wide swath for a man without a gun," Bowdine said.

Hood looked coldly at Bowdine. "No need for a gun to get the bulge on you."

Bowdine flushed. His arm jumped, and Thompson quickly put his hand on Bowdine's arm, calming him.

"Take it easy, Art. There's no reason for gunplay here. Besides, it wouldn't look right you shooting the preacher."

"You're lucky," Bowdine said to Hood.

"Maybe so," Hood said.

"You may have a point, preacher. I always prided myself on being a reasonable man. I'm willing to work with the good folk," Thompson said. "Tell you what: You may have a point about the citizenry. I'll pass them by. But Tent City's paying nothing and they're getting the same benefits as the town members. And that goes for the mine owners, too."

"The mine owners are helping to foot the

bill for you," Hood said.

"Well, they can foot a little more," Thompson said. "I'll give you the town, but the rest of it is mine."

Hood started to speak, but Thompson cut him off.

"That offer's nonnegotiable, preacher." He looked over at Williams and Packer. "And take your men out of here, or tell them to shuck their guns and give them to the barkeep."

Hood sat quietly for a long moment, studying Thompson. Then he rose.

"I hope you don't come to regret your decision, Mr. Thompson," he said, then turned and walked away from the table and out of the saloon.

Packer and Williams followed silently.

"You're going to have to kill that man," Bowdine said.

"Maybe," Thompson said. "Maybe."

20.

Hood took a deep breath when he left Bowdine, and headed back to Mrs. Hargrave's barn. He walked into the corral and Sheba tossed her head, eyeing him for a moment, then came across and nudged him with her nose.

"Well," Hood said. "So you think you're going to get more with honey than vinegar, eh? You're right. We're going for a little ride."

Hood saddled Sheba and stepped into the saddle. The moment the seat of his pants hit the saddle, Sheba began to buck, jarring Hood's teeth every time she came down. Sam skedaddled out of the corral and crouched behind the water trough, peeking around the corner.

Finally, Sheba stopped and blew air out of her nose and looked back at Hood.

"So that was my punishment?" Hood laughed. "All right. I'll try to do better in the future."

He rode out, turning toward the north road leading to the upper reaches of the valley. The sun was warm upon his back and he took a deep breath, enjoying the Indian summer. Sam flushed a rabbit and disappeared, chasing it through the brush. A Gambel's quail flew up heading off to Hood's left. Overhead, a golden eagle soared in widening circles.

He glanced behind him, and saw Crease and Packer following easily over the road, about a half mile back. He waved and they both waved back.

Hood passed Turnbull's and Campbell's places, and paused when he came to Hayes's before turning off the road and heading northeast. Soon, he came to Harris's range, and rode thoughtfully across the range until he found what he was looking for. He took his rope and shook out a loop, then tossed it around the head of a calf. Sheba backed away, keeping the rope taut while Hood followed the rope down to the bawling calf and took it to the ground. He kneeled on its head and looked closely at the J-Bar-H brand, tracing it with his fingers.

Satisfied, he rose and released the calf and stood thoughtfully for a long moment, his hand upon his pommel, staring north toward Gannon's place. Then he mounted and rode north, soon passing onto the range controlled by Gannon.

Again, he roped a calf and studied its brand, then nodded to himself and rose, mounted, and turned Sheba back toward town.

He'd gone barely a mile when a bullet snapped past his ear, followed faintly with the sound of the gunshot. He clamped his heels against Sheba's side, pushing her into a gallop while he bent over her neck. Sheba stretched her neck out and raced down the road. Another shot whipped by them, and Sheba reached down inside and galloped faster.

Hood chanced a glance behind and saw the shooter on a ridge on Gannon's place. He wore a blue-washed shirt and sunlight reflected off the silver conchos of his saddle.

Hood came to Turnbull's place and turned up the lane toward the ranch house before easing Sheba to a stop. Sam came up, panting, and sprawled in the shadow cast by the porch.

Turnbull came out of the house and grinned at Hood.

"You're about three days early, preacher," Turnbull said amiably. "Our meeting ain't until Saturday."

Hood nodded, taking his hat off his head

and mopping his forehead while he led Sheba to a water trough.

"I know," he said, taking a deep breath, trying to still his thudding heart. "I was out for a ride when someone took a couple shots at me. Thought I'd better find a place for a spell."

Turnbull's face hardened. "On my range?"

"No, I was up on Gannon's range. But I have a hunch he followed me down the road until I turned in here."

Crease and Packer rode up, both looking grave, and dismounted by Hood.

"You all right?" Packer asked anxiously.

Hood nodded.

"You boys get a good look at who tried to shoot the reverend?" Turnbull demanded.

"No," Crease said. "Not really a close one. But we were hanging a half mile or so behind Mr. Hood to cover his back. The shots came from in front of where he was."

"I got a quick look, and I feel that I've seen that shooter somewheres before," Packer said, rubbing his chin thoughtfully. "In fact, I know I've seen him or at least his horse somewhere. Just don't know where."

Turnbull turned to Hood and said, "Well, if you were up on Gannon's range, it could have been any of his riders. Remember, you had a run-in with two of Gannon's riders

— Wilson and Wade. Cowboys have long memories. Any one of them could have shot at you."

"Maybe," Hood said.

"What were you doing up there anyway?" Turnbull asked, frowning.

"Just having a look around," Hood said.

"It ain't healthy riding across a man's range without his by-your-leave," Turnbull said. "If you'd been shot, Gannon could claim that you were fixin' to steal some of his steers. 'Course, no one would believe him, but no one could prove any differently either."

"I'll be careful in the future," Hood promised. "Right now, I think I'll ride back to town. I've got some thinking to do."

"Sure you won't stay for dinner?" Turnbull asked. "Long's you're here, you might as well."

"Yeah, Reverend," Crease said. "My belly button's stuck to my backbone."

"And my stomach thinks my throat's been cut," Packer added.

Hood laughed. "All right. I guess there's not that big of a hurry to get back to town."

"Now you're talking!" Crease said as the cook came out of the kitchen and, picking up a crowbar, began whacking a bell hung on a post.

21.

Friday came and went. Hood spent the time working on the converted stable, visiting with Elizabeth when she wasn't teaching or going for a ride with Ellis. Several times, Hood noticed Bowdine scowling as they rode by in Skeeter's buggy, laughing and talking.

Once, Hood was close enough to see the ugliness in Bowdine's eyes when Bowdine turned away to stomp back into the Crystal Palace. But Hood gave it no thought.

On Saturday afternoon, Hood saddled Sheba and, calling Sam, rode out to Turnbull's place.

The others were waiting for him when he arrived — Turnbull, Hayes, Campbell, and McKellon.

"Harris said he couldn't make it," Turnbull said.

"Craven?" Hood asked.

Turnbull shook his head. "Crease said that

you'd just as soon he wasn't notified. So, I didn't send a rider out to find him. I expect he's around, though."

"All right," Hood said. He removed his hat and stood facing the others. They looked back at him curiously.

"All of you have been losing cattle to rustlers. And, unless I miss my guess, the rustling hasn't stopped much since Jack Craven's come to town. At least for you, Jed, and J. R. If I don't miss my guess, you're no better off than you were before you all hired Craven."

"We're a little better off," Turnbull said. "Craven is making a little difference, but not as much as we'd hoped for."

"And he's getting a little careless," McKellon said. "The Gordon boy he shot isn't going down too well with folks around here."

"And I don't know about you, but it seems like *we're* losing the cowboys and not Gannon," Campbell said.

"Well," Turnbull interjected, "remember that we told him to chase down the rustlers. Maybe not all are from Gannon's spread. Fact" — he appeared a little uneasy — "given everything, we really don't know if Gannon's that involved or not."

"Damnit, Jed," Hayes said. "You know as

well as I do that Gannon's involved. He's got more cattle now than he ever did and he ain't made a raid down into Mexico in some time."

"Still don't mean he's guilty," Turnbull said stubbornly. "You gotta have proof before you can call a man out."

"That's why we're here," Hood said softly.

The others gave him their undivided attention. Hood smiled thinly.

"The other day when I was out riding, someone shot at me when I was up on Gannon's range. You warned me about that, Jed."

Turnbull nodded.

"Well, I wasn't just up there by happenstance," Hood said. "I had a hunch about how you were all losing cattle, and I think I've found out."

"How?" Hayes demanded.

"Do you have a pencil and paper?" he asked Turnbull.

Turnbull went to his desk, removed a couple of sheets and a pencil, and brought them back to the table where Hood was standing. He gave them to Hood.

"Now, I can't speak for you, Jed, or you, J.R., but I think I can tell you why you, Ira, and you, Josh, have been losing cattle."

All eyes were on Hood as he drew on the

paper and held it up for all to see.

"Now, this is your brand, Josh, the Circle C. And yours, Ira, the I-Bar-H. Now watch."

Carefully, he made the C on the Circle C into a G, the Circle G. And the I on the I-Bar-H became a J-Bar-H.

"You recall, Crease, and you, too, Vince, that I was asking if anyone had found branding irons the day someone shot me?"

Crease and Vince nodded.

"And the branding irons were gone, Crease, when you found me and brought me back?"

Crease nodded.

"I was on Circle C range at the time," Hood said, nodding at Campbell. "And I'd swear the branding irons were Circle G. I rode up to Harris's place and found a calf that looked as if it had a brand worked over the old one. The same up at Gannon's."

"Damn!" Hayes said softly. "I know Gannon is no friend of ours, but Harris?"

"Like Jed says, Amos," McKellon said, "we gotta have proof."

"The only way we'll be able to tell for certain is to check under the hide of the calves. The old brand will show clearly," Hood said.

"And I'll supply two calves for the ones we kill," Turnbull said, his face red with anger. Campbell sighed. "Well, let's get to it. A sharp knife cuts cleanly."

The others nodded and with grim faces, walked outside and mounted their horses. "What you gonna do, Amos?" Crease asked.

"I'm going along," Hood said. "Maybe if I'm along, there won't be any bloodshed."

"Let's do it then," Packer said grimly.

Turnbull glanced at Packer and Crease. "You two come with us, but get Smith first. We might need him. You'll find him down at the corral, I think."

"On the way, Boss," Vince drawled and left, spurs jingling musically.

Panhandle Smith was not what Hood had in mind when he rode up on a dun. He was thin, but seemed like rawhide stretched over bone. His clothes were clean, but showed wear. His shotgun chaps were worn smooth. The two pistols at his waist, however, gleamed with care.

"Don't think we've met before," Hood said, stretching out his hand. "I'm Amos Hood."

A tiny smile slipped across Smith's face as he took Hood's hand.

"Uh-huh," he said. "I reckon our trails crossed somewheres in the past. Up Kansas way, I'd bet."

A chill set upon Hood, and he looked at him sharply. "I've heard about you, Panhandle, but as far as I remember, we never met."

"Didn't say we met exactly," Smith said easily. "But I've seen you before and it shore weren't wearing preacher clothes."

Hood cast a quick look around, but no one appeared to have heard the exchange.

"I'd appreciate you keeping that quiet," he said. "That's in the past and I'd like to keep it there."

"It's okay with me," Smith said. "The way I see it, a man's got the right to be what he wants when he wants. A lot of folk would like to change what they are, but just haven't the nerve to give it a try. Fact, I've heard you have. Leastways, that's the way people are talking who've come to your church. Don't worry, preacher. Ain't nothing comin' from me to spoil your deal. I just wish I had something to fall back on." His voice lowered. "I'm gettin' up there in years. Ain't got too many left if I have to keep using my gun. Shore would like to just ride the range. Maybe do a few drives. I'm tired, preacher. Plumb tired. But" — he shook his head — "there's still a need for me and I just can't let folks ride roughshod over others. Sticks in my craw. But know

301

this: Someone finds out who you were, ain't comin' from me."

"Thanks," Hood said meaningfully. "You'd do to ride the river with."

Smith gave him a strange look. "Yer the first man to ever say that to me. Maybe there's hope left."

"You two gonna keep jawin' or we gonna get this goin'," Turnbull bawled.

Hood and Smith rode up next to Turnbull. The others fell in with them, and they made little talk as the ranchers rode up to the J-Bar-H. They had started to swing across Harris's range when Harris and another cowboy rode up to them. Harris gave a smile to the others and said, "Welcome, boys. I'm sorry I couldn't make your little meeting, but we have some fall calves that need branding."

"That's what we're here for," Jed said soberly.

The smile slipped a notch off Harris's face. His hand dropped casually to his gun.

"I'm afraid I don't get your drift, Jed," he said.

"We want to do a little brand inspecting," Hayes said, watching Harris intently.

The smile slipped fully off Harris's face.

"I reckon you'd better spill all of it," he said quietly.

"Amos here showed us a possible reason for me missing all those cattle," Hayes said. "It seems that there's a possibility that my I-Bar-H is being made to make a J-Bar-H."

"That's nonsense," Harris said bleakly. But he looked nervous as Smith pushed his horse next to his.

"Maybe," Turnbull said. "But we have an easy way to prove it. We'll look to find a brand smudged — if we can find it — then we'll kill the calf and skin the brand. The underside will show the old brand."

"You ain't gonna kill one of my calves!" Harris said furiously. His hand slapped at his pistol, but Smith's suddenly appeared, cocked, under his nose.

"No reason to be alarmed," Turnbull said. "If we're wrong, I'll replace the calf. You'll be out nothing."

"No!" Harris said, his hand going to his pistol. But Crease and Vince already had theirs out along with Smith's, centered on Harris and the cowboy.

"Let's have your pistol, Jess," Turnbull said.

Smith gigged his horse forward and silently took the pistol from Harris's holster. Crease took the other cowboy's pistol and they made him come along.

"Now," Turnbull said harshly. "Let's see if

we can find a calf."

It didn't take long. Within a mile, they found a calf bearing a suspicious brand. Hayes shot it and dismounted, pulling a knife from his pocket and opening it. Within seconds, he had peeled the skin and brand from the calf and held it up. Everyone there could see how the brand had been altered.

"Reckon that does it," Turnbull said coldly. "I take this badly, Jess. We been friends for a long time."

Harris licked his lips, his face ashen. "Come on, boys," he said. "That's obviously a mistake. And it don't mean I put that brand there."

"Who else?" Hayes said. His eyes glittered angrily. "Who else would put your brand on one of my calves?"

"What I don't know is how you think you would be gettin' away with it all the time," Campbell said.

"Gannon came up with the idea," Harris said in a panic. "We combined our cattle on drives over to Kansas and the cattle towns. First to Dodge City, then to Abilene. That way, no one would get suspicious. We thought." He looked bitterly at Hood.

"At least we thought no one would," Harris said.

Turnbull gave a big sigh. "You know what

this means, don't you, Jess?"

Harris shook his head. "You can't do it, boys. We been friends for too long. I'll make it right. I promise!"

"There's a cottonwood down by the creek," Hayes said, pointing.

"That'll do," McKellon answered.

"No! Please! Don't!" Harris pleaded.

"Don't do it, men," Hood said. "Take him over to Durango for trial."

Campbell smiled thinly. "You know what kind of trial that would be, Reverend. Gannon or Harris here will have boys come over to load the jury, and we can't trust Futterman not to let them escape from jail."

"It's the unwritten law, Amos," McKellon said. "I'm sorry, but that's the way it is."

"No," Hood said desperately. "Don't put blood on your hands!"

"The blood won't be on our hands," Turnbull said. "Harris did that when he started to rebrand Hayes's cattle. This law's been here longer before any other came into the country."

"Crease? Vince?" Hood asked desperately.

"Sorry, Amos," Crease said coldly. "Afraid we're gonna have to side with Mr. Turnbull and the others."

"Ain't nothing else for it," Packer said.

"Please, Reverend!" Harris said. "Make

them stop."

"You form the loop, Ira," Turnbull said. He rode behind Harris, pulling piggin strings from his saddle. "Put your hands behind you, Jess."

"I'll be damned!" Harris said, and dug his spurs into his horse's sides.

The bay whinnied and started to run away, but McKellon caught the horse by the bridle while Campbell tossed a loop over Harris, pulling him from his saddle. Harris lay dazed in the dust.

Turnbull jumped to the ground and rolled Harris over, expertly knotting the piggin strings around Harris's wrists. Crease and Vince dismounted and awkwardly put Harris back in his saddle.

McKellon took Harris's reins and the group rode toward the cottonwood.

"What about him?" Campbell said, nodding at the nervous cowboy who'd ridden with Harris.

"What's your name?" Turnbull asked belligerently.

"Rhodes. Dusty Rhodes," the cowboy said.

"You don't wanna join your boss, you'd better whip leather out of here."

No sooner were the words free from his mouth than Rhodes had his sorrel in a run, racing north away from the party.

"Well," McKellon said as Hayes tossed the rope over a thick branch about fourteen feet from the ground. "Let's get on with it. Waiting don't make it any easier."

Hood tried to gig Sheba forward to stand between the ranchers and Harris, but Vince caught his reins and said, "No, sir. This is the way it's gotta be."

Hayes ran the rope around the thick trunk of the cottonwood while Turnbull fixed the noose around Harris's neck, carefully positioning the knot behind Harris's right ear.

"Preacher!" Harris squealed.

But Hood could do nothing to stop the hanging.

"Dear Father in heaven," he said. "Please forgive these men for what they are about to do."

Hardly were the words from his mouth when Campbell laid his quirt over the backside of Harris's horse. The horse leaped forward as Harris gave a loud cry of despair. Then his neck broke loudly and his body swung back and forth limply beneath the cottonwood tree, his weight making the rope saw back and forth, creaking.

All sat quietly on their horses, looking at the swinging body of Harris, who had once been their friend. Then Turnbull removed his hat and wiped his sleeve over his forehead.

"All right, boys," he said quietly. "The first one's over. Let's take him back to his ranch and bury him. He may have been a rustler, but he was also our friend and I for one don't want to leave him for the buzzards."

"I agree," Hayes said. He reached down from his saddle and loosened the knot around the cottonwood tree. Harris slipped to the ground while Vince retrieved Harris's horse. McKellon stepped down from his horse and removed the noose from his neck.

Together, Campbell and McKellon lifted the lifeless body and draped it over Harris's saddle.

Turnbull looked at Hood. "I'd appreciate it greatly, Reverend, if you'd say a few words over Jess."

Hood nodded. "At least we can give him a Christian burial."

"Wouldn't have it any other way," Hayes said, gathering the reins of Harris's horse.

They took Harris's body back to the ranch house and laid it on the porch. Several cowboys came running, shouting to each other at the sight of their dead boss, grabbing angrily for pistols. Turnbull and the others quickly pulled their rifles from their sheaths and leveled them at the cowboys.

For a moment, it looked like a massacre was about to begin, but Hood rode Sheba between the cowboys and ranchers.

"Put up your guns!" he shouted sharply. His eyes danced with anger. "There's been enough bloodshed! Put up your guns! Now!"

Reluctantly, the cowboys sheathed their pistols, muttering dark imprecations against the ranchers. Then a couple climbed the stairs to the porch and shouted, "He's been hung!"

"For rustling!" Turnbull shouted back. "We have the proof. And what's more, some of you might want to shag tail out of here within the next twenty-four hours. Harris couldn't have stolen all those cows without some help from some of you. Maybe," he added, his face a grim mask, "all of you."

"What if we don't!" a voice taunted.

"We have lots of rope," Turnbull said quietly. "There's little lower than a man who steals from his neighbors."

"Tomorrow morning I'll come by to read over him," Hood said. "About ten."

"He'll be ready," a burly cowboy with a bushy beard said. His eyes snapped black fire. A black-handled pistol was belted at his waist halfway between his right wrist and elbow. Hood knew instantly that this man wasn't an ordinary ranny to ride fence and push cattle. "We appreciate your concern, preacher," the man said.

He shifted his gaze to Smith, sitting his horse quietly to the side.

"Good to see you again, Panhandle. Don't like the circumstances, though."

"Know what you mean, Jubal. But I think this valley's gettin' to the point where there ain't gonna be much use for you or me."

The man named Jubal nodded, studying his boots for a moment, then looked up. His eyes shifted back and forth between Smith and Hood. He nodded at Harris's body.

"Wouldn't want you to think I had anything to do with that," he said.

"I know," Smith said quietly. He slipped from his horse and stood facing Jubal. He dropped the reins and took a wide step from his horse. His thumbs slipped the leather loops off the hammers of his pistols.

"But I do ride for the brand," Jubal said, stepping clear of the others. "You know how it's gotta be."

"I know," Smith said gently. "But you could ride on outta here. Go north. Or west."

A rueful smile spread over Jubal's face,

taut now with strain.

"Would you? Things reversed?"

"No," Smith said.

"Well, then," Jubal said. His hand darted down for his pistol and he almost had it level when Smith's gun boomed. A great hole appeared in Jubal's chest, then blossomed into a red flower an instant before blood spurted.

Jubal dropped his pistol and used his hands to try to staunch the flow of blood.

"Never thought you were faster," he said. Blood spurted from his mouth. He hawked and spat. He looked at Hood. "You do the rites, preacher?"

Hood nodded. "Yes," he said gently. "I'll do the rites."

Jubal nodded, then said to Panhandle, "Never thought we'd cross."

"Me neither," Smith said.

Jubal coughed again, blood gushed from his mouth, and he pitched forward into the dirt, dead.

Smith sighed, and slipped the spent cartridge from his pistol and replaced it with a fresh one before slipping it back into its holster. Tiny lines of regret appeared on his face.

"Well, I reckon that finishes that," Smith said. He stepped back into his stirrups and swung aboard. "I take it Gannon's next?"

Turnbull nodded. "Yep, I guess he is."

"He ain't going as easy as Harris and Jubal," Smith said.

"Never reckoned he would," Turnbull said. He turned his horse north and rode away, followed by the others.

Black clouds suddenly appeared overhead as the party rode up the road toward Gannon's Circle G. Hood and Smith rode, as if by consent, at the rear of the party, taking comfort in that strange bonding that links two people who respect and admire each other.

They didn't get far off Harris's land when a small band of cowboys rode down to meet them.

"I'm Jim Wall," the cowboy in the lead said. He smiled pleasantly enough, but Smith turned his horse out a short way from the party. Instinctively, Hood followed.

Wall studied them humorously for a moment; then his face hardened as the riders with him fanned out on either side.

"You're on Circle G land," Wall said, his eyes narrowing. His bay shifted her hooves nervously, then quieted under Wall's hand.

"I know," Turnbull said, his jaw jutting out belligerently. "But we got business with your boss."

"Gannon ain't here right now," Wall said. "You got a message you want me to take to him?"

Turnbull made as if to speak angrily, but Hood rode in front of him and sat, addressing Wall.

"We have a problem," he said. "It seems as if Gannon's Circle G has been placed over quite a few Circle C brands."

Wall studied them for a moment; then his eyes lit on Panhandle.

"What do you have to say about this, Panhandle?"

Smith shook his head. "I don't know what to say, Jim. 'Cept I've seen the proof of Harris turning Hayes's I into a J. It don't seem far wrong to say that it's possible Gannon's been overbranding Campbell's stock."

Wall set his bay quietly for a long moment; then he shook his head.

"I ain't seen any of that," he said to Hood. "But if'n you think that's possible, then I'll go along with you while you inspect."

"I appreciate that, Mr. Wall," Hood said.

Turnbull rode up beside Hood. He addressed Wall. "And if it proves false, I'll reimburse Gannon for all expenses."

"Fair enough," Wall said. He glanced over his shoulder at the other riders. "There ain't no need for all of you to follow. You have chores to do. Get to them. Blake, you're in charge. And if Kevin comes around, you keep him with you, understand? We don't need that hothead stirring things up."

"I got it," Jim Blake said. "But you know Kevin. He doesn't take kindly to someone ordering him about." He looked at the ranchers in front of him. "Especially when you all are looking for his brother."

Wall gave Blake a hard look and said, "I don't care if you have to hog-tie him. Keep him up by the ranch house."

"All right," Blake said. "Come on, boys."

The riders hesitated for a long moment, studying the ranchers and Smith and Hood. Then they deliberately turned their horses and headed back up the valley toward Gannon's place.

Wall fell in beside Smith and said, "This is queer doings, ain't it? You ever think that Harris and maybe Gannon would be doing something like that?"

"What's stranger is that they kept it from others. The best I can figure is that they had a few brand artists they could trust and they handled that while others, like you, Jim, handled the honest part of their ranching. This valley is big enough that they could carry on their business. But I reckon it smarts some to realize that your boss has been dealing false while you've been working at the honest trade."

Wall rode in silence beside Smith for a while, then sighed.

"I shore hope you all are mistaken, Panhandle. I shorely do."

"I do, too," Smith said. "But they weren't mistaken at Harris's place, and I don't think that they are going to be mistaken at Gannon's."

"What'd they do with Harris? Send him back to town with someone?"

"They hung him," Smith said curtly.

"*Hung him?* Sweet Lord! I thought they'd send him back with Jack Craven or someone."

"Ain't seen Craven in two, three weeks now. Far as I know, he might not even be in the valley."

"Oh, he's in the valley," Wall said. "He's been spending a lot of time with Gannon,"

"With Gannon, eh?" Smith said, raising his eyebrows. "Seems like there's more than one Indian in the woodpile. You know I'm gonna have to tell Turnbull and the others, don't you?"

"Well, however this turns out, I figure on leaving the country. I don't think I wanna work where this sort of thing is going on.

Where there's smoke, there's fire. Least-ways, how I'm thinking. An' I have no desire to get my neck stretched by mistake."

His face darkened. "I saw that happen up in Wind River country. It got so's in the end they didn't care who they hung, even if someone was given up as being a thief or rustler 'cause someone else had it in for them. I ain't saying that's gonna happen here, but it's got similar earmarkings."

The ranchers abruptly pulled up and sat, studying the side of the calf in front of them.

"Looks like it might have been reworked," Turnbull said. "What do you think, Reverend?"

Hood shrugged, then nodded reluctantly. "I'm not much of a cowman, but I've been around enough that I'd say that brand has been altered."

"I agree," Campbell said. "The circle looks overbranded and the seven changing the C to a G looks newer."

"All right," Hayes said, cocking his rifle. "Let's get it over with."

He sent a bullet through the calf's head, then stepped down from his horse and drew his knife. Four quick slashes and the flap of hide was free. He turned it over, studying it, then nodded and handed it up to Turn-bull.

"It's been altered," he said quietly. He wiped his knife on the hide and replaced it, then dusted his hands.

"I reckon we gotta search for Gannon," Campbell said. He looked at Wall. "Any ideas?"

Wall shook his head. "I ain't seen him for a while. I thought he might be going over to Durango for a spell to gamble and drink and whatever else he might take a fancy to. But he could just as well be up there."

He nodded at the steep walls covered with lodgepole pine. "He likes to hunt and when he gets the urge, he just takes off for a week or two."

"And if he's up there," Turnbull said thoughtfully, "chances are that he's seen what's going on down here and knows that we're onto him."

"There's something else," Panhandle said, looking at the others. He jerked his head toward Wall. "Jim here tells me that Craven has been spending a good amount of time with Gannon lately."

"Craven?" Turnbull frowned. "What would he be doing that for?"

"I'd say that Gannon probably made him a better offer than you folks," Hood said slowly. "He'd be able to make more than your Association would pay him by turning folks away from Gannon's land and maybe even Harris's. I'll bet he's the one who bounced a slug off my head."

"Campbell, how many men can you break loose to help hunt down Gannon?"

"Maybe eight or nine," Campbell said.

"I can match that," Hayes said.

"And me," McKellon said.

"And I can add to that, too," Turnbull said. "That gives us about thirty-five riders who can set off after Gannon. And Craven," he added darkly. "We know he wouldn't go south or east. So if we divide the men up into two parties, we should have a good chance of bringing him in."

"I hope you mean that," Hood said.

"What?"

"Bring him and Craven in instead of lynching them."

Turnbull shrugged. "It's really all the same. Here or there. But I figure if we hang them in town, they'll serve as a warning to others who might get the same idea. And" — he gave Hood a wintry smile — "I want to see their faces before they swing."

McKellon suddenly reined up and stood in his stirrups, shading his eyes with his hat.

"Hey, ain't that Thompson up there?" He pointed at a ridgeline to the north where a man sat his horse, apparently studying them.

Hayes looked and said, "I'll be damned. I think you're right."

"I wonder what he's doing out here," Campbell said.

"Whatever it is, I don't like it," Turnbull said. "I got a funny feeling about him being out here. He's been a town man all along."

"Appears to be alone," Hayes said.

"That worries me even more," Turnbull said. "It's almost like he's keeping track of us."

"Maybe it's just someone who looks like him," Hood said.

McKellon shook his head. "Nope. That's him. And if I ain't mistaken, that's Craven riding up to him."

The others looked and grimly agreed.

"What do you say, Jed? Should we go after him?"

Panhandle shook his head. "Our horses need resting. He's better mounted than we are. And that long gun of his could pick off a few of us if we get into its range. Let's just go back home and let tomorrow take its place."

Reluctantly, the ranchers booted their horses forward, riding toward their homes. A darkness seemed to settle over them as each was caught in his own misgivings about why Thompson and Craven were watching them.

22.

The next day, Sunday, Hood stood behind his podium and stared soberly at the congregation. He took a deep breath and began.

"My friends, a terrible justice has been brought down upon some who once we numbered as friends. That justice was swift and terrible, and the kindness and the truth by which all lived together have been broken, leaving only pain and anguish, hatred and anger, in their place. We are told in Proverbs that those who delight in doing evil and rejoicing in evil, those whose paths are crooked, will walk forever in that land where those paths shall lead them. They will not walk in the way of good men, for those who live upright in the good land are the peacemakers. The wicked will be cut off from the land and the treacherous will be uprooted from it.

"In our frenzy to bring justice to the land, we forget that the Lord will by no means leave the guilty unpunished. No one can stand before His wrath that is poured out like fire upon the sinners and those who were trusted once but who have broken that trust.

"I fear that this land will soon be covered with blood. We need at this moment to help bring peace and prosperity to the land, and by the goodness that we stretch forward to those who sin against us, to bring those sinners deep into our fold.

"I beg you to let the law handle what we would do for ourselves. It will be hard to turn that other cheek continually, but regard the jar of honey and the bottle of vinegar. Which draws the more flies?"

There was a general shuffling of feet along with furtive glances at one another while Hood continued with his sermon, begging that more people would not be judged and executed by irate citizens who were intent upon taking the law into their own hands.

When services were over, many left with surreptitious looks at Hood and the few who stood around him visited about what had happened in the Upper Valley. Elizabeth stood beaming beside him, performing the duties a wife normally would have undertaken in her husband's parish.

Suddenly, Bowdine appeared in front of

Elizabeth and Hood, his face dark with anger.

"I have come to take you for a ride," he said to Elizabeth, ignoring Hood and the others.

A deep blush rose into her cheeks. She shook her head.

"I'm sorry, Art, but I have already promised Mr. Ellis that I will go for a ride with him."

"Break it," Bowdine said bluntly. He reached out to take her arm, twisting it in his hand. She gasped and jerked back, only to be pulled forward even harder by Bowdine.

"Mr. Bowdine!" she said. "Behave yourself!"

"You've been leading me on long enough," Bowdine said harshly. "Now, I'm calling for a reckoning."

He turned to walk away, jerking Elizabeth after him.

A low growl came from beside Hood; then a gray wolf streaked through the air, paws landing on Bowdine's back, driving him to the ground. Quickly, he rolled over, but Sam leaped upon his chest, anger rumbling from his throat, his muzzle locked on Bowdine's throat.

Bowdine jerked his hand and pulled at his

gun. Sam released his hold on Bowdine's throat and clamped down hard with his teeth upon Bowdine's forearm.

Bowdine howled with the pain and tried to jerk away, but Sam's teeth were locked tight, and blood began dripping down from Bowdine's forearm. He tried to bring his pistol to bear on Sam, but Sam shook his head vigorously and Bowdine's pistol flew from his hand.

"Enough, Sam!" Hood ordered.

Reluctantly, Sam slowly relinquished his hold and stepped back from Bowdine, crouching, growling.

Suddenly, Ellis appeared, standing a short way from Bowdine. His eyes were hard, his features gaunt with tension. He kicked Bowdine's pistol to him.

"Pick it up, Bowdine," he said softly. "I'll give you that before I draw."

"Mr. Ellis!" Elizabeth burst out. "Please. Let's just go."

"Bowdine?" Ellis asked coldly.

Hood stepped between them, kicking Bowdine's pistol away from him.

"Let it go, Ellis. Please? This is not the time or place."

"As you wish," Ellis said, tipping his hat. "Don't push this any further, Bowdine."

"When I do, you won't have the help you

do now," Bowdine snapped.

Ellis gave a short ugly laugh and offered his arm to Elizabeth. She took it, and he walked her to the buggy standing a short distance away and helped her in. He paused to give Bowdine a short smile, then climbed in the buggy, picked up the reins, and drove off.

Bowdine stood white-faced with anger, and painfully slipped his pistol back into his holster. The bleeding had stopped and as he tried to wipe the blood from his clothes, he turned to walk rigidly away to the buggy he had hired. He mounted, took the reins, then whipped the horses savagely into a gallop.

"I think this is just the beginning of trouble," Bledsoe said regretfully from beside Hood. "Very bad trouble."

Hood nodded, watching Bowdine as he rode off.

"I do believe that you are right," he said to Bledsoe.

He called Sam to him and squatted, petting Sam and thanking the wolf for keeping an ugly thing from becoming uglier. Sam stretched his head, letting Hood's hand slide down his neck and back.

Nelson Futterman, the county sheriff, came down from Durango after hearing about the lynching of Harris, but more to complain to the Citizens Committee than to seek to take anyone into custody. He blustered around, talking to people, but it was obvious that he was hoping that no answers would be forthcoming that would force him into a duty that he really didn't want to perform.

After a couple of days, he rode back to Durango, leaving Gold Town to its own devices.

An uneasy peace fell over the town. Thompson arrested four miners for brawling in the street. He also took in Jim Blake and Kevin Gannon, who got drunk and, after reclaiming their pistols, proceeded to shoot up the town. Thompson fined them thirty dollars and told them never to come back in town. For a moment, it looked like Kevin was going to draw his pistol, but Blake talked him into riding out.

Panhandle and the men riding with him brought five men in for taking part in Gannon's and Harris's scheme. One of the men was shaken and ashen-faced. A crude bandage was wrapped around his left shoulder. Another's face looked as if he'd fallen headfirst into a beehive.

Thompson locked the cowboys into the jail while the riders had a drink in the Crystal Palace. Panhandle came to see

Hood and shook his head.

"It ain't good, Reverend," Smith said. He took his hat off and slapped dust from his shotgun chaps with it. "Everyone's toting guns up there" — he nodded toward the Upper Valley — "and they ain't hesitant about using them. There's been a couple of killings and more coming, I expect. Those we brought in were seven to start with, but they decided to try and shoot their way out. We killed two — one of them was Jim Blake — and winged that other one and the rest gave up readily enough."

"Gannon and Craven?"

Smith shook his head. "Nope. Nary a sighting. But they're up there. No doubt about that. And now it's official that Craven has started to ride with Gannon. They came down outta the hills to get supplies and such from Gannon's house. We pinned them in there for two days, but when the second night came, it was moonless and they managed to slip away."

"What are you going to do now?"

Panhandle sighed and ran his hand over the top of his head. "Well, go back out, that's for certain. But this whole thing is looking like flaring up into a range war."

"Over two men?" Hood asked.

"It just ain't them anymore," Smith said.

"Seems like some of the miners are deciding that ranching beats the hell out of trying to wash enough color out of the creeks to make things profitable. You know that's all open range out there, and some of those miners are staking claims. Of course, they're staking claims around the water, and that ain't setting right with folk who have been sharing water for the most part. Turnbull has water close enough to the ranch house that the few miners who have tried to squat on it have been easy to drive off. Gannon has water in the side canyons, but McKellon, Campbell, and Hayes are going to be hurtin' if something can't be done to drive them off. I think we're seein' the end of open range, Reverend. I know that Turnbull and McKellon have ordered Glidden wire, and I have a hunch Campbell and Hayes aren't gonna be far behind."

"But if they fence off the range, what about water?"

Smith shook his head. "There is water close by, and it would be theirs if they already had the wire up. But some of those miners have already moved in and placed their stakes, enclosing the water by squatter's boundary. It ain't right, Reverend. It just ain't right."

"I know," Hood said. "But it's the coming

times. There isn't much we can do about it. Have the squatters registered yet?"

Smith shrugged. "I don't know. I expect not as they are goin' around banging their chests like they're some he-bull, bragging how they're gonna close those ranchers off and buy their spreads for a song after they go under."

Hood pursed his lips, frowning. He scuffed the toe of his boot in the dust and arched his back to get a crick out of it. He reached down and ruffled Sam's ears, then looked up at Smith.

"All right. Here's what you do. Ride over to Durango and claim the Upper Valley under rough survey. That means you are the one who is gonna set the spread limits of anyone who wants to use the land. It's unusual, but I've known it to work back in Kansas. And, if *you* do it, there'll be less chance of flimflamming going on when you set the valley under rough survey. The land office will have a map and you make them produce it, then draw a line ten miles north of Gold Town clean across the valley, marking out the upper reaches."

"This legal?" Smith asked, then grinned rakishly. "Hell, I guess it don't matter much to me."

Hood laughed and stood, running a forefinger under the brim of his hat to remove sweat. "I don't think it means much to anyone out here right now. I wouldn't say that there's really much law in the valley what with Nelson Futterman staying up in Durango close to the saloons and eating houses."

"Well, I'll do it. I'll leave right now. I should be up at Durango by morning and be first for the land office when it opens." He smiled grimly and touched the handle of one of his pistols. "Even so, I reckon I can persuade him to let me go first. Thanks for the advice, preacher."

Hood sighed and took Panhandle's hand and shook it.

"I hate deceit and wish there was some other way of doing this. But I can see where it might stave off shootings and murders. One thing, though: You'll have to use your name as the representative of the Cattlemen's Association. And you'll have to sign the land transfers once the survey is accomplished. I'll try and get to Turnbull and the others and let them know what's going on so they won't get their ire up any."

Panhandle grinned and flicked his finger against the brim of his worn, sweat-stained hat.

"And I'm off, Reverend."

He turned, hitched his gun belt, and walked briskly down the street to his horse, mounted, and galloped off.

"I hope this works," Hood murmured. He looked down at Sam and scratched behind his ears. Sam sighed deeply in contentment. "There's going to be a lot of mad people if they haven't registered their claim. And I do feel sorry for them. But the ranchers have earned the right to that land."

He sighed. "I reckon we'd better ride out and let Turnbull and the others know what's happening so there aren't any surprises when Panhandle comes back."

He rose and walked down to the corral to gather Sheba.

For once, Sheba didn't protest her saddling, and waited patiently for Hood to step into the stirrups. Hood touched her ribs lightly with his heels and trotted out of the corral and town. Once free of the town limits, he relaxed the reins and let the filly pick her own gait while Sam moved smoothly beside her.

23.

The evening star was shining brightly when Hood was met by Turnbull in the ranch yard. Turnbull grinned up at him as he caught Sheba's bridle.

"Well, Reverend, it appears that you've come just in time for supper," Turnbull said easily. "Come along and join us."

"Us?" Hood said as he swung down from the saddle.

"Yep. I decided to have the men over for dinner and a talk. McKellon's here. And Campbell and Hayes just rode in. You're surely welcome, too."

Turnbull reached to pet Sheba on the nose, but she jerked her head away and Sam made an unwelcome growl from beside her.

Turnbull's eyebrows lifted. "Good Lord! I've heard about one man's horse, but never knew that one man to have his horse protected by a wolf!"

"Sam," Hood said quietly, taking Sheba's

reins. "That's enough."

Sam walked stiff-legged to the porch and climbed up on it. He sat, yellow eyes gleaming as he studied Turnbull.

"I think," Turnbull said solemnly, "that your horse is as safe as if she was in the bank vault."

Hood smiled and draped Sheba's reins loosely over the hitching rail. "If you think Sam is bad, try to mount Sheba. She's got quite a temper. Sometimes — most times — she barely tolerates me."

"Uh-huh," Turnbull said thoughtfully, staring from Sam to Sheba and back. "Let's go inside. And bring your wolf. He's as welcome as you. People talk about some things he's done in Gold Town."

"I appreciate that," Hood said, removing his hat and smoothing down his cowlick. He snapped his fingers for Sam, fell in next to Turnbull, and entered the room with Sam at his heels.

The ranchers were sitting on horsehide chairs and a sofa in front of a fire dancing in the cobblestoned fireplace. The walls had been paneled with knotty pine and gleamed from waxing. A magnificent elk head was mounted over the fireplace and black walnut mantel. On the mantel stood two small frames with pictures of a woman and a small boy in them.

"That's my wife and son," Turnbull said when he caught Hood studying them. "They died of diphtheria a few years back."

Hood nodded. "I'm sorry to hear that."

Turnbull nodded and turned away as Hood considered the rest of the room.

Small pine tables, their surfaces glowing like soft gold, stood beside the chairs and sofa, and upon the tables were green-shaded oil lamps. Indian blankets had been thrown over the chairs and sofa, and the fur of a silver-tip grizzly covered the floor in front of the fireplace.

Around the room were several paintings showing life on the range. Against one wall was a gun cabinet with the well-oiled gun barrels standing like the pipes of a pipe organ. A drinks cabinet stood next to it, the shelves in the cabinet shining with expensive crystal, the marble surface covered with several liquor bottles.

At the far end, which served as the dining room, stood a polished limestone table with a small crystal chandelier hanging above it. Places had been set, and Hood could smell beef cooking in the kitchen. His mouth watered.

"Boys," Turnbull said, "the reverend's gonna join us. What will you have to drink,

Reverend? We're having a little Tennessee sippin' whiskey."

"Why, then, I think I'll have the same," Hood said. "I haven't had good Tennessee whiskey since leaving the Tennessee hills quite a few years ago."

"Well, we'll see if we can change that," Turnbull said, turning to the drinks cabinet and taking a heavy crystal glass from a shelf.

"What brings you here, Reverend?" Mc-Kellon asked, coming forward to shake Hood's hand in welcome. The others followed him.

"I heard from Panhandle about some problems that are happening on your ranges," Hood said.

The atmosphere in the room grew chilly and heavy. The men shook their heads, grim-faced.

"I hope you didn't ride out here to try and tell us to turn the other cheek, Reverend," Hayes said. "We've gotta find some way of stopping those miners from homesteading our range and cutting us off from water."

"I know," Hood said, taking the glass from Turnbull and trying a sip. His eyebrows rose in appreciation.

"Now that's sipping whiskey," Hood said. "No, I haven't come out to try and talk you out of anything. Yet. I just want you to know what I've been doing."

"Oh?" Campbell asked.

Hood took another sip. "I know that you've all had some miners trying to become homesteaders by staking out land that you've managed for years. As I rode out, I didn't see any buildings on the land others than yours. Has a homesteader built anything on your lands?"

"No," Hayes answered. "No, they've just staked out the land."

"And it is useless," McKellon said. "No one can farm over four thousand feet. At least in this day and age. Maybe later someone will figure out a way, I don't know, but this land right now is good only for cattle and sheep. Frankly, I think the only reason they staked out the land is to hold us hostage for the water. I can sympathize with them for wanting a home, but they're only allowed a hundred sixty acres and that ain't enough for running cattle or sheep even with a single-loop operation. I ain't in favor of bloodshed, but by God — excuse me, Reverend — it ain't right for land we have been using all along to be taken from us. And it sure isn't right that water be taken away from other people who need it."

Hood took a deep breath and let it out

slowly. "Then, I think we can settle this without bloodshed. I sent Panhandle into Durango today to claim the Upper Valley under rough survey."

The ranchers exchanged looks.

"Rough survey?" McKellon asked. "I've never heard that before."

"I'm not certain that it will work out here," Hood said, "but back in Kansas I know that it did and I understand that it is federal law. The area hasn't been surveyed yet for statehood, and that leaves it open for someone to survey it and assign homesteading if any. Now, Panhandle is going to claim the land in the name of the Cattlemen's Association for rough survey. That means that he is the owner for the Association and will be responsible for settling claims *and previous claims of people who have already proved on the land.* And that," Hood added, "is everyone here."

Silence met his words as the ranchers looked back and forth at each other. Then a shout of relief came and they all came forward to shake Hood's hand and pat his back thankfully.

"My God!" Turnbull breathed. "You're a genius!"

"Will assigning land also be granted to the homesteaders?"

Hood shook his head. "No. No, it shouldn't, as all of you have been using the land steadily, taking care that none of it is overgrazed, and making small stock tanks here and there, which is improving the land."

"This isn't going to go down well with those miners," Hayes said grimly.

"We'll cover that bridge when we come to it," Turnbull said. "Right now, this dinner has turned into a celebration. Reverend, brace yourself. You ain't riding home tonight."

He turned away, took the crystal decanter from the table, and refilled everyone's glass. He lifted his aloft and said, "To the Reverend Amos Hood."

"To Reverend Hood," the others chorused.

24.

The moon came up blood orange when Hood made his excuses, despite the objections of the ranchers, and bade them good night. He started back to Gold Town. He rode easily with Sam trotting by his side. Bullbats darted overhead, catching night insects, and the shadow of an owl swept silently over the moon in search of rodents. A wolf howled in the distance and Sam lifted his head, ears pricked forward. He loped off into the darkness a short distance off the trail and lifted his head in an answering howl. Silence followed his howl and he trotted back, satisfied, to Sheba's side.

"Right proud of yourself, aren't you, boy?" Hood said. "You hearing the call of the wild?"

Sam sneezed from the dust kicked up by Sheba's hooves. He moved off a short distance to get in front of Sheba. Hood laughed softly.

He was passing a small stand of lodgepole pines when something shone on the ground in front of him. He reined in Sheba and bent down to look at it just as a bullet whistled past where his head had been just seconds ago and smacked into one of the trees.

Hood clamped his heels to Sheba's side, rode swiftly into the lodgepole stand, and slipped the Spencer .56 from its sheath on his saddle and levered a cartridge into the bore. He glanced around for Sam, but the wolf had disappeared.

He heard the shot this time, and flinched as the bullet slapped into one of the trees away from him, followed by a heavy *boom!*

A Sharps rifle, he thought automatically. *Maybe a Winchester .44-40. Probably a Sharps, though. Maybe a fifty-caliber. There's more time between the shots than a Winchester could make.*

He slipped forward, trying to take a steady line toward the shooter. Another shot, this one disappearing through the pines.

Hood crossed the road swiftly and weaved his way rapidly through the pines, moving toward a slight hill that looked as if it would be high enough for a shooter to wait for his victim.

He was almost there when he heard a

scream and snarling. Hood dashed forward over the crest and saw Sam, feet holding the shooter's shoulders down, his muzzle buried in the shooter's throat. The shooter's hands gripped the ruff around Sam's shoulders, trying desperately to push the wolf away.

"Sam!" Hood snapped. "Back!"

But Hood was too late. Even as he ordered Sam to back away, the wolf gave a savage shake with his head and blood spurted from the shooter's throat. The blood looked black in the moonlight.

Hood knelt beside the shooter, but the shooter's eyes glazed. He shuddered once, then lay still.

"Kevin Gannon!" Hood said. Then a feeling of loss and sorrow came over him. "You should have stayed away from your brother, son."

Then the thought of Frank Gannon being around made him stiffen, and he stepped quickly from the body and merged into the pines and stayed silent. He watched Sam as the wolf calmly cleaned himself, but Sam gave no notice that there was someone else in the area.

Still, Hood waited, patient in the dark, listening to the night noises around him. At last, he knew nobody else was around and went back to Kevin. He knelt beside him and started going through Kevin's pockets.

He found a folding knife, a few coins, and from an inside pocket of Kevin's vest, a large wad of bills. Hood looked at them closely — all fifties and hundreds. Maybe a thousand dollars, he thought. Kevin had been riding for his brother for a long time. *But what are you doing with this much money?*

He shoved the wad of money in his pocket, took Kevin's ivory-handled Colt .44 from its holster, and headed back into the trees to find Kevin's horse. He found the sorrel tied off to a tree and brought the gelding back to Kevin's body. The sorrel snorted and tried to dance away from the smell of blood, but Hood held the reins tightly and talked soothingly to the sorrel until he settled down.

Sighing, Hood bent and lifted Kevin and draped him over his saddle. He picked up Kevin's Sharps .50 rifle and shoved it into the saddle sheath.

"Come on, Sam," he said, and led the horse back to where Sheba stood, waiting patiently for him. He mounted and took the sorrel's reins and rode back onto the road, turning toward the town lights a short distance away.

■ ■ ■ ■

A small group of miners was standing around under the Sampling House's over-hang when Hood rode into town, leading Kevin's horse with Kevin draped over his saddle. A couple of them slipped back into the saloon, and by the time Hood got down to Doc Martin's place, a crowd had gathered behind him.

"Who'd he get?" someone asked from the back of the crowd.

"The reverend shot someone?"

"It's Kevin Gannon."

"Jesus! Look at his throat!"

"The reverend didn't do that. I'd reckon it was that wolf pet of his'n."

"Lord have mercy!"

Ignoring them, Hood climbed the stairs and knocked on Doc Martin's door.

Doc answered the door and glanced down the stairs. His bloodshot eyes came back to Hood's.

"Anyone I might know?"

"Kevin Gannon," Hood said. "He tried to dry-gulch me on my way in from Turnbull's place."

Doc nodded. "You shoot him?"

"No," Hood said, shaking his head. He

indicated Sam sitting beside him. "Sam took him in the throat."

Doc scrubbed the knuckles of his right hand over the top of his head.

"This is not going to settle well with the Circle G boys," he said. "I imagine that there are some in town right now. Well, have a couple of those miners take him down to the undertaker. If his throat's gone, I don't need to see him."

Hood nodded and went back down the stairs. Cacklejack and Hank Wooten had pushed their way to the front of the crowd. Hood nodded at them. "Appreciate you two carrying him down to the undertaker."

Cacklejack and Hank exchanged glances and nodded, and took Kevin by the arms and legs and plodded down the street with him.

Hood stepped into his saddle and turned toward Mrs. Hargrave's boardinghouse. The crowd parted silently as Hood rode through them. Halfway down the street, two cowboys stood in the middle of the street, blocking his way, their hands not far from their pistol butts. Hood recognized Croak Stone on the left and Johnny Crane on the right.

"Heard you brought in Kevin Gannon," Croak said. "Heard it was your wolf that ripped out his throat."

Hood nodded, his eyes watchful on the pair.

"You don't do that to a Gannon," Crane said.

"He shouldn't have tried to dry-gulch me," Hood said quietly. "It was his call, he paid for it."

"Don't make no difference to us!" Crane said. He nodded at Hood's Spencer. "I imagine you ain't carrying a pistol. We'll let you get that Spencer out before we draw."

Hood reached under his coat and brought out Kevin's pistol. He held it easily by his saddle horn.

"That looks like Kevin's gun," Croak said.

"It is," Hood said quietly.

"You planning on using it? You a reverend and all?" Croak asked.

"No," Hood said, tossing the gun at their feet. "Take it back to Gannon. It's only right he should have something of his younger brother's."

"Maybe we'll use it to finish the job," Crane said, bending to pick up the pistol. "I'm gonna collect that wolf's ears for what he done to me."

"Leave it lay," Thompson ordered from behind Hood.

Hood turned in the saddle to see Thompson standing a short way off from Sheba's withers.

"This ain't your affair, Thompson," Croak said. "This is between us and Hood."

"And that wolf pet of his," Crane added.

"No, it's my business," Thompson said. "Outside of the town limits may be your business, but not in my town."

"Your town?" Croak asked. He gave an ugly laugh. "Taken on a bit much, haven't you, Thompson?"

Thompson shrugged. "You heard me. Now unbuckle your gun belts. You're going to jail and the judge in the morning. After that, I'm posting you both out of town. What are your names?"

"I'm Croak Stone," Croak said. "This here is Johnny Crane. He's got a problem with that wolf. That wolf damn near tore his hand off."

"Well, Croak, Johnny, you'll have to work that out some other time. Right now, unbuckle your gun belts and drop them. I'm taking you both to jail."

"Where's Bowdine, your partner?" Croak asked, looking around in the shadows.

"He's not here," Thompson said. "Now, I'm not going to tell you again. Go to jail."

"Be damned if I will!" Croak said furiously. His eyes glinted wildly.

"You'll be dead if you don't," Thompson said softly.

The two cowboys stared at Thompson for a long moment; then suddenly, as if both shared a single thought, their hands stabbed down for their pistols. As they raised them, two shots rang out. Croak twisted sideways as he fell backward. Crane staggered backward, but kept his balance. He started to raise his pistol again. Another shot rang out, and Crane's legs seemed to leap straight from the ground as he fell backward with a neat hole in the center of his forehead.

Croak's legs twisted and he brought them up tightly against his stomach, trying to ease the pain there. Then his legs twisted three times and he lay still.

Hood looked over at Thompson as the marshal calmly thumbed the three empty shells from his pistol and replaced them with fresh cartridges. He slipped the pistol into the black sheath hanging on his hip and looked up at Hood.

He read something in Hood's eyes and gave a thin smile. "I offered them an out, Reverend. They could have taken it. Instead, they chose this." He waved his hand, indicating Croak and Johnny. "It was a fair fight."

"Was it?" Hood said thoughtfully. "I wonder."

Thompson's eyes narrowed. "What do you mean?"

"For all their loud talk, they weren't in your class."

Thompson shrugged. "I just saved your life, Reverend. If I wouldn't have killed them, you would be lying in the dust right now. And so would your wolf," he added, nodding at Sam.

"For that, I thank you," Hood said. "But I wonder if you couldn't have taken them to jail by covering them with your pistol. Neither of them could match your draw. We just saw the proof of that."

"Maybe I could've," Thompson said. "I guess I just didn't give it a thought."

He turned and left Hood sitting on Sheba, the cowboys dead in the middle of the street.

"I wonder if you did," Hood said softly to himself as Thompson mounted the steps to the Crystal Palace and pushed his way through the swinging doors.

Cacklejack and Hank appeared beside Hood.

"You want we should take them two up to the undertaker, too?" Hank asked.

"Appreciate it if you would," Hood said.

"All right," Cacklejack grumbled. "I reckon the undertaker's gonna be real busy for a while now."

The two miners bent and picked up Croak. Cacklejack nodded at Johnny. "We'll come back for him soon's we drop this one off."

"No hurry," Hood said. "He isn't going anywhere."

"Ain't that the truth," Cacklejack said.

Together, the miners moved awkwardly down the street, carrying the limp form of Croak between them.

25.

The dining room was empty when Hood entered it with Sam. He pulled a chair out and sat as Mrs. Hargrave bustled in.

"You got a soup bone back there, Sam," she said, indicating the kitchen behind her.

Sam rose and trotted out to the kitchen.

"He's the easiest to feed among all my boarders," Mrs. Hargrave said.

Hood laughed. "I imagine he is."

"Well, now," Mrs. Hargrave said. "I got steaks, eggs, and fresh bread baked this morning."

"I'll take it all," Hood said. "I seem to have worked up an appetite."

Mrs. Hargrave put her hands on her wide hips and said, "That's the word going around. I imagine some of those old biddies are going to have their tongues a-waggin' about how it ain't right for a preacher to be mixing in with the trouble."

"You can't stop people from talking,"

Hood said easily.

"Isn't that the truth," she sniffed. "But I think you should take heed of the talk."

"Where should I be but with those who need to be brought into the church?" Hood asked.

"There are some here who don't think that way. That church is for those who are the so-called 'good folks' in town. Frankly, I figure they're so prissy that they can't smell fresh manure on their shoes. Just watch yourself, that's all I'm saying."

"And I thank you for that," Hood said.

Mrs. Hargrave eyed him suspiciously, then heaved a great sigh. "Easier talking to a fence post than a preacher set in his ways. I'll get your breakfast."

She went into the kitchen, and Hood listened to the sound of skillets and pans being placed on the stove. He resolved that he would make more house calls, which, he admitted to himself, he had been lax in making.

But first, he had to find out if Panhandle had made it back and how things were setting with the ranchers and others. If he didn't miss his guess, trouble was going to come to a head soon enough.

Hood felt the sun on his back as he rode

into the Upper Valley, but there was a chill beneath the warmth as well, and he knew Indian summer was coming to a close. If that wasn't enough, he had noticed that Sam's fur was thickening, as was Sheba's. It wouldn't be long before the first snow came.

His eyes wandered to the upper mountains at the far end of the valley. Already, they appeared white on top with early snow. The ranchers would be wanting to bring their cattle close into their home pastures in preparation for the winter. And some of those pastures were near water where, he realized, some of the miners had staked out homesteads.

He turned into Turnbull's lane and rode up to the ranch house. Turnbull came out to greet him, Seldon and Panhandle by his side.

"Come on in, Reverend," Turnbull said, waving generously. "We got coffee on and something stronger if you feel the need."

"Coffee will do," Hood said, removing his gloves and shaking hands.

"Then, coffee it will be," Turnbull said. "And you'll stay for dinner. I won't take no for an answer. Seldon, why don't you ease his horse's saddle and give her a bait of oats? And maybe Cookie has something for his wolf?"

Seldon grinned. "Take care of it right away," he said, taking Sheba's reins.

Obediently, she followed him as he led her over to the barn corral. Sam trotted along with them.

"Well, how'd it go, Panhandle?" Hood asked.

A broad grin came to Panhandle's face.

"None of those would-be homesteaders had been in to file before I got there. I did what you said and lopped off the northern part of the valley for rough survey. At first, the ranny running the land office didn't want to do it, but I did a little persuading and he decided that it would be a good thing if I was given survey rights."

Turnbull stepped aside to let Hood go first into the house.

"The others are coming over this evening so we can mark our ranges on the survey map Panhandle brought back. Why don't you stay over and go out with us in the morning? We're gonna move those miners out then."

"Maybe it would be better if I went first," Hood said. "There's less confrontation that way."

Turnbull led Panhandle and Hood over to the easy chairs and called for coffee. The cook came out, holding three cups and bearing a pot of coffee. Sourly, he poured each a cup of coffee, muttering all the time about why he was told to do this and that and never given time to finish what he'd started and if the boss wouldn't leave him alone, there wouldn't be much for supper except leftovers. And if it wasn't hard enough to keep the men eating, now he had a wolf taking up space in his kitchen.

Turnbull laughed as the cook left and said, "Old Cookie wouldn't feel things were right if he didn't have something to complain about."

"Ain't that the truth," Panhandle said, blowing across the surface of his coffee to cool it. "Never saw a man complain so much about so little."

Turnbull sat back contentedly in his chair and sipped his coffee. He studied Hood for a moment, then said, "I don't think it's a good idea for you to go alone out there. Some of those miners are more than a little touchy, and just because you're the preacher doesn't mean that they won't try something with you."

"There is that chance," Hood said, sipping his coffee. It was strong and black and just to Hood's liking. "But still, I'd like to give it a try."

Panhandle said, "I agree with the boss. It

ain't a good idea for you to go out there by yourself. Seems to me that's a pretty reckless thing to do. A couple of us with you might help keep the peace. Besides, I'm the surveyor and I'm the one who has to tell them to move off and show them how they missed their chance by not gettin' to Durango and filing their claims. I ain't sure it would be legal if'n I don't do that."

"We'll leave it to the others when they come," Turnbull said, deciding. "But I go along with Panhandle. It would be better if he goes with you, and if he goes, a couple of us should go as well to help keep the peace while he explains things to them."

The other ranchers unanimously agreed with Turnbull that night at dinner, although Hood objected with grave uneasiness, fearing that the Upper Valley would explode in a deadly conflict between the homesteaders and ranchers. Finally, reluctantly, he agreed that the ranchers would accompany Panhandle and him the next day when they rode out to the staked sites.

Early the next morning, the group mounted and rode out, heading for the nearest staked site. When they arrived, they found that no permanent shelter had been built nor was there any indication that such a shelter was in the planning. A tent had been erected and that was it.

Hood breathed a deep sigh of relief. Even if the ranchers weren't right in their claim about land usage, the would-be homesteader had not complied with the law for claiming land.

A man, filthy beyond all definition, came out and watched them ride up. He carried a Henry .44 rifle in both hands and held it in the general direction of the riders.

"Close enough," he snarled. "What d'you want?"

Panhandle eased himself in the saddle and said pleasantly, "Just thought we should let you know that you're on this land illegally and will have to move."

The man laughed. "This here land is staked and mine," he said. "That's according to the law."

"Nope," Panhandle said, shaking his head. "This land is under rough survey and is already claimed through constant usage by Mr. Turnbull here. That goes for the others as well. You all are gonna have to move off."

"We're entitled to a hundred sixty acres," the man said stubbornly. "And that's what I got staked out."

"You have illegally staked a claim on another man's property," Hood said, breaking in. "Additionally, even if this wasn't so, you have not built a permanent structure, which is needed to claim the land. *And* you have not filed your claim with the land office over in Durango. In fact, none of the others have filed either and they all will have to move."

The man waved his rifle threateningly. "I'd like to see the man who's gonna move me off'n my claim."

"If necessary, *I* will," Panhandle said softly, his thumbs loosening the thongs around the hammers of his pistols.

Hood hurriedly butted in.

"What I would like to know is why you thought to homestead this range," he said.

The man studied him sourly, then said, "None of us was panning enough gold to even buy supplies. We held a meetin' and the town marshal told us our rights and said we should stake out the land we wanted."

"Oh? Do you mean Ben Thompson?"

The man nodded vigorously. "That be he. And he said if we wanted to, we could sell out to him oncet we had been on it for six months and paid the . . . ." He frowned, trying to remember the term, then said, "Preemption entry. That's a dollar and twenty-five cents an acre. He said he would give us the money for it and then buy it from us. A few of us went through the War Between the States and we can use that money for moving elsewhere."

"I'll be a dirty skunk," Campbell said softly. "It appears Thompson's planning on going into the cattle business."

"That it does," Hayes said grimly.

"Well, I reckon Thompson's gonna have to find another way to get land here in the Upper Valley," Panhandle drawled. "Since I am the legal representative for a land survey and division of property, I reckon I'm gonna have to give you just twenty-four hours to pack and get off this land." He glanced around and said, "And it looks like once you take that tent down, you're pretty well packed."

"You just come and try and push me off," the man said, threatening.

"Twenty-four hours," Panhandle said softly. "That's all." He stared hard at the miner until the miner dropped his eyes. Then Panhandle turned his horse and rode away, Hood by his side, the ranchers loosely trailing. Panhandle glanced over at Hood.

"I don't think it's gonna go well, Reverend," he said. "I think this is shaping up to be a pretty bloody affair."

"I hope not," Hood said. "I sincerely hope not."

Panhandle's pessimism turned out to be right as all the other "homesteaders" were equally as threatening and boasted that no one was gonna drive them off their claims, and certainly no rancher or group of cow-boys was going to do the job.

Panhandle held his temper, though, and quietly informed one and all that they had twenty-four hours in which to move off the land as the land was undergoing a rough survey and would be reapportioned to those who had prior use of the land. And, he added to each, none had conformed to the Homestead Act by recording their claim or establishing a permanent structure.

As the grim ranchers rode back to their ranches in the early evening, a foreboding fell over Hood as he contemplated what was going to happen if the squatters would refuse to follow Panhandle's orders.

Turnbull rode up beside Hood and looked at him. "What do you think, Reverend?" he asked.

"I don't like it," Hood said. "I don't like it one bit."

"You know it's gonna have to be done, don't you?"

Hood nodded. "Yes, I know it has to be done. But I don't have to like it."

"None of us do," Turnbull said. He shifted his weight in his saddle, the leather creaking. "But we're in the right and they're in the wrong."

"Is it as simple as all that?" Hood said.

Turnbull nodded. "It's as simple as all that."

"May God help us," Hood said.

26.

The next day, the ranchers met again at Turnbull's place. It was a grim party that rode out, retracing their path from the day before. Panhandle again took the lead with Hood riding beside him. A tiny knot began to work at the corners of Panhandle's mouth. His eyes were gray and flat. Hood glanced down at his Colts; they had been freshly oiled.

Panhandle caught Hood's look and said, "Can you figure out anything else to do? You know the territorial marshal ain't gonna do anything. Fact is, I don't even know where he is right now. And as for Futterman, well, might as well send a flea-bitten hound dog to do the job."

"I would like to talk to them before you push them off," Hood said.

Panhandle rode in silence for a moment, considering, then said, "Well, I can't see where it'll harm anything. If'n you think there's a chance that we ain't gonna have to fight them, then go ahead. I'm for it."

"Thanks," Hood said. "Maybe I can talk some sense into them."

They topped a small rise and reined in. Down below, a group of homesteaders stood around the man who had arrogantly faced them the day before. Daylight gleamed from their rifle barrels and shotguns. Panhandle turned his horse so he could face the ranchers.

"I'd say you all should wait here while the reverend and me ride down and see if we can't put a peaceful ending to all this. I know you're my boss, Mr. Turnbull, but I say we should give it a chance. 'Sides, if you all come down in force with your rifles in hand, I think that might just be the spark to set off the powder keg."

Turnbull nodded. "I agree."

The others followed Turnbull's lead, and Panhandle turned his horse back again and looked at Hood.

"You ready, Reverend?"

Hood took a deep breath and let it out slowly. "Let's try it," he said.

Slowly, the two rode down the small rise to meet the angry group below, Sam padding patiently beside them. When they got closer, Panhandle whispered to Hood.

"I think you'd better resign yourself, Reverend. This don't look promising."

"I know," Hood said grimly. "But I have to try."

Wordlessly, Panhandle slipped the thongs off the hammers of his pistols and turned his attention to the crowd as they approached.

They pulled up in front of the crowd. Sam sat down, ears pricked forward, yellow eyes intent upon the men in front.

"I told you that you ain't gonna move us off'n our land," the leader said. His Henry was held in both hands, the stock tucked under his right arm.

"Men," Hood said, "you don't want to do this. In the first place, you're in the wrong. In the second, there's no use for bloodshed. None of you are farmers. You're all hard-rock miners who've come upon bad times. But you could hire out to the mine owners and make a living that way without shooting your fellow man."

"Go away, Reverend," a voice shouted from the rear of the crowd. "This'n ain't your affair."

"That's right," the leader said. "And what you doing siding with those ranchers?" He indicated the group on top of the rise with his chin.

"There are other ways," Hood said. "You could take your claim to the federal courts."

The leader snorted and said, "And where you think we gonna get the money to hire a shyster to do that for us?"

"There's open land in the Lower Valley," Hood said. "You could move down there and take up land without anyone challenging you. You can't farm up this high, but you could give it a try down there."

"Reckon we like it right here," the leader said. Others muttered angry agreement.

"It's your call," Panhandle said, moving his horse to the left of Hood. He looped the reins around the pommel of his saddle and rested his hands lightly upon his holsters.

"Now, move!" he ordered harshly.

"I'll be damned!!!" the leader shouted hoarsely, and tried to bring the Henry to bear on Panhandle. But Panhandle palmed his pistols and shot the leader in the throat and turned his guns upon the crowd. A man brought up his shotgun, but a bullet from Panhandle's pistol struck him in the chest, knocking him backward.

A third and a fourth fell to bullets from Panhandle's guns; then a hail of bullets from the top of the rise struck the mob, killing many.

And as soon as it began, it was over, the

rest of the men throwing down their weapons and raising their hands. Panhandle kept his guns trained on the crowd.

"All right," he said tightly. "You made your try. Now, I see you all have your horses tied up back there" — he nodded at the trees — "so I reckon there's no need for you to go back to your places. Mount up and ride on outta here. And I mean now!"

The men turned sullenly toward their horses. A couple made a halfhearted attempt to collect their guns, but a hard word from Panhandle stopped them.

The crowd mounted their horses and turned south toward town.

Panhandle sighed and placed his heavy pistols back in their holsters, took a bandanna, and wiped his forehead.

"I reckon that was touch and go, Reverend," he said, turning toward Hood. His eyes widened in surprise as he saw Hood had drawn the Spencer from its sheath and had the hammer rocked back.

Slowly, Panhandle nodded and said, "I reckon there's somethin' else inside you other than a preacher, Reverend. I got a hunch that coming up against you a-shootin' wouldn't be a good idea."

Embarrassed, Hood lowered the hammer

on the Spencer and slipped it back in its sheath.

"I don't know what got into me," he said, shaking his head.

"Habit, I'd say," Panhandle answered. He turned to watch the ranchers ride up to them.

"I figure that's about it," Panhandle said to them. " 'Course, I think we're gonna have to ride around and make certain that no one hung around after this morning's doings, but I think that's gonna be it. Those men will tell others what happened here and there'll be few others who will want to come back in their footsteps. Those boys were miners, not farmers or ranchers or gunmen."

McKellon heaved a deep sigh. "Thank God," he said shakily.

"Yes," Hood said quietly, dismounting. He began to check the downed miners to see if any were wounded. Panhandle dropped to the ground to help him. All were dead.

"I say I send a rider in for the undertaker," Turnbull said. "I got a place where we can bury these folks after Doc gets them ready. And I got a carpenter who can make the coffins. I don't think we should take them back into town. Some folks seeing them might get riled up."

Hood nodded. "Yes, I agree. If you let me know when you're ready, I'll ride back out and bury them."

Turnbull nodded, then said to Panhandle, "Why don't you ride in with the reverend and bring the undertaker back?"

Panhandle nodded and, together, he and Hood rode slowly back toward town, leaving the killing ground behind them.

27.

Hood and Panhandle rode into Gold Town in the early afternoon, the sun beating down hard and merciless on their backs. Hood reined in in front of Mrs. Hargrave's and nodded at Panhandle.

"I guess this is where we part company," he said.

"Reckon for a while anyway," Panhandle said, sitting easily in the saddle. He took the makings from a shirt pocket and began to build a cigarette.

"You know that what was done back there is going to follow you, don't you?"

Panhandle laughed bitterly and said, "Other things in my past have been following me for quite a spell. I guess I can handle a bit more."

Hood nodded and turned to walk into Mrs. Hargrave's boardinghouse while Panhandle ambled down the street toward Doc Martin's.

Inside, Hood's flesh began to prickle as he sensed something wrong, out of place in the otherwise cheerful house. He paused just inside the doorway, looking around carefully, feeling the familiar warning that he had felt countless times when he had been the sheriff back in Walker, Kansas. Sam stood beside him, half-crouched, growling softly, his fur standing on end. A low mumble of voices came from upstairs. He climbed the stairs, staying next to the wall and testing each step to prevent it from creaking. Sam ran lightly up the stairs and waited for him.

"Hello?" Hood ventured cautiously. He kept his balance, ready to throw himself downstairs if someone emerged with a pistol.

But it was Mrs. Hargrave who emerged, her face tight, eyes flashing mad, lips pressed into a thin line.

"We've been needing you," she said darkly. "Come on up. This is bad. Very bad."

Hood mounted the stairs and followed her into Elizabeth's room. Doc Martin turned away from the bed and Hood looked dumbly at Elizabeth, lying on the bed, her face battered. Both eyes were black and swollen. Bruises appeared on both cheekbones, her nose was broken, and her lip was split badly. Dried tears had cut a path through the fine dust on her pale face.

Hood went to Elizabeth, knelt, and took her hand. It was cold and damp.

"Elizabeth?" he asked softly.

She didn't respond, and Doc Martin said tiredly, "I gave her enough laudanum to knock out a horse. She'll sleep a long time. Maybe even until morning. She needs it right now."

"What happened?" Hood asked.

"She's been raped," Mrs. Hargrave said harshly. "Cacklejack found her when he went to the church to deliver a few more benches he'd made for her school. He fetched Doc and brought her here."

"Who?" The words came thickly from Hood.

"She told Cacklejack Bowdine caught her in the church after school had been dismissed. He beat her, then raped her. He did that, plus cracked a couple of ribs."

"I've wrapped the ribs," Doc Martin said. "But she won't be moving around for quite a spell."

Hood nodded and rose, wild thoughts spinning darkly in his mind.

"Where's Bowdine now?" he asked, his face a dark mask that made the others step back from him.

"Probably down at the Crystal Palace," Doc Martin said.

Wordlessly, Hood turned toward the door, but stopped when Mrs. Hargrave asked, "What are you going to do?"

"Have a talk with Bowdine. And tell Thompson what has happened and demand that he arrest Bowdine."

"You really think he'll arrest his friend?" Mrs. Hargrave asked.

Hood shook his head. "We have to try. He is the town marshal. The only law we have here."

"I think you are wasting your time," Mrs. Hargrave said grimly. "It'll be Bowdine's word against hers."

"Maybe," Hood said. He left, stumbling down the stairs and out the door.

He met Panhandle walking through the gate.

"Doc Martin here? Bledsoe told me he had come up here." He frowned as he caught the look on Hood's face. "What's wrong?"

"Bowdine raped Elizabeth. The schoolteacher," he said when Panhandle frowned.

Panhandle's face darkened. "She . . ."

"Yes," Hood broke in. "He beat her badly. *Very* badly."

"She gonna live?"

Hood shrugged. "Doc has given her laudanum. I don't know."

"Where you going?"

"To ask Thompson to arrest Bowdine."

"You want company?"

Hood shook his head. "No. If you come along, there might be a killing."

Panhandle nodded. "All right. I'll wait here. Doc ain't goin' anywhere for a while, I expect."

"I doubt it," Hood said.

He left and walked down toward the Crystal Palace, his steps kicking up a small cloud of dust. A band tightened around his head as he walked into the saloon. Immediately, he smelled stale beer and smoke. A few miners were at the bar, drinking. He looked down the bar and felt his muscles tightening. Sam growled softly beside Hood.

Bowdine was standing at his usual place, by the bar where he could see who entered. He held a glass of whiskey in his hand and grinned mockingly. Frank Gannon and Craven stood next to him.

Hood paused, his eyes locked on Bowdine's. Then he noticed Thompson playing cards, his back to the wall. Ellis was playing solitaire at the table next to him.

Hood walked down to Thompson and stood across the table from him. Thompson ignored him for a moment, then sighed and looked up.

"Something wrong, preacher?"

"Yes. I need to talk with you."

Thompson shrugged. "Spill it."

"Alone."

"What's wrong with here?" Thompson asked.

"Alone," Hood said.

Thompson studied his cards for a second, then threw them in the deadwood and stood.

"That hand was a bust anyway."

He walked around the table and followed Hood as he moved on the other side of Ellis.

"Get your partner over here," Hood said harshly.

Thompson raised his eyebrow, then looked at Bowdine.

"Art, would you come over here?"

Bowdine placed his glass on the counter and joined Hood and Thompson.

"What is it?" he asked, his eyes intent on Hood. Amused lights danced in his eyes.

"Thompson, I want you to arrest Bowdine here."

"On what charge?" Thompson asked.

"Rape. He raped Elizabeth. I figure he did that because she wouldn't ride out with him anymore."

Hood became aware of Ellis gathering his cards, placing them neatly in the middle of the table, and listening quietly.

"That's serious," Thompson said, his face hardening. "Art? What have you to say?"

Bowdine shook his head. "Not me. I've been here all day. Doing accounts in the office until just a short while ago when I came out to have a drink."

Craven and Frank Gannon appeared beside Bowdine's shoulder.

"I can vouch for that," Craven said, a cheerful smile on his face. "We were talking in the office while he finished up his accounts, then came out here to have a drink. Just like he said."

"I was with them," Gannon said.

Thompson nodded and looked at Hood. "You got any witnesses?"

"No," Hood said.

"Did she name him?"

"I don't think so."

"Then, it's just gonna be her word against theirs. Art's and Jack's and Gannon's. Right?" Thompson shook his head. "That'll never hold up."

"You're going to do nothing, in other words?" Hood asked quietly.

"No. Not with Art's alibi being proven."

"I guess I should have figured as much," Hood said. He looked from Craven to Bowdine, then back to Thompson. "I guess law around here is numbered according to your wishes."

Thompson's face hardened. "The law's mine. I made that clear the day I took this job. You know that. You were there."

"You wouldn't do anything even if Craven hadn't lied."

The words made Thompson's face fall into a stony mask.

"Those words are pretty harsh, preacher," Thompson said. "I reckon you'd better leave before I arrest you for makin' false accusations."

"Get out of my saloon, preacher," Bowdine said, hard on Thompson's words. "You ain't welcome here anymore."

Hood stood silently for a long time, then turned on his heel and stalked across the floor and through the swinging doors. Shaking with anger, he stood on the boardwalk as the others laughed behind him in the saloon.

He became aware of Ellis standing beside his shoulder and looked at him.

"What are you going to do?" Ellis asked.

"Go back to Missus Hargrave's to check on Elizabeth," Hood said.

"I reckon I'll go down to Missus Hargrave's with you," Ellis said.

Together, they started down the street, Ellis limping along on his club foot.

"You knew what would happen even before you came down to the Crystal Palace, didn't you?" Ellis asked.

Hood sighed and nodded. "I think I did. But I had to try."

"What are you going to do now?"

"I don't know," Hood said.

"I think I do," Ellis said calmly. "I think it's time you leave Amos Hood out of it and bring Tom Cade back."

Hood stopped and looked at Ellis.

"You knew all along, didn't you?"

Ellis nodded. "I was in the saloon that day you took on the two Johnsons who came hunting you. Something about a feud begun back in Tennessee. I put it together when Long Johnson braced you here. Later, I was forced to kill a man called 'Carmady' over a card game. Unfortunately, he was popular and I was a gambler. Talk came fast about lynching me, but you took me to jail and let me out the back door. I lit a shuck out of Walker then."

"You kept it all to yourself." It was a statement, not a question, but Ellis answered it anyway.

"I figured you needed to put it behind you." He shrugged. "Besides, it wasn't my fight."

"Is that why you killed Long?" Hood asked. "Because it wasn't your fight?"

Ellis shrugged. "I guess I just had a loose moment when my conscience got the better of me."

Hood started walking again toward Mrs. Hargrave's.

"And now, you're mixing in this?" he asked.

"I don't know," Ellis said. He smiled thinly. "That's up to Tom Cade, I imagine."

They mounted the steps and walked into the boardinghouse. Panhandle sat at the dining table, a cup of coffee in front of him.

"I heard," he said.

"Panhandle," Ellis said, touching the brim of his hat.

"Ellis," Panhandle said and nodded. "How have you been?"

"Sixes and eights," Ellis answered.

"This is bad," Panhandle said, his face hard and formidable.

"I'm going up to check on Elizabeth. Want to come on up?" Hood asked Ellis.

Ellis nodded. "Indeed. Let us see what hell hath wrought."

When they entered Elizabeth's room, Mrs.

377

Hargrave stood, staring wrathfully at Ellis.

"What are you doing here?" she demanded. She indicated Elizabeth still sleeping quietly. "This is all your fault. If you hadn't started courting her, Bowdine wouldn't have done this to her."

Ellis studied Elizabeth calmly, then turned and said to Hood, "I'll wait for you downstairs."

"It's your fault, you hear me?" Mrs. Hargrave said furiously. "Your fault!"

Hood placed a calming hand on her forearm.

"No, it's not his fault. Bowdine would probably have done this anyway if Elizabeth had refused his advances. And I think that she would have. She was too decent for Bowdine."

Slowly, Mrs. Hargrave's face began to sag. She dropped into the room's chair. "This town. This town," she said in despair. "This town is bad to the core."

"No," Hood said. "There is good here. The good may have relaxed a little when they brought in Thompson and Bowdine, but it is still here. If given a chance, I think it will eventually become a decent town."

"Then the town committee better get rid of that Thompson and Bowdine," she said.

"Easier said than done," Doc Martin said

sourly. "Those two have made the town pretty much theirs. I reckon the committee will have to bring in another gun to get rid of them."

"Maybe," Hood said hollowly. "Maybe."

"There's no change," Doc Martin said when Hood's eyes returned to Elizabeth. "She's still sleeping."

Hood nodded and left the room. He went down the stairs and turned down the short hallway to his room. He stood for a long time, thinking.

A new start for the town, he thought. *Maybe. But first law has to be set. Law for everyone and not a few. Not leave the town in the hands of someone like Thompson and Bowdine. Yes, Bowdine. Might as well include Bowdine, too. There's nothing else for it.*

And it is a decent town. Once the riffraff is driven out or at least kept in Tent City. The committee will learn by its mistakes. But they're only human. No, they are afraid. They were afraid and are still afraid. And that does not necessarily make them good. Frightened, yes, but not good. Not at the moment, for they are still frightened.

His glance fell on his saddlebags. Slowly, he crossed to them and took the ivory-handled Schofield, still in its holster, out of the bottom of one. He unwrapped the cloth around it and took it from its holster. The pistol came easily into his hand, curving into it familiarly like a plow handle does to a farmer's hand. Curved as if it had been made for it.

He opened the pistol and checked the barrel, clean and glistening with a fine coat of oil. He closed the pistol and checked the action: smooth, almost like liquid.

The old feeling came back to him, tightening his shoulders. Calmly, he loaded the gun and replaced it in its holster. Then he removed his coat and buckled the black gun belt around his hips. It settled on his thigh in the old place as if it had memory of when it had last been there.

He turned and walked down the hall. Panhandle and Ellis looked up at him. Their eyes fell to his hip and the Schofield.

"So," Ellis said, "Tom Cade's back."

Hood nodded and glanced at Panhandle.

"Tom Cade," Panhandle said slowly. "Yes, I've heard about you."

Together, the two men rose and took their pistols from their holsters and checked them before dropping them lightly back into their holsters.

"Reckon we'll come with you. Right, Ellis?" Panhandle drawled.

Ellis smiled thinly. "I think my hypocrisy

has been stretched far enough."

The three of them left the boardinghouse and turned their steps toward town. Sam trotted beside them, ears perked alertly.

"You know Gannon and Craven are going to be there," Ellis said. Cade nodded.

"Gannon and Craven?" Panhandle repeated. "This should be interesting."

They walked slowly down the street, staying in the middle. A stillness seemed to fall over the town. Overhead, an eagle circled high in the sky. The smell of dust rose, and Ellis began to whistle "Lorena."

People stopped and stared at them, then disappeared indoors. A couple of men ran down the street and into the Crystal Palace.

"I do believe the message has been delivered," Ellis said from Cade's right side. "Who do you want, Tom?"

"Thompson," Cade said harshly.

"Then I'll take Bowdine. How about you, Panhandle?"

"Craven. He'll be better than Gannon."

"Then whoever finishes first takes Gannon?"

"Sounds like a working plan," Panhandle drawled. "You, Reverend?"

"That's as good as any other plan," Cade said.

"Then, by all means, let us proceed," Ellis said.

The door of the saloon swung open and Thompson, followed by Bowdine, Craven, and Gannon, stepped out and walked to the center of the street to face Cade, Panhandle, and Ellis, all of whom stopped a short distance from the four.

"You boys are violating the law. You know wearing guns in town is forbidden," Thompson said. "I reckon I'm going to have to take you in."

"I don't think I'm going to let you do that, Thompson," Cade said.

Bowdine smiled recklessly. "Well, lookee here. The reverend's wearing a pistol. How interesting. You any good with that, Reverend?"

"I'm Tom Cade," Cade said. "And if any arresting is going to be done here, then it'll be by me and Panhandle and Ellis."

"Tom Cade?" An excited light appeared in Bowdine's eyes. "Well, I'll be damned!"

"You may well be," Cade said. "Now why don't the four of you drop your guns and come with me to jail?"

"So, you're in this, too, Ellis?" Bowdine asked.

"Seems like the thing to do," Ellis said.

"I'm looking forward to killing you," Bowdine said.

"You must be the biggest toad in the puddle," Ellis said, smiling. "I'm just the one to dance with."

"One more warning," Thompson said. "Drop your guns."

"Well, I reckon I'd feel plumb naked without them," Panhandle said.

"Better than feeling dead," Thompson said.

"What about you, Craven?" Panhandle asked. "I thought you were riding for the cattlemen."

"Why, I was," Craven said cheerfully. "But Gannon here offered me a better job."

"Too bad you took it," Panhandle said.

"Cut bait or ride out," Gannon growled.

"Say 'when,' " Ellis said mockingly to Bowdine.

Suddenly, Bowdine's hand slapped down for his pistol. Thompson drew swiftly, trying to bring his pistol up to bear on Cade. Craven's pistol cleared its holster; then he staggered back and fell on the ground, holding his stomach. Gannon fired just before a gray form blurred across the distance and knocked him sprawling to the ground. Sam sunk his teeth into Gannon's forearm and Gannon shrieked as Sam's powerful jaws crunched the bone there. He tried to shake

Sam free, but Sam dropped Gannon's arm and went for Gannon's throat. Instinctively, Gannon dropped his chin to his chest, trying to block Sam, but Sam caught half of Gannon's face in his jaws and bit hard. Gannon screamed and, ignoring the pain, pushed Sam away. He half-rose, firing as he came up, and Panhandle felt the breeze of the bullet fly by his ear and fired back, knocking Gannon to the ground.

Thompson had gotten his pistol half out of its holster when Cade fired twice rapidly, both shots centering on Thompson's chest. From beside Cade, Ellis's pistol fired three times quickly, the shots rolling into one as Bowdine twisted and fell forward onto his face. Craven raised his pistol and fired at Panhandle. Two bullets jarred Craven, slamming him back on the ground. Gamely, he tried to rise again, but Panhandle put a finishing shot in his forehead.

Bowdine staggered to his feet, holding his stomach, firing blindly at Ellis, who coolly took aim and shot Bowdine in the middle of the face. Thompson tried to rise, but then a gush of blood splashed from his mouth and he fell face-forward into the dust. His hand twitched his pistol twice; then he shook and slowly relaxed. Gannon got to his knees, only to be hit by three bullets instantly. He jerked, his pistol flying up into the air. Another bullet hit him and he fell back into the street beside Craven just as Sam locked upon Gannon's throat, ripping it apart.

And then, it was over. Cade's ears rang from the gun blasts. He took a deep breath, automatically reloaded, then sheathed the Schofield. He looked at Ellis and Panhandle.

"I reckon I've done my good deed for the day," Ellis said, placing his pistol in its holster under his coat, after reloading.

Panhandle followed his example, reloading and easing his Colts back into their holsters. He left the thongs off the hammers.

"Think that finishes it?" he asked Cade.

"Yes, I believe it does," Cade answered.

Doc Martin appeared and bent over the four figures on the ground. He rose and looked at Cade and shook his head.

"I knew about Panhandle and Ellis," he said. "But I never expected a minister to be hell on wheels with a pistol."

"Men are but gilded loam or painted clay," Ellis said. "We are what we are despite the shield we carry."

He touched the brim of his hat, then sauntered in to the Crystal Palace. Panhandle nodded at Cade and followed Ellis into the saloon, and after a moment's hesitation, Cade pushed his way through the swinging doors and let them slap closed behind him.

EPILOGUE

The days that followed seemed to blur into one for Hood. People walked wide of him when he happened to stroll down the street, and he found himself spending more and more time with Ellis. Elizabeth healed rapidly, but did not return to the school. Hood or Ellis often took her for a drive out in the country. She wore a long black veil to hide her face. Curious people stared at her for a while when she rode by in the carriage driven by either Hood or Ellis, but soon the curiosity waned and she became, once again, simply one of the people in Gold Town.

Turnbull came into town and visited with Elizabeth at Mrs. Hargrave's, vainly trying to talk Elizabeth into going back to teaching. But she refused, saying she could not step into that building any more for the bad thing that had happened there.

One not to be deterred, Turnbull had a

schoolhouse built on the opposite side of town and after a few weeks of hesitation, Elizabeth returned to teaching, always wearing the veil.

About that time, Crease began to visit her more and more on a regular basis, until finally she agreed to go on a buggy ride with him. After that, they rode regularly while visits by Ellis and Hood became fewer and fewer.

One Sunday, only half a dozen families appeared in church, and Hood knew his time in Gold Town had ended. A man just can't go back from a killing — especially if that man had the people's trust as a minister. The next day, Monday, he stopped in to see Howie in his store and Howie appeared embarrassed to wait on him.

"You know, uh, preacher, people are wary of a man like you. Now," he hastened to add, "I don't mind it. I think you did what had to be done. But . . ." His voice trailed off.

"I know," Hood said gently. "I know."

"There's another minister coming . . ." Howie's voice trailed off. He fidgeted with a bolt of cloth.

Hood smiled, and walked from Bledsoe's store and crossed the street to the Crystal Palace. Ellis was dealing stud poker in the back to five gamblers. He looked up as Hood entered, and excused himself from the table and crossed to the bar to stand beside Hood. There was a new bartender behind the bar.

"A drink," Ellis said to the bartender. "From my bottle."

Silently, the bartender put tumblers in front of each and poured generous measures into both, then moved down the bar.

Ellis picked up his glass and said, "To what could have been."

Hood picked up his glass and clinked it against Ellis's. "To what could have been," he repeated.

They drank and placed the glasses back on the bar.

"What are you going to do?" Ellis asked.

Hood shrugged. "Might try Arizona."

"I see," Ellis said. He refilled their glasses. They drank.

"I'm leaving in the morning," Hood said. "Just came by to say adios and to thank you again for what you did."

"Panhandle left Turnbull and went over to Texas somewhere," Ellis said. "He said to tell you good-bye. I guess he wanted to be away from the shooting. He knows that once word travels about what we did, there'll be young ones coming to try and build a quick reputation."

"What about you?" Hood asked.

Ellis shrugged. "I haven't decided."

"Well," Hood said, slapping the bar and holding out his hand to Ellis. "I might be seeing you around."

"Might at that," Ellis said, taking Hood's hand.

Hood walked from the saloon and down to Mrs. Hargrave's.

The next morning, he was up early and saddled Sheba as Sam waited impatiently at the door. Hood wanted to be gone before Elizabeth awoke. It would be better that way than a tearful farewell.

He mounted and rode west out of town. The sun was warm on his back, but he could smell the coming change of weather hanging in the air.

A whistle sounded behind him.

He turned and watched as Ellis rode up.

"Reckon I have decided," Ellis said.

Hood nodded and turned back to ride Sheba away from the rising sun as Ellis fell in beside him.

The employees of Thorndike Press hope you have enjoyed this Large Print book. All our Thorndike, Wheeler, and Kennebec Large Print titles are designed for easy reading, and all our books are made to last. Other Thorndike Press Large Print books are available at your library, through selected bookstores, or directly from us.

For information about titles, please call:
(800) 223-1244

or visit our Web site at:
http://gale.cengage.com/thorndike

To share your comments, please write:
Publisher
Thorndike Press
295 Kennedy Memorial Drive
Waterville, ME 04901